The Sixth Man

The Sixth Man

A Thriller

Ron Lealos

Skyhorse Publishing

Skyhorse Publishing books may be purchased in bulk at special discounts for sales promotion, corporate gifts, fund-raising, or educational purposes. Special editions can also be created to specifications. For details, contact the Special Sales Department, Skyhorse Publishing, 307 West 36th Street, 11th Floor, New York, NY 10018 or info@skyhorsepublishing.com.

Skyhorse® and Skyhorse Publishing® are registered trademarks of Skyhorse Publishing, Inc.®, a Delaware corporation.

Visit our website at www.skyhorsepublishing.com.

10 9 8 7 6 5 4 3 2 1

Library of Congress Cataloging-in-Publication Data is available on file.

Cover design by Laura Klynstra

Print ISBN: 978-1-5107-0188-5
Ebook ISBN: 978-1-5107-0189-2

Printed in the United States of America

The number of people out of the more than nine million citizens of Ho Chi Minh City who didn't want me dead was probably somewhat bigger than the paltry sum of true communists in our Stalinist paradise. The total was limited to other half-breeds like me. We were the sons and daughters of whore mothers and syphilitic fathers who had been foolish enough to believe Chinese and Vietnamese blood could mix. Or too drunk on snake wine to care. The only reason I was allowed to walk the suffocating streets was my position in the city's security force. But that didn't protect me from the barrage of insults shouted at my face and whispered behind my back, the least offensive being labeled "gookinese." Since I couldn't kill the mothermockers, or even carry a pistol, my defense was to sharpen my tongue and give back even more than I was given. I was a Master of Insults, my only weapon against the bigots. At least today, the lowlander I was viewing was lifeless and couldn't give me any *cuc*. Shit.

The missing ears had to be a clue. Three murders in a week and all the victims unable to hear their ancestors in the afterworld. There must be a connection. Solving mysteries was how I had risen to the exalted height of "detective captain" after thirty years with the Ho Chi Minh City police. Normally, it took only ten and a few hundred million dong in bribes. Now, I was surprised to carry the name Captain Chyang Fang, detective, and chief homicide inspector in a people's utopia where even speaking of murder was politically incorrect, since our happy, healthy citizens wouldn't think of such atrocities.

Crumbs from the toast the third dead man ate as his last meal hung to his permanently unsmiling lips. On the table above him, a plate held eggs curdling from the morning's breakfast in humidity thick enough to wear as a robe. He was naked, and his protruding belly showed he hadn't missed many meals since reunification. This lifeless one had been doing his thinking in the politburo. The newly familiar tin cobra was lying on the murdered man's chest, along with an old black and white photo. No one at my level of the ruling bureaucracy could fail to recognize this stiffening body.

The name was Danh Nguyen, formerly the Saigon chief of the North Vietnamese Ministry of Public Security, shortened to the An Ninh. He was, in his just-ended cycle of life, a high-ranking government official and one of the secret puppet masters who truly ruled the country. He'd been the lead commissar of the police during much of the American invasion. Since 1976, Comrade Danh had held the lofty title of head of the central military commission office in Ho Chi Minh City. He'd only recently retired to the old French villa on Hoa Da Street where I now watched the flies drink from the side of Nguyen's head like it was a puddle of Sting cherry pop.

"How do you think he died, Captain?" Lanh Phan, my assistant, murmured, seemingly fascinated by a roach drowning in the small pool of blood stagnating beside Nguyen's skull.

"No need to whisper, Phan," I said. "As you can see, someone got away with his ears. He can't hear you."

Careful to disturb as little as possible before the forensics team arrived, I pushed Nguyen's head to the left with my gloved hand. An entry wound gaped in the matted hairs at the back. It was a hole no bigger than a two-hundred-dong coin, the puncture made from up close by a small-caliber pistol, probably a .22 like the other victims.

"I'd guess it was a bullet," I said, pointing to the hole. "And someone assassinated him, unless he could reach around his head and shoot himself after he cut off his ears. Then dispose of the gun, the ears, and the knife before he fell on the floor and dropped a cobra and picture on his chest." I stood and sighed. "But I'm just a lowly half-caste Chinese detective, not fortunate enough to have the intelligence of a racially pure Vietnamese."

Sergeant Phan was used to my stereotyping and rarely commented, even if he understood the sarcasm. He'd risen in rank among more worthy candidates for homicide division positions in the Ho Chi Minh City police department because of my limited influence, not his abilities at detection. In a city with a greater unreported murder rate than that of New York City, he was one of the few I could trust to hear what would be considered "traitorous remarks." Like refusing to call my birth town after the name of the country's esteemed father and communist apologist. I preferred to use the more historic name, Sai Gon, roughly translated in Mandarin as "cotton forest," because of the groves of cottonwoods that previously surrounded the city. Besides, no one other than Phan could work with a yellow bandit. Chinese were the Jews of Vietnam. Even my mixed blood couldn't keep me from being considered a chink rather than a gook.

Phan bent forward and reached for the toy cobra.

"Don't touch that," I said. "If it doesn't have real fangs, I do. Why do you think I have the name? I've told you enough times not to soil a crime scene that your dead parents must have heard the words." Slowly, Phan stood. "Even if someone stuck chopsticks in their ears."

Besides his deafness to my heresies, Phan had many uses. Like making sure a cab picked us up when drivers were reluctant to rent themselves out to a lone Chinese if Phan wasn't chauffeuring me in one of the station's Toyotas. And getting us seats in the noodle shops. Phan was nearly six feet tall and had the look of a big, surly cop, even if he couldn't hit the Cao Dai temple at twenty meters with a bullet from his Russian-made Makarov pistol. He would faint if a street urchin threatened him by taking a Cuong Nhu martial arts stance and growling.

Phan quickly straightened, looking as if he'd been caught sucking face in the Samsora Club on Dong Khoi Street, the only lady-boy bar in the city still allowed to stay open by the commissars.

"I'm sorry, Captain," Phan said. "I wanted to see if the tin piece was the same as the last two."

"Again," I said. "I would guess a third man killed with a shot to the back of his head, ears cut off and missing, and a toy cobra and photograph left on his chest would be somehow related to the other two. Of course, my inherently weak Chinese mind struggles with obvious relationships." I watched as Phan wiped the sweat on his brow, the beads ever-present in a city that will surely drown in its own humid air if global warming isn't just another Western plot to subvert our glorious proletarian society.

"Have you called Ngo?" I asked.

"No sir," Phan said. "I was awaiting your orders."

Outside, the never-ending traffic roar and blue-tongued exhaust mixed with the devil's breath heat to stir a cocktail only the most fanatical Vietnamese would call "paradise." Citizens of Sai Gon were treated to the stench of bubbling garbage that seemed to gurgle on every corner, making the rats dance with happiness. I sighed, remembering my ever-evolving Buddhist belief that I should "conquer the silly with enlightenment" and not focus on poor Phan's weakness.

"Was your mother an ox, Phan?" I asked. "Do I have to tell you Buddha is fat? When I say, 'We'll check the body and call Ngo,' who do you think will do that when you are the only one the colonel will honor with a cell? You know my kind are not to be trusted. I might be phoning Beijing. Or selling the information to the American devils."

Ignoring me, Phan took his iPhone from his pocket and hit a number on the speed dial, but not before he again admired his picture that I had loaded on the screen. It always caused him to smile in wonderment at the magic. He turned and walked to the window overlooking the Sai Gon River, iPhone to his ear.

Dr. Ngo was the physician who passed for a coroner and head of the forensic team that was a millennium away from the standards of the *CSI* television reruns now being shown on Channel 34. A wide-screen Sony on the living room table and a sister set in the in his office were the major institutions where Dr. Ngo received his training. Of course, he could only dream of the equipment the actors had at their disposal. In the small darkroom that passed for a laboratory, he was limited to a few Bunsen burners and years of experience with corpses, many burned to crispy critters by American napalm manufactured by that global provider of all that is unnaturally fertile: Dow Chemical.

The Communist Party of Vietnam had just recently admitted that murders did take place in our perfect society. Despite the growing hush-hush statistics, they were reluctant to fund modern forensic techniques. Nonetheless, with Dr. Ngo's help, my closure rate on homicides was so much higher than the rest of the squad's that I was begrudgingly named captain, even if, behind my back, they called me "Comrade Viet Cong" and chuckled at their hilarious joke. Only the Americans drew on the VC description, since it loosely meant "yellow savage" and was not a category used by Vietnamese. Except when referring to a Chinese-half-breed evil spirit like me.

Returning to my side, Phan snapped the iPhone case closed with a flick of the wrist like he was Edward G. Robinson closing his lighter. I could almost imagine Phan groaning in pleasure as the nicotine from his cell hit lungs already made into a tar pit by the deadly fumes he breathed everyday just walking down Hoa Da Street. The move was one of the many small gestures that made Phan a serious detective in his own mind. Like squinting at a suspect and asking solemnly, "Where were you at the time of the crime?"

"He's on his way, sir," Phan said.

"And you remembered to give him the address?"

"Of course."

"Good. That's better than the last time when he had to call back."

To say I had a chip on my shoulder and took it out on Phan was like saying the traffic in Saigon was dominated by motorcycles that caused the city to suffocate on its own black-dragon emissions. Much too simple. Not even my Vietnamese sometimes-girlfriend, Thien, could stand my tirades and sent me out to Ma Jing's for a ball of tar opium to calm the devils when I started to rant.

"Sir, shouldn't we cover the body?" Phan asked, staring down at the corpse. "Or, at least make his lips into a smile?" The communist regime had failed to eliminate much of the popular Buddhist folklore. It was believed the dead should have a grin curling their mouths after passing so they could arrive in heaven with their happy face on, joyously prepared for the next circle in their journey of incarnation. Phan began to look around, as if he were searching for a tablecloth or sheet to put over Nguyen.

"Don't you dare, Phan," I said. "If you so much as touch the body, I'll have you transferred to schoolgirl patrol." The city had recently seen an outbreak of second-level girls fighting in the streets as their classmates cheered them on. The shrieking battles were videotaped and posted on You-Tube. Hair was pulled and kicks to the groin were favored in the adolescent matches that often ended in minor injury. Much publicity had been given to the fights, and a national debate was occurring in the press and on television concerning the collapse of the culture and deteriorating values. If only Uncle Ho was alive and not turning in his vault, he could guide his children to enlightenment on this and all issues including eating, walking, and screwing.

On the other hand, I sometimes wondered if Phan was a child of Agent Orange. Over twenty million gallons of the dioxin-laden herbicide had been sprayed on Vietnam by the Americans from 1961–1971, another gift to my ancestors provided by Dow and other multinational death machines. Agent Orange didn't just kill plants. Humans coming in contact with the defoliant developed an extremely high rate of cancer. Women gave birth to deformed and retarded children at over twenty times the percentage in a normal population. Phan's mother came from an area of the Mekong where the spraying was the heaviest. From one day to the next, I didn't know if Phan would remember what we had done even minutes before or anything I had said. In a way, he had given his mind to help overcome the Yankee imperialists. Reaching up, I patted him on his bony back.

"Why don't you stand right here and make sure no one disturbs the crime scene until Ngo arrives," I said. "You can play the SpongeBob game I downloaded on your phone. I'll take a look around the house." I started to walk away across the hardwood floor, turning back when I reached the door to the next room. "And don't touch the body or I'll have to send Mara to visit." Mara is the Buddhist Devil God. My words seemed to be enough to scare Phan into a SpongeBob orgy, with no further thoughts of violating the corpse on the floor.

What I did understand was that Phan would step in front of a tiger if it threatened me. I had dragged him along and into the police force after rescuing the boy during another murder investigation that included wild dogs and the human meat used to feed them. This was usually reversed, since the Vietnamese liked the high protein and vitamin C value of puppies especially. There were many restaurants in the city that featured doggy stew as their main dish, the most famous "BowWows" on Tran Khac Chan Street. I had tracked the killer to one of the local Triad gang's puppy mills and discovered Phan bound to a post with a leash that allowed him to feed and water the dogs. He was filthy and starving, his eyes deep black and flashing with insanity. It had taken considerable effort and lies to get Phan as my quasi assistant after years of prodding. Now, my superiors believed he was more loyal to them than to me. That was questionable, but I wanted him close by. I was now responsible for his soul.

"Yes, Captain," Phan said, reaching for his phone. Once I gave him permission, it would take a tsunami to tear him away from his quest to find the bubble in the Lost City of Atlantis.

First, I went to the door that opened onto a bougainvillea and banana-draped section of Hoa Da Street. I wanted to walk in as if I were a guest. Or the murderer. This was a trick I'd learned from old *Colombo* reruns. While it might be a violation of strict Buddhist thought, placing myself in another's mind helped assure I kept receiving my monthly salary that was barely enough to feed me let alone my mistress.

Several uniformed policemen were on the terrace, smoking Black Vidana cigarettes that smelled like burning wet clothes. The cancer sticks were made in Danang and fell apart if the smoker didn't grip tight. And pray.

One lane of Hoa Da had been blocked. Cyclists beeped their horns, frantically trying to keep from being swarmed by the hive. A man peddling a pushcart filled with oranges couldn't get up enough speed to enter the chaos. He stood high on the bike, straining his skinny legs, and screamed, *"May an long dai cham mui!"* You eat pubic hair in salt dip.

Looking through the open teak front door, it was apparent the house-keeper had yet to make an appearance today. Or else the killer had forgotten to dust and made more of a mess than just murder. Nguyen would have at least one cleaning lady, as well as a cook and in-house masseuse for rub-and-tug. I already knew his wife had died a year ago. All police officers were required to attend the funeral ceremony before she was cremated, fortunately only one day of the three. The nauseating drum and cymbal music brought on one of my frequent migraines while I tried to look solemn for a woman I'd never met. The constant clang of the tinny instruments sounded more like screeching cats than a song. Of course, I was culturally and ritualistically ignorant in this land of ghosts and spirits.

Somehow, in a communist fairyland, the dead Nguyen had accumulated enough dong to restore this villa to its original splendor. The mansion was built nearly a hundred years ago. His money and position had assured the ticks and tree worms hadn't been able to have their way with the wood. Louvered and arched windows opened from all of the outside walls. Overhead fans stirred the porridge air. Light-colored paint contrasted with vases of lush, green indoor plants and freshly cut orchids floated in bowls sitting on the surface of antique mahogany furniture. Buffed floors with a few carpets covered the dark polished shine of the grain. Portraits of old Vietnamese peasants and French aristocrats mixed with the requisite landscapes, water lilies the primary theme. Jasmine in the air. It smelled of newfound fortune not shared with the other workers in this people's Eden, a country only just discovering the rewards of free enterprise. What that meant was the rulers of our closed society could more easily enjoy their villas in the south of France, while the rest of us tried to squeeze the life out of every dong that crossed our fingers.

Three floors. I made my way slowly through the many rooms, all in perfect order. Rifling the drawers in the master suite, I found a new Sig Sauer P226 pistol and a wad of five hundred thousand dong notes. I put both in my pocket, knowing full well they wouldn't survive the next search by the police and military, not feeling in the least guilty that a hybrid Chinese charity could benefit rather than a homegrown corruption that would be spent at the brothels in the Thu Duc District. Since I wasn't officially allowed to carry a weapon, I would keep the gun for what I already sensed was going to be a dangerous investigation and turn over the currency to the AIDS hospice newly opened on Mi Lam Street.

In the roll top desk, a scrapbook. Nguyen in most of the black and white grainy pictures. Smiling in some, he was often dressed as a North Vietnamese soldier. Floppy rubber tire sandals and black pajama pants. A fatigue blouse. An AK-47 in his hands and bottle grenades tied to his waist. It was easy to see he was in command by the way the others looked at him or shrunk in his image. The photos were organized in a time progression. As the war grew old, so did Nguyen. The peasant fighter transformed into an officer. Next, a high-collared bureaucrat and Uncle Ho look-alike, wispy silver beard and all. More recently, in a dark suit, white shirt, and tie. I went back to the beginning.

It was a photo taken in the jungle. Five men standing in front of a banyan tree as wide as one of the ancient Peugeots that whined and coughed in the streets. The print was almost identical to the one that now rested on Nguyen's stiffening body downstairs. It felt as if the picture were the second snapped by the photographer to make sure at least one came out right. All the soldiers were heavily armed, and the snapshot had to have been taken somewhere around 1970. Three bodies were at the men's feet. Young girls. Corpses mutilated and the remaining clothes torn filthy rags. Three pure-bred Vietnamese.

One of the soldiers was holding a girl's head up by the hair and smiling. The grinning NVA was Le Dian Phu, a recently murdered politburo member. Besides Phu, I only recognized a young Nguyen. But I could guess who at least one of the other men in the picture was. A few days ago, I'd been to his house too. The .22 slug that passed through his skull hadn't been as tidy as the one that killed Nguyen, rendering the man's face unrecognizable. Tran Huy Phong, the second politburo official to be shot in the back of the head. We now had a dead Nguyen, Phu, and Phong, all with toy cobras and this photo on their chests, ears amputated, and .22 bullets in their scrambled brains. That meant two to go if the killer was aiming for a clean sweep. I put the picture in my vest pocket and went down to the first floor, wondering if I really cared whether these murderous, ruling-class thieves had been executed by someone who probably deserved some peace. I patted the photo and walked out of the muggy, ghost-filled room.

Downstairs, in the small dining room open to the veranda, Dr. Ngo was crouched over Nguyen's body. Phan stood above him, the cell phone in his hand, entirely focused on the chirping SpongeBob calls.

"Put that away, Phan," Dr. Ngo said. "It sounds like a cricket fight. And you know gambling is now illegal."

Bent over the way he was made Ngo's hunchback even more pronounced. Standing, he was shriveled and barely half the size of Phan. The one attempt he'd made to disguise his ugliness was to grease his longish hair so tight it sat on his head like he'd drenched his locks with a quart of congealed motor oil. It didn't help. Once anyone moved on from remarking about his gelatinous coif, they gasped in pure dread at his face. It was as if one of the street waifs who begged and played in the sewers had found a pan of dough and stuck wads together in an approximation of a human. Nothing was related to the next, just globs of pitted flesh.

A source had once told me Ngo had been in a Central Highland tunnel, crawling toward an underground field hospital, when a running dog Yankee rolled a grenade on top of him. Not able to turn in the tight dirt space, he was trying to swat it away when the charge exploded. What was left behind was a series of clumped scars that barely resembled a person—and certainly not a highly educated and experienced physician with a hook for a left hand. He was shaking his vile head from side to side and making "tsk, tsk" sounds as he examined the carcass.

"This reminds me of that old joke," Ngo said, staring closely at the entry wound in the back of the dead Nguyen's skull. "Why does an esteemed member of the politburo have a hole in the end of his penis?" Ngo didn't bother to look up or wait for a response. He continued to examine the bloody gash. "So he can get oxygen to his brain, comrades." Ngo moved his good hand toward the corpse's mouth, trying to force the teeth open.

"This old one used another method to breathe. A bullet. He seems to have gotten lots of air inside."

He chuckled at his own macabre, nonsensical joke. By now, being in his seventh decade, the demons that haunted him were beyond what even I could imagine. "Too bad he swallowed his tongue or he might be able to tell us who shot him." He chuckled again, knowing full well I wouldn't inform on his heresies and Phan was paying little attention, under the spell of SpongeBob.

Ngo tried to stand, and I stepped forward, attempting to steady him by holding his arm. He always looked as if he were about to fall over from the weight of the hump glued to his back that seemed to weigh ten kilos, pushing him toward the earth. He hated it when anyone touched him.

"*Du ma*," Ngo hissed. Motherfucker. "Leave me alone." He pushed my arm away, nearly ending up sprawled across the hardwood floor as he struggled to get to a standing buckled posture. I didn't let go until he was on his feet.

"Yes, grandfather," I said. "But I never knew my mother. She died when the French came into her village. I think they believed she was a Viet Minh cadre leader. From what I know, she was a rice ball eater, like everyone else in the family. Most likely she didn't know a rifle from a fishing pole."

"Do I look like I give a shit, Captain?" Ngo asked, now standing. "Your mother was a whore and the French dined on her bowl many times."

Phan seemed to find this hilarious. He understood words like "whore," "rice," and "shit," since they had few letters in them. Beyond that, his head was made of rotting chicken lungs. I turned the anger disturbing my spirit toward him, regretting the words as soon as they left my lips.

"When eating, chew well," I said to Phan, who was now unwrapping a Chupa Chups mango candy and popping it into his mouth. "When being stupid, know you are the maggot on the pig's ass." It was simple enough to hurt his feelings. It was like tormenting a retarded three-year-old.

Somewhere I'd read you couldn't say "retard" anymore in the supposedly civilized western countries. It was politically and societally incorrect. Not so in the socialist republic where I live. We aren't nearly as delicate as the blue-eyed heathens with the pasty milk skin. At least that's what I'd learned in the re-education camp. Besides, the Vietnamese had made an industry of teaching the nuances of what is politically acceptable. Poor students often don't survive.

"Now look what you've done, gizzard lips," Ngo said to me, nodding his revolting head toward Phan. "I think that's a tear in his eye." Ngo started to make a noise that might have passed for a laugh if it didn't sound more like an infant having an asthma attack. "Or it could be what's left of his brain leaking out like the last drop of sesame oil from the dumpling."

That night, I would have to light an extra joss stick for my sins. I was tiring of all the insults and apologized to Buddha under my breath. "For current slanderous thoughts, words, and actions, let me no longer want to have them for anyone." It was time to become more enlightened and less cruel, especially to those who were less fortunate than I. I turned to Phan, bowing to him like he was the master incarnate.

"*Me cua ban da co benh giang mai va cha cua ban song trong am dao cua co*," I said to Phan. Roughly translated, it meant "your mother had syphilis, and your father lived in her vagina." Before I could say another word, I remembered the guidance of my Lord. I would have to find a starving beggar on the street and treat him or her to a meal of *chao tom*, prawn paste on sugarcane, in order to atone for my sins.

Too late. Phan began to tremble. Within seconds, he left the room, scuttling outside into the traffic noise and smell of ten thousand rotting cabbages. I looked at Ngo, watching while the mush balls on his face morphed into something he must have thought resembled a grin. It didn't. It was more like a batch of baguettes that hadn't risen and were stuck to the pan.

"Well done, comrade," Ngo said. "Now we can talk without that *dan tu cu* recording every word to take back to TC2 for disassembly. And our hanging." Ngo had called Phan a "dickhead" and was happy Phan was now gone so he couldn't make a tape of our conversation for dissection by the Mandarins back at General Department No. 2 of Military Intelligence, the agency that lived only to spy on the citizens of this worker's heaven. A discussion with those dragons would lead to our dangling from the meat hooks at Chi Hoa Prison. I smiled back and bowed to Ngo's great wisdom.

"I found this upstairs," I said, handing him the jungle picture of the five men with their dead trophies at their feet. "It was in a scrapbook and is nearly the same as the one on his chest." I nodded toward the stiff.

Ngo took the photo in his good hand and held the snapshot close to his face. I would have liked to say he studied it closely, grimacing at the picture of barbarity in front of his eyes. But who could tell? His face was white molten lava that had cooled and hardened to approximate a face. He glanced back and forth between the two photos.

"*Chung nao tat nay*," Ngo said. These leopards can't change their spots. "Someone altered their lives for them. Then someone ended it. Do you think it might have something to do with the ears?" He gave the picture back to me.

"Of course, uncle," I said.

"*Tai sao?*" Ngo asked. Why?

"I think the three dead ones served in the NVA together with the two others who might still be alive."

"Go on. Your detective skills are quite astounding."

"Someone else has a copy of this picture or another nearly like it. At least, the murderer is aware of their association."

"It must be the Chinese part that makes you so inspired."

"Leaving the toy cobra and picture and taking the ears have significance to the killer and are a message of sorts."

"Please continue. I can barely breathe being in the presence of such genius."

"The murders are related to actions that occurred during the American invasion."

"Our leaders should award you the Civil Actions Medal First Class for your powers of deduction."

"Now, someone who was involved with that US aggression is seeking vengeance."

"Your radiant skills have been unappreciated by your department and you are truly worthy of promotion."

"As you know, esteemed cousin, that will only happen for the half of me that is Vietnamese. I wonder which half that is?"

"It's not the half below your waist. The girly-men on Pham Ngu Lao Street say that part is as useless as your mother's dry hole."

It took a while for Ngo to arrive at the true way he felt. That meant something I'd said had some tiny bit of value or the abuse would have started sooner. We were within a decade of the same age, but this game was as old as the years I'd known the troll. I bowed low and respectfully to Ngo.

"Thank you, revered elder, for the sincere compliments to both me and my mother," I said. "She will be pleased the two of us have finally achieved your acceptance and love."

"*Con di me may buoi,*" Ngo barked. Your mother sucks goat dick. "Hearing chickens fart is as likely as my 'acceptance and love' for either of you shit eaters."

"Admired brother," I said, bowing again, "we now have three murdered government officials in our current case load. Respectfully, do you think we can stop the name calling and try to find the avenging ghost who has appeared from the past?"

"Don't tell me what to do," Ngo said. "I'm not finished, you anal wart. Until I am, the entire politburo can drown in their own pus."

This made me laugh. Vietnamese were not used to having themselves and their entire family verbally assaulted in public by nearly anyone passing with a mouth, especially friends and relatives. Openly degrading others didn't include government personnel or anyone in an official position, least of all members of the national assembly, known by the common people as the Politburo. Few Sai Gon inhabitants, other than Ngo and me, would dare call our leaders "pus buckets" even when alone. For me, it was the one way I could battle the socialist machine.

The fan above our heads was motionless. I could barely restrain myself from flipping the switch on the teak doorjamb that would make the blades slowly cut through the heavy air like a dull butcher knife through a victim's ear. For now, I couldn't show any weakness or Ngo would belittle me until I was as shell-shocked as I would be standing under a B-52 Archangel raid. He was a feral species and smelled fear through the holes in his face where a nose should be.

Ngo rarely attacked my looks. They were so average he could not refrain from calling me *com,* boiled rice, the most common and innocent name for a five-and-a-half-foot-tall Sai Gon resident with mixed blood. Not much distinguished me as either Vietnamese or Chinese. I had black hair and skin more yellow than my fellow citizens. The exception to the blandness was the uptick in the corners of my eyes, giving away the poison in my genes. I was neither fat nor thin, tending more toward the skinny description, but with enough *banh tieu* jellied doughnuts in my belly to make me seem fit. I dressed as if I were normal, while feeling alien. I had no idea if I would be accepted on the streets of Beijing. I doubted it.

We'd been informed of the crime early enough that the stench of rotting flesh had yet to reach the unbearable coat-the-nose-with-Eagle-Brand-menthol peak. Still, the smell was nearly as strong as the skinned and gutted dogs hanging in the meat market stalls in Ban Thanh Market that were covered by flies and waiting selection by one of the local four-star-restaurant chefs. Why serve the meat of a cow when much cheaper canine steak could be fried up, layered in onions, and dished to the unsuspecting? Again, another example of our national discourse. Below me, the fly count on Nguyen was about equal to that of any gutted mongrel for sale in the shops. I hoped Ngo would eventually tire of the game, realizing there could be more joy in finding a murderer than vilifying me. I brushed one of the tiny airborne bloodsuckers off my face and waited for the next onslaught from Ngo.

Other than the smothering heat, the space where Nguyen had died was not anything close to palatial for someone in the ruling class more used to air conditioning and Waterford crystal. Of course, if he sold Chiclets and slept in a cardboard box on Le Loi Street, this would be a palace of unbelievable decadence, never before witnessed except on the *ti-vi*. Television. The one remarkable feature was the incredible number of orchids that covered most every flat space. Obviously, Nguyen was a connoisseur and collector. There are nearly seven hundred varieties of orchids grown in Vietnam; several are very rare. Nguyen had cultivated the rare and leafless *Gastrodia theana*, its salmon-pink knurled flowers on display next to an expensive Blaupunkt high-fidelity music receiver.

Ngo continued to study the dead Nguyen, spittle leaking from the corner of the slit that passed for the coroner's mouth. At least his focus was on someone else for the moment. Ngo used his hook to turn Nguyen's head back and forth like he was examining a durian fruit for ripeness. I relaxed and allowed my eyes to travel slowly around more of the room, trying to let my spirit fuse with the killer's, a trick that was supposedly real in the mind of Western crime detectives in the movies and books. They were my main source for criminal investigation techniques besides intuition, a trait totally dismissed in advanced police departments. I needed a sucker to lick the way Kojak did. Not to mention his contacts in the after world.

While no faces materialized, I did recognize the quality of knickknacks that adorned Nguyen's villa. That included several paintings that could easily pass as original Gauguins. Maybe they were. I would put no amount of audacity beyond the ruling class. My fellow countrymen had become expert forgers. Kind of like the way when passing a nightclub with live music in District One, you might swear the Beatles had re-formed and were playing for cold 333 beer. The excuse for the fake art was, as always, the barbarian Yankees, who, bent on our destruction, raped not only our women but our museums too. In order to keep evil whites from getting greedy hands on our treasures, we learned how to copy the great masters we'd collected, developing skills that existed to this day and could be seen flourishing in the Binh Tay Market stalls. If Nguyen's were phonies, they were still worth a lot of dong, they were that exquisite.

Maybe the motive for this crime was simple burglary. Any of the trinkets left behind would feed legions of our street people for months. But that was just a silly, lazy thought. This one had been murdered because he'd killed someone whose phantom haunted the victim until he was joined in death. Displaying my proficiency at homicide inquiry and mentalism, it was simple to deduce that the toy cobra and amputated ears didn't have anything to do with robbery. Ngo was right, I was a genius. Chuckling, the thought almost made the morning's noodle and rice broth soil my sandals. Charlie Nguyen strikes again.

Several of the *hoang vu* orchids made the room smell like passion fruit, but soon their flowering efforts lost the battle to the fumes from the street that came in through the louvered windows. The constant, shrill *beep-beep* of the cyclos and cars made it hard to talk to Ngo unless I was closer than a few feet away. I surveyed the room again, not in the least believing there was any chance I'd find a shell casing that Phan and I had already searched for. Whoever executed the three politicians and ex-Viet Cong left behind plenty of clues and another kind of road map. There was no need to tempt with spent bullets when the amputated ears, photo, and snake toys should point us in the right direction, unless I was as slow and distracted as Phan.

My mind continued to drift back to the cobra. When I was much younger, a mythical beast had crept through the paddies, cities, and villages of the south. Mothers scared and threatened their children with stories of the *Gan Con Ran*, the Night Snake. Bad behavior meant using his signature move. It was a silenced shot to the back of the head with a pistol. The bullet leaves wounds like the three murders I was now probing. But the Night Snake didn't only use a .22. Often, he nearly decapitated his target with a garrote, tightening the handles on the oiled and sharpened wire firm enough to cut through the vertebrae if he yanked hard. It was whispered he named this move "The Herky Jerky," because of the way his victims flailed in their final dance, spurting blood. The number of his victims was estimated to be in the hundreds. Back then, before the dong, we used piasters in the south. There was a one-hundred-thousand-P bounty on the Night Snake's head. Now, I couldn't shake the old legend, especially with the combination of a probable .22 entry wound, the snapshot, and the cobra on the chest. No one the policemen had interviewed outside had heard a shot. Secretly, I was proud of my homicide closure rate. This one seemed almost too easy, but I knew it could be my most dangerous and difficult case. Someone was guiding me. And I didn't like it.

By now, Ngo had finished his inspection of Nguyen's head. My thoughts weren't following enlightened Buddhist teachings. Mostly, I wasn't able to summon any sympathy for Nguyen and his fellow political tools, a sentiment I couldn't speak aloud. Ngo might feel the same. Still, there was no way we could let an opinion like that out into the universe without ending up hung by our toes in a Chi Hoa interrogation cell. I was barely able to enjoy stroking my penis when the American barbarians scrambled away in their helicopters from the roof of the Sai Gon embassy. I don't remember anything except my mother wailing, knowing the life of a Chinese woman and her half-breed son would forever be changed for the worse. While there were claims of racism leveled continually against the Yankees, no culture is more bigoted than the Vietnamese, who despise anyone who isn't a descendent of the dragon king Lac and his wife Au Co, who bred and hatched one hundred eggs that held one hundred humans, the origin of the superior species.

Ngo was watching me. At least I thought he was. It was hard to decide if his face was even turned in my direction. I had to focus on his black eyes, nearly encased in a roll of lumpy flesh that couldn't even come close to being called "cheeks."

"You look like a monkey eating ginger," Ngo said. "Time you quit being a vomiting cat and get to work. Put your dick down and get your hands out of your pockets for once."

"Repulsive" was a word I'd learned in my English classes and from the war survivors who treated their guilt with massive amounts of whiskey in the *Apocalypse Now*–themed bar on Thi Sach Street in District One. While Vietnamese weren't welcome there, my People's Police ID card got me inside, where I practiced my English and listened to drunken ex-GIs drown in their guilt. Ngo was repulsive, and I couldn't keep these unkind thoughts from my head. I tried not to wince, risking only a glimpse at Ngo's battered face. It was time to relent and listen to this honored uncle's wisdom. I bowed.

"You eat the flies from your mother's pussy and lick the wings," I said.

Ngo attempted a smile, and I cringed, almost ready to make the sign of the cross I'd seen on *The Exorcist*.

"Good, nephew," he said. "One day, you might get the boy seed out of your ears and become a real man."

I took this as a compliment and, encouraged, ventured forth.

"First," I said, "we need to discuss the obvious."

"You mean the air conditioning in this citizen's head?" Ngo said, nodding toward the corpse. "He won't be tasting the Cayenne spice in his fish ball dinner."

"When the tree falls," I said, "any child can climb it. We need to look past what is visible. Someone is trying to send a message."

"Sometimes, I watch the evil empire's TV shows," Ngo said, stating the obvious. "There always seem to be these young women with huge breasts, an attribute I do not understand as a target of lust." He shook his pot sticker head back and forth. "Anyway, these girls often say 'duh' when the question is so elementary it is beyond comment." He studied my face as if I were a gecko on his pillow. "Duh."

"When eating a mango," I said, "think of who planted the tree."

"*Du ma nhieu,*" Ngo snapped. Go fuck yourself. He stood up, pushing off the teak floor with his hook. "You state what is clearly in evidence. We have three murdered commissars, and you continue to coat me in the vomit of your worthless proverbs." He took a step forward, forcing me to back away. "How about this one?" he asked, his black eyes shooting streams of napalm into mine. "A frog living at the bottom of the well thinks the sky is as small as a cooking pot lid." He stopped only long enough to take a breath. "Your thinking had better expand beyond the pot. You need to start coming up with answers or our masters will find a camp where you can be permanently re-educated."

Threats. Another pastime for those in power. Just as cheap as insults and far less expensive than a bowl of noodles. It didn't matter if the warning had no teeth. Once, when I had eaten nothing but grubs, swamp grass, and mud for a month in a Delta camp, one of my wardens had blustered, "If you do not acknowledge there is nothing more important than independence and freedom, I will be forced to cut off your food ration." Unfortunately, I barely had the strength to laugh. Regardless, my grin was enough for him to beat my skeletal shoulders with a bamboo stick, while I could only dream of what a real "food ration" would be like. This time, I smiled, knowing full well Ngo wouldn't hit me with a tree limb using his one good arm.

"A man's tongue is more poisonous than a bee sting," I said, laughing and holding up my hand before Ngo could spit out more venom.

Both of us knew it was time to move from proverbs to action. For me, it was more that I couldn't concentrate when the deformed gnome was nearby. I closed my eyes and took a cleansing breath, folding my hands and concentrating on my personal mantra. *Asato ma sad gamaya.* Lead me from ignorance to truth.

"Earth to stupid Chinese captain-soon-to-be-relieved-of-duty-and-disappeared," Ngo said, nudging me with his hook. "We'd better start making some progress or a real Viet will be in your position by daybreak."

"*Vang,*" I said. Yes. I turned toward him, but still couldn't make eye contact with his Play-Doh head. "I'll summarize and you tell me if my opinions are as out of place as an elephant in a minefield."

"Hurry up before Phan slithers under the door," Ngo said. "There could be some delicate thoughts rattling your brain. I'd hate for it to be recorded and analyzed tonight at Public Security Police headquarters."

He was right. Some of what I was thinking might land me in a chair with electrical clips attached to my balls and my feet in a puddle of water to help the juice flow easier toward my prick. The problem was trusting Ngo. He hadn't betrayed me in the past. This time, we were in the swamp without mosquito netting. Ignoring my instincts for protection, I went ahead, wiping the sweat bubbling on my forehead with the sleeve of my white shirt.

"You will remember better than me the Americans' practice of leaving cards on their victims," I said. "I was too young to witness this, uncle, but I know it to be true." I pointed to the toy cobra. "I think that snake is what the Yankee soldiers said was a 'calling card,' meant to leave a message they would be back, were everywhere, and should be feared."

"I see you are a student of our history," Ngo said.

"More than the snake trinket," I said, "it's the way the three men were killed. And the picture."

"Go on."

"All were shot in the back of the head in broad daylight. No one heard a gun. I believe it was a .22 bullet. Fired from a pistol with a silencer."

"I agree. So far."

"The photo shows three of the five former NVA we've found bled out in the last few days. Now, the motive."

"And that is?"

"Revenge."

"Well, I didn't think it was sex. Or even dong."

"The pictures I showed you provide much information."

"Such as?"

"Three murdered. Two probably still alive. It appears they were posing. Proud of the bodies below them."

"Go on."

"In the picture, the dead ones seem to be a Montagnard and two flat-landers. The Montagnards were hunted then by the NVA and are still outcasts in our modern, progressive society. The other two, I'll have to give more thought. But they were all too young to be soldiers."

"That Degar was ugly too. With those sloped foreheads, they all look like rock apes."

"Thank you for that esteemed wisdom. May I continue?"

"*Lam on.*" Please.

"Early in my police training, I became fascinated with the story of the *Gan Con Ran*. The techniques the Night Snake used to hunt and kill his prey were intriguing. Part of what I remember was he had a Montagnard sidekick and guide who helped him move around the south."

"And you think this Night Snake is back to avenge some wrong?"

"No. Not necessarily. It could be the Montagnard. We need to find out more about him."

"How do you plan to do that?"

"First, we must decide if these clues are herding us like the old woman and the water buffalo."

"Not me, *lo dit.*" Asshole. "My job is to collect the dead. Yours is to discover why they became that way."

"*Da.*" Yes. "Still, I may need your vast intellect and connections to assist me." I bowed.

"*Thang nguc lon.*" You suck dirty vaginas. A simple slur that meant Ngo was softening. "I'm not crazy enough to get involved in this kind of political case. I want to keep my *cac.*" Penis. Ngo tried to smile, the result something nearly as hideous as a dog hit by a freight train. "It's the only part of me that still works." He reached for his belt. "Want to have a looky-look?"

"*Khong.*" No, I barked, backing away, waving my hands in front of my face like I was trying to ward off a waterfall of leeches.

"*An cac tao ne.*" You can eat my dick. Again, he was trying to be nurturing. "When they have hanged you by your eyelids from the bamboo rafters, I will remember you as the foolish half-breed you are."

"In the meantime," I said, "can you find out if any foreigners who might meet the description of the Night Snake have recently entered the country?"

"There are hundreds of Yankee devils arriving every day," Ngo said. "They come out of shame for the atrocities they committed. Somehow, fucking one of our *con di* (whores) in Dong Khoi seems to make the nightmares disappear for a few minutes."

"I seem to recall the name Morgan. Try that first. He was supposedly involved in that nighttime assassination of Comrade Ky not long ago. I will hunt for the Montagnard. I believe our Central Research Agency will have a dossier on the Night Snake and his accomplice."

"Don't call me," Ngo said, shuffling toward the door. Over his knurled hunchback, he said, "I'll call you. Remember, my job is the dead, not old wives' tales." He stopped. "Oh, that's right, yellow demons like you aren't given phones. I'll call the retard Phan. The code word will be *lon.*" Pussy.

Before I could blink, Ngo had limped outside and Phan was coming toward me, still engaged in his SpongeBob screen, the mongoloid smile on his lips.

"Did you make it to the Goo Lagoon?" I asked.

"No, Captain," Phan said. "But I got the Bubble Blower twice."

Behind him, one of the uniformed officers came into the room, scowling to see the department half-caste in charge.

I sighed, realizing full well there was no way the next few moments would be calming to my inner peace.

"Captain," the man said, "can we take the body away or will you be using it to stuff spring rolls in the Chinese Quarter? I hear you chinks like human flesh even better than puppies."

Phan couldn't help himself. He laughed as if he'd reached Bikini Bottom unassisted.

The prejudices were never-ending. Often, I felt the Vietnamese suffered from an inferiority complex that caused them to respect, fear, and hate the

Chinese all at the same time. Starting with the Ming Dynasty, their Northern neighbors had dominated every aspect of Vietnam's government, society, and commerce for over five hundred years. The scars had not healed, and it seemed many of my countrymen thought the next invasion would happen any day. And I was possibly the reincarnation of Mao, sent to eat their children.

"If the coroner has released the body," I said, "go ahead. If I find you have had sex with the corpse like your kind is known for, I will be forced to inform your superiors. They will surely demand pictures."

This caused another outburst of giggling from Phan and didn't gain me any points with the scowling sergeant in front of me. I moved aside, letting the man approach the body. The officer was short even by Vietnamese standards, and Phan towered over him like a king cobra stalking a mongoose. The sergeant's fangs would sink deep if I told him how I thought his brain didn't work any better than the dead one at his feet. I stayed still, knowing any further comment from me wouldn't be taken well.

"On the street," I said, "it is told that policemen eat so much rat *rac ruoi* (shit) they have their babies in the gutter beside the garbage. Is that true, officer?"

There was no reason to give the speech about "contaminating the crime scene" that seemed to be required in every episode of the *CSI* dramas. We didn't have yellow tape, gloves, smocks, or those cute little booties. All I could hope for was that one of the policemen didn't put his cigarette out in Nguyen's head wound before Ngo was able to dig out what fragments he could. At some point, we might be able to verify what we already knew. Nguyen died from a silenced .22 caliber bullet, the pistol forced against the back of the politician's head.

Stepping outside onto the small porch, ignoring the nasty Chinese stereotypes sputtering from the mouth of the policeman, I inhaled the essence of Saigon. Today, the heat had cooked up what must be a shipment of overripe hog that was now simmering from the butcher stalls in the nearby Ben Thanh Market. Many of the pedestrians wore masks like the city was in the middle of a SARS breakout, but I doubted the filthy mesh had any success against the reek of rotten pig. Two more policemen pushed by, headed inside to help the sergeant load the carcass onto the old Renault meat wagon parked a few yards down the street.

Across the way, an old Montagnard woman held a baby to her chest, the infant wrapped in the colorful weave mountain people sold alongside the winding Central Highland dirt roads. The woman squatted against the wall separating two shops, one selling dumplings, the other Coca-Cola, flip-flops, and fresh fruit. This scene would normally be unremarkable, repeated a thousand times around the city. But the wrinkled woman was staring at me, behavior neither the Montagnards nor purebred Vietnamese normally practiced. Gawking at another was considered rude in our society. An invasion of privacy and theft of a soul. Nonetheless, she watched every move I made as if I were a scorpion crawling toward her sleeping mat. I stared back, trying to understand the significance of her disrespectful actions.

In decadent western crime novels, there seemed to be an attention to the chance of the "perp" returning to the scene of the crime. That wasn't part of the Sai Gon culture as far as I knew. It was better to flag down a taxi and get hundreds of kilometers away before the national police began arresting everyone within blocks of the area. Nonetheless, I didn't see this old Montagnard woman as an assassin.

The police had barricaded one lane of traffic and the cyclo horns and ringing bike bells caused by the congestion drowned out any other sounds. Like swatting at a ghost, I reached in my pocket for a Gitane, a thoughtless, empty gesture since I hadn't had a smoke for over twenty years. The only thing I touched was the Sig Sauer. I was trying my best to be relaxed while I put together the Montagnard's scrutiny with the dead commissar inside. In the next few seconds, I chewed over the possibilities like a wad of betel nut. The woman continued to watch, no sense of peace or love drifting across the road from her black eyes and wide, squashed mountain-people head. The baby on her lap was quiet and motionless.

Scoffing at my old, fake loafer-like sandals bought for a few dong and advertised as "Authentic Guchii" in the Cholon Market, I continued to attempt nonchalance while I analyzed the absurdity of the beggar woman across the street being involved in these murders. She gave me the answer with a cell phone. There was no call, only a photo op. I was the subject and barely saw her take the picture. Her hand was hidden under the multicolored quilt. Still, she had to expose the lens to capture my image.

Immediately, I started across the road, trying to thread my way through the swarm of cyclos, cars, pedestrians, and bicycles. When I stepped into the street, the woman rose and began to shuffle down the sidewalk. Within a few strides, she dropped the blanket and baby, increasing her pace. The infant bounced hard on its head and lay motionless on the filthy sidewalk.

One of the oldest tricks in modern Sai Gon. Wrinkled, raggedy women with dolls. At least, the way this plastic one rebounded on the concrete, I could tell it wasn't a real dead baby. I had seen too many of those pulled from the river or sewers. The ruse happened often enough to call it "doggy style," because the third-world mongrels that populate the city will play with a dead baby more than a live one. They get tired of chewing the fakes into shreds with no protein content. Locals knew the trick, but tourists never seemed to stop being fooled, cooing over the "cute, sleeping child" while they dropped their dong into a dented tin bowl made from old canteens.

For a supposedly-starving elderly beggar, the woman moved amazingly fast through the stalls and around the crowd of shoppers and strollers on the street. Still, I was gaining, until I found myself on the pavement, staring face-first at a puddle of chicken blood, the intestines, feathers, and lots of other colorful items I didn't want to know about staining my recently clean shirt and poking into my nose.

Someone in the crowd had tripped me. The beggar woman was escaping. I sighed and tried to get to my feet, needing a helping hand from a young man dressed in the uniform of working Saigon. Dark slacks, a short-sleeved white shirt, open at the neck, and no tie. At least his shoes were polished and buffed.

"Are you OK, *ong*?" grandfather, he asked. I tried to peer over his shoulder and spot the woman somewhere in the chaos of the street. Nothing. She'd melted into the mixing bowl.

"I'm no more your grandfather than any of the other thousands who fucked your grandmother like she was a street bitch in heat," I said, pulling away. I was ashamed of the blood and guts on my shirt, the way I had fallen, and the old age that was causing me to shamble more like a one-legged cripple than a man. I'd lost sight of a woman who appeared at least as old as me. There was no one else to take it out on other than this poor comrade who'd helped me stagger upright. I felt the guilt of my harshness surround me like the white shroud before cremation.

"*Cam on*," I said, thank you, bowing low in my shame. I tried to brush the slime off my knees, watching the young man's face and wondering, harshly, if he had anything to do with keeping me from catching the old woman.

"I would compliment you on your strong facial features, but that might be misinterpreted in these times," I said. He was astoundingly handsome, with strong cheekbones and a hairstyle that must have cost him more dong than I made in a month. He bowed back, a smile curling his lips.

"No problem, uncle," he said, grinning even wider and forgetting I'd been his grandfather less than a minute ago. "Somehow, I feel we're related. Or our karma would not have merged."

Before I could tell him he wouldn't want an old Chinese half-breed exile in his family no matter how the stars were aligned, a pistol shot echoed down the street. It sounded like it came from a Norinco Type 54 9 mm, a Chinese knockoff of the popular Russian Tokarev TT-33 handgun. There was the distinctive *click* after the firing that could be heard meters away. It was the automatic most of my colleagues carried and practiced firing on the department range in the basement of police headquarters off Tran Hung Dao Boulevard. My first thought was that one of the policemen had shot the old Montagnard mamasan. I hurried through the crowd to find out.

With still a block to go, the screams and wailing were already louder than the *meep-meep* of the cyclos and growl of the old Citroen taxis. A cluster had formed, everyone looking down at something on the side of the road. Being the practiced sleuth I was, it was fairly easy to surmise by the clothing and size that the crumpled heap was the aged woman I'd been chasing.

As I shoved through the mass of stunned gawkers, I caught sight of two flip-flop-covered feet sticking out at angles that could only mean death. Or too much Son Tinh rice liquor. They were the calloused feet of a hill tribe woman. I pushed the closest civilians aside, barking, "*Canh sat, canh sat.*" Policeman, policeman.

The dead one wore the typical black slacks and silk shirt with gold and red stripes on her shoulders. Other than the fact that there was a bullet hole in her forehead and blood leaking onto her cheeks, she looked like any one of the other thousands of hill people trying to eek out a grain of rice in the cities of the Republic.

Dead. I had the odd thought she looked healthier than the deceased policeman I'd examined a few days ago. That one was a sensation on You-Tube and other Internet sites where gruesome videos could be posted. It showed a male officer on his back, his upper half completely detached from his lower, the parts separated by four feet of pavement and a few liters of blood. Absurdly, he was talking. He reminded me of a ventriloquist dummy. By the time I got there, he was already lifeless, but the digital recording was shoved gleefully in my face by nearly everyone I spoke to about the accident. He had been cut in half by a truck that lost control on a highway where he directed traffic. Today, I shook my head, trying to release the demon of that vision and focus on the fleeing spirit of the woman below me.

It wasn't so much I wanted to discover what had killed this old one. The more important goal was to contact my Taoist side. The metaphysical region where I could, somehow, put myself in the victim's spirit and listen to her soul tell me who had done this horrible deed. I tried anyway, using more empirical reasoning. Like, did the size of the hole in her skull indicate she was shot from close range? What was the probable location of the shooter? Had she been robbed? What did it have to do with me or the dead guys without ears? Questions I would have to resolve myself without the help of a true forensics team or even a capable assistant.

As the sirens got closer, I knew I wouldn't have much more time with the body, no matter my rank or position. Someone had been murdered in our socialist, crime-free, tranquil society, and that always made the security forces nervous and angry. They'd start swinging their batons before separating out the innocent. If I objected, I'd have to hold up my papers or I'd be kicked to the gutter, especially being part-Chinese, a feature I couldn't disguise.

The most important finding so far had nothing to do with the corpse. It was the handsome young man who had helped me up from my unwanted taste of chicken guts a few minutes ago. He was staring intently at me, not the woman with a new eye in her forehead. I noticed only because I was trying to work out the angle of the bullet and where the killer might have stood. If I could figure out where, the police who decided to listen to me would harshly interrogate anyone who might have been in the vicinity when the shot was fired. No lawyers would be present during the questioning, and of course, no one would have seen anything suspicious. No need to complicate life because of a murdered old Montagnard.

Now, the good-looking man moved behind one of those typical ageless Vietnamese women. She wore the conical peasant hat and full-length pink *ao dai* like she just stepped off the set of 1940s a French movie production. Modern Ho Chi Minh City females wore jeans and a T-shirt, unless they were going to the office in a skirt and blouse. His attempt at concealment was almost laughable, since such striking features would stand out in any Vietnamese crowd. Something didn't fit, especially with the way he stared at me and paid no notice of the dead woman.

The flies had arrived, along with a few roaches and even a starving dog trying to push between legs to get a lick. Every surrounding building was inscribed with the squiggly snakelike Vietnamese cursive and English translations, hocking products from lizard skin gloves to crunchy spider candy. All sold prepaid phone cards. Some of the watchers clutched rags or handkerchiefs to their faces, fighting a losing battle against the car fumes and festering trash. In a tangle of electrical wires above the nearest shop, sparks were popping close to the stucco sides of the two-story building. As the first whooping police car arrived, signal at full blare, the crowd began to melt away into the shops and down the nearby alleys. No one would want to answer questions. I stayed where I was. So did the handsome man.

The first security officer ran up to me, his gun drawn and about to bury a polished black boot in my gut. The kick would be mainly because I was Chinese, a sin worse than kneeling next to a woman who'd been shot. He was shouting, "*Ve lai, ve lai.*" Get back. I reached into my pocket to pull out my ID card. Before I could open it to show him my picture and official credentials, the good-looking man stepped forward and grabbed the policeman's arm, hissing something firmly into his ear. The traffic noise and my advanced years kept me from hearing what he said, but it was obvious he was a man of powerful words and high-placed friends. The security officer immediately stopped and came to attention, looking as if he might faint. The other policemen were close behind. Seeing the man holding their fellow officer and the way he was reacting was enough to slow all of them down. I stared, enjoying the rare treat of witnessing Ho Chi Minh City Sai Gon police, who thought they were gods, being treated as if they were ordinary worthless citizens.

In hindsight, I should have recognized this too-pretty man for what he was. Tall, attractive, confident Vietnamese men were movie stars, politicians, volleyball players, or agents of TC2, the Second Central Commission of Military Intelligence, our own CIA, Homeland Security, and FBI all-in-one. He was the latter, and I could guess why he was following me. It had to do with dead politburo members and missing ears more than protecting me from these goons.

The man must have told them who I was and given me some room to examine the body because all the police stood rigidly, watching to see what I would do next. It was time to astonish them with my detective skills. I looked back at the woman, reaching down and turning her head slowly back and forth, almost groaning at her singular brown tooth and an astonishing mole the size of a swiflet egg with long hairs hanging down tickling her chin. I made a few *cluck* sounds and then lifted her gently to her side, this time groaning a long "hmmmm." I took her hand in mine, marveling at the dirt under her fingernails and the calluses on her palms, expressing my surprise with a loud "oh." All of these sounds were for the benefit of the princely man and the cowed police officers. I didn't have a plan or much reason to continue my inspection, even though I'd viewed hundreds of murdered victims. I stood, wiping my hands on my trousers, not having the luxury of latex gloves.

Immediately, I stepped to the fine-looking man of mystery, a smile of gratitude on my face. I bowed slightly.

"*Cam on,*" I said. "It was very kind of you to keep these thugs from kicking in my face." I nodded to the policemen. "May I please know your name?"

No smile. He didn't even look at me, continuing to scan the crowd.

"*Truoc,*" he said. First. "What did you find out about the dead woman?"

"I believe that is police business," I said. "Can I see your ID card?"

He chuckled, no teeth showing. It sounded more like a grunting ape.

"No," he said. "But we can go down to Hung Dao Street and have a quiet chat. You know. Share a cup of jasmine tea and get acquainted, ignoring the screams from down the hall."

Hung Dao Street was the headquarters for the internal intelligence division of the Socialist Republic of Vietnam. Lots of invited citizens had crossed the threshold. A few had even come out scar-less and with all their fingers. On the rare occasions I had visited the well-guarded sand bagged offices, there was a lingering scent of fear, sweat, and gallons of cleaning fluid. Worst of all were the ghosts. The Ho Chi Minh City rumor mill told of the many bodies buried below the building. I had no idea if that was true, but I did easily sense the torment of lost souls as they tried to escape the evil place. Their spirits screamed in agony as I walked the halls. I never wanted to go to Hung Dao Street again. I smiled and stood, hoping I hadn't gone too far.

"Maybe we could just go across the street to Quickly Bang Thanh," I said, nodding to my right. "I hear they have an excellent *tran chau* milk."

"Are you finished with the corpse?" he asked.

"Yes," I said. "I believe she's dead."

"Any orders for your comrades before we leave?" he asked, motioning toward the policemen still standing at attention. Now, there were at least a dozen, none daring to interrupt our friendly talk.

"The size of the bullet hole means she was shot from very close range," I said. "It could've been anyone walking by. Whoever did it is far away by now. The police should try to find out who she is. There was no identification I could find."

He turned to the officers and barked a few commands, then back to me. Taking my elbow, he steered me through the few remaining onlookers. The normal chaos of Ho Chi Minh City traffic was already stalled because of the police presence. Now, it was *du tai hoa*, a fucking disaster. The man said something, but it was completely drowned by the *meep meep* of a hundred stuck mopeds and the horns of the Korean-made minivans that crowded for space. He guided me between the Hondas and Vespas, all jockeying for a slim chance of negotiating through the mess.

Inside the Quickly Bang, the striking man took a seat opposite me on a black-lacquered chair that faced one of the green Formica tables. It was cool inside, a testimonial to the sign on the window written in English, claiming it was "Air Conditional." Of course, the shop also advertised "Free Parking," as if they impossibly had a lot somewhere in this district customers could use rather than the few open inches of space in front that weren't occupied

24/7. Looking at the menu while I tried to compose myself for what was to come, I decided on a "Fruit Juit," made from mangoes and bananas. The man ordered a "Frothy Tea" from the waitress in a pink miniskirt and inspected me like he was trying to find a landmine in the dead leaves of a jungle floor.

"My name is Nguyen," the man finally said. "I have a story to tell you. Then, I want your help." All of this was said with the utmost of seriousness making ruts in his forehead.

I nodded, knowing full well there was no choice but to sip my juit and listen to "Nguyen" spin his tale. At least he could have picked a better alias. Every Ton, Dinh, and Huynh in Ho Chi Minh City was named "Nguyen," including one murdered commissar. I stirred my drink with the thin straw and waited.

"Please do not ask questions," Nguyen said. "Know that I am aware of your history and work." He bowed. "And your file is quite impressive, grandfather."

Again with the old man *cut*, shit, but he couldn't have offered me a much greater compliment, especially given to a half-breed Chinese and coming from a pure-blood Viet. Still, I was tiring of the "grandfather" description and the bouncing back and forth. I wasn't yet an elder, even if my knees hurt like I was when I made the daily walk to the noodle shop.

"*Vang*," I said. Yes.

"During the war with the American imperialists," Nguyen said, "the Montagnards sided with the Yankees. These inbred traitorous hill people, mostly called Degar, have always hated the flatland Vietnamese and found a way to get even for the supposed harm, exploitation, and murders allegedly committed by those from the cities below. They joined the Americans, bringing with them their tracking and jungle skills, becoming some of the most fierce and unforgiving troops in the Yankee military."

Stifling a yawn, I put my hand to my mouth, letting Nguyen know he was telling me something every first-level schoolchild in Ho Chi Minh City had been indoctrinated into at an early age. That was fifty years ago for me. The Montagnards were already hated, well before the American invasion and long after the hated Yankees scuttled away with their Satan's tail between their legs.

"Are those the same hill people our infinitely wise government has tried to exterminate over the last sixty years?" I asked. "I believe some foreign devils have called it 'ethnic cleansing.' Or a few say 'genocide.' But I don't claim to understand the delicacy of the situation and the threat of these vicious Montagnards to our revered socialist society. I'm sure they have WMDs like Saddam."

Even in my small, isolated country, we're aware of global news, especially when it is embarrassing to the lapping dog Yankees. Mostly, the ruling class in this Republic is concerned with keeping power in order to drive the newest model of luxury Mercedes. Threatening their position is defined as treason, and I could tell Nguyen was about to remind me of that reality. He was scowling, neck stretched and chin pointed well above my head.

"*Ngu nhu heo*," Nguyen said. You're being stupid as a pig. "I won't save you when your words are repeated. Even the rice balls can hear in this city. And I'm not on your side. Not even slightly. Remember, *thang cac be*, grandfather."

Nguyen was telling me I was stupid and had a small penis. In reality, he was letting me know who was in charge and that I'd better watch my bent backside. I'd lived too long and suffered too many pretty boys like him to be politically correct when it involved murder. I sipped my fruit juit and gave him my most sincere smile.

"What do you want to tell me, nephew?" I asked. "We're not here sharing a frothy tea for no reason. You must have some idea what's going on with the earless bodies. And I don't think you give a *cuc* about the murdered woman." Shit.

Outside, the neon lights were flickering on, filling the street and walls with colored shapes. Dragons were the most popular theme, followed by rats, vipers coiled to look like the regular Vietnamese writing, and Coca-Cola advertisements. It was usually hard to distinguish rush hour from any other time of the day or evening, but the traffic had now found freedom and increased in speed to the point it was difficult to hear anything above the whine. One upside was the number of young women peddling by on their bikes or steering their cyclos, a meter of thigh showing from the slit in their tight skirts. The more modest girls rode side saddle on their motor-cycles, even though that made things difficult when it came to shifting and turning and actually gave a better view of the tunnel of love. At least sundown cooled off the boiling smells of the suffocating afternoon and made it easier to breathe without gagging on the fumes of fly-blown chickens, pigs, cats, and dogs.

My ruminations of the street noise and almost bearable aroma gave Nguyen time to gather his thoughts. He needed me, or I'd already be arrested for my subversive remarks. So, I waited, wanting to hear how the next chapter was written and if he was an idiot puppet of the pseudo-communist regime. Sipping my fruit juit, I admired the short skirt on the waitress who was scrambling to service the room, now nearly full with after-work tea seekers.

The conflict raging inside Nguyen's head was obvious. There was no doubt he was clever, as well as tall and good-looking. I could guess at the pressure he was under. He was clearly torn by the decision to recruit me or send me to the notorious dungeons on Hung Dao Street for further re-education.

Unfortunately, I had work to do and wasn't about to get involved in the dramas that came out of police headquarters. Besides, no one had ever praised my diplomacy, only the results of my investigations. I looked at Nguyen, tiring of his indecision.

"Excuse me," I said, "but I sense conflict in your thoughts. Let me give you a small piece of advice that came from the Imperialist Secretary of State, Henry Kissinger, during the war for reunification. He said, 'The illegal we do immediately, the unconstitutional may take a little longer.' Whatever you need to find the killers will be acceptable, even if it means employing a wormlike Chinese detective. Or even the possibility of killing an old woman." I bowed, demonstrating more respect than I felt, a gesture well practiced over years of subservient ass licking.

At this last prospect, Nguyen looked as if I'd insulted his grandmother by saying she ate vomit and not chicken broth. He flinched, snapping his head back like he was trying to avoid a bullet.

"Talk like that could get you a private cell in Hung Dao, sharing your stale rice with the rats," Nguyen said, shaking his head. "I had nothing to do with the death of that unfortunate woman."

"Which one was that?"

He was about to take a sip of his frothy tea. Instead, he set the cup back down and scowled.

"No more poking like I'm a *con nhen*," he said. Spider. "Believe me, I bite."

"Then tell me what your eminence wants from a poor peasant like me," I said.

"A story," Nguyen said. "One I started before, but was rudely disturbed. Your words have stirred my memory like a stick in an anthill. Again, the tale begins in the Phuoc Long Province of the Central Highlands, the ancestral home of the Montagnards. The spies from the CIA recruited Degars to help the American fish bellies against the Viet Cong, especially to harass the shipment of arms and supplies south on the Ho Chi Minh Trail. The Degars were ruthless and fought with a vengeance and brutality grown from centuries of supposed discrimination by the various Vietnamese governments, always directed from the lowland capitals."

Watching the clock on the wall being attacked by a gecko was more interesting than listening to this propaganda that every first-level schoolchild in Vietnam had heard many times in an attempt to ensure the ruling class continued to be able to squeeze every last dong out of the workers. Besides, he'd already recited this fable. I pulled at my ear and sighed, letting Nguyen know it was, once more, time to move on.

Nguyen wasn't pleased. That was obvious by the way he clucked his tongue on his teeth. He stopped his lecture and glared.

"It must be a myth you chinks have learned patience," he said. "Again, I would advise you to keep your thoughts to yourself. I have much to say." He motioned the pink-clad waitress over and ordered another frothy tea, this time with extra milk and pearl tapioca.

Maybe he could read my mind. Or it was the way I acted as if there were a nest of subterranean termites in my slacks. Two murders today and I was forced to sit and listen to political disinformation. I needed to get back to work. I smiled, in case my voice became too sharp, having decided a gentle approach would be more productive.

"You're about as interesting as watching a water buffalo chew on rice shoots," I said. "Tell me what you want from me before I get too old to hear. Or care."

"I will ignore you for now only because you could be useful. Be quiet or I will send you screaming to visit your ancestors."

I bowed, motioning him to go forward with a wave of my fingers and a slight nod of agreement.

"December 1967," Nguyen said. "The Viet Cong, along with our comrades from what was then North Vietnam, were trying to establish transportation routes through the mountains along the Cambodian border. A few hundred brave soldiers came into Dac Sun and were attacked by the villagers. The freedom fighters retaliated, and the entire hamlet was destroyed. Three hundred Montagnards died. Old men, women, and children hid in bunkers they had dug out, but the mortars and machine guns found them. Everyone was killed. It was meant to send a message to all the other Degar communities in the Highlands. It was regrettable that nearly every able-bodied man was already away helping the American devils. This incident, no matter how unfortunate, helped pacify the locals and open up the trail." He stopped and looked over my shoulder as if he were watching someone out on the busy street.

Following his eyes, I noticed a man staring at us while he squatted on the sidewalk. Even from this distance, I could tell he was obviously Montagnard. The watcher made no attempt to conceal himself, his boxy face, or his concentration on the Quickly Bang's customers.

"Maybe you better get to the point and stop with the history lesson," I said, turning back to Nguyen. "It seems there's someone very interested in us. And I think it has to do with the dead comrades and the unlucky woman. Is that a fair guess?"

He brought his eyes slowly back to me.

"You Chinese seem to be in a great hurry," he said. "I'll try to finish before the next dynasty."

"Why don't you focus on what I don't know," I said. "The massacre at Dac Sun is common knowledge. The important point is what it has to do with the murdered Politburo members and the woman we just left bleeding on the street from the new hole you put in her head. Mostly, what any of this has to do with me. I feel like the monkey in the banyan tree, watching the tigers battle below."

"Why do you believe I shot her?"

"Every time you take a sip of your frothy tea, I smell the gun powder on your fingers."

"I came directly from the firing range."

"No one ran. I was right there, and the gun was fired from exactly where you appeared."

"There were many standing or walking around that could have done the shooting."

"I would guess none had your information or motivation. Or a pistol. I think the Degars may have come down from the mountains and you might be a tool in the cleansing."

"And I'm a target for surveillance?"

"Maybe now that you're involved in the investigation, you are. Or, it could be me."

Nguyen laughed. The first time his face had creased into a smile. He was truly worthy of his own TV series.

"You? Why would anyone be after you?"

I grinned, too, making sure it was obvious to the man outside we were having a jolly good time.

"Pardon me, but I would like to continue your fable myself. It will become clear to you." I bowed my head and waited for Nguyen's consent.

Nguyen only blinked. I took it as a sign of his approval.

"After the end of the war with the American running dogs," I said, "I met a Montagnard who called himself Luong. He told me a story. One that involved a man nicknamed Night Snake. And the slaughter of Luong's village. Twice. He started his tale with a few highlights of his days with the Night Snake." Nguyen didn't look in the least interested in the Luong and Night Snake saga, making me wonder if he already knew the highlights. The Viet Cong had a long memory and the Saigon police was still largely run by ex-black-pajama'ed soldiers, meaning this young officer would have read the files.

❧

The man was asleep. Beside him, a woman snored softly, while two young children next to her sucked their thumbs and imagined full rice bowls. The family was curled into thin burlap blankets, even in the stifling heat of Delta summer darkness. The Night Snake was closest, his silenced Hush Puppy .22 already pressed against the man's head. He pulled gently on the trigger and the victim's skull bounced, rising an inch off the pillow made of rags stuffed into an old T-shirt. The woman and children didn't stir, continuing to spend time in a dreamland that would never be the same.

The assassin's real name was Morgan. Frank Morgan. The Viet Cong had given him the title *Gan Con Ran,* Night Snake, and a reward of one million piasters for his capture. Dead or alive. Morgan's weapon of choice was the silenced pistol or a garrote, both capable of killing with little noise. Besides killing, his talent was a ghostlike ability to sneak into a room unheard and unseen, vanishing after he left at least one target dead. That was why he was feared across the Mekong Delta and into the Central Highlands. If you were on his list, sleep would soon be suddenly eternal.

This starless night, the target was a supposed local Viet Cong cadre chief. The space where the family slept was the back of a two-room hootch in a tiny hamlet a few klicks south of Can Tho. No one would ever know if the rumor about the now-dead man supposedly confirmed by the Rand computer in Saigon was true. It only took a single wrong word and it was a death sentence. A slap of a punch card and no judge. No jury. Just wasted.

Morgan wasn't alone on this op. Covering his back at the door to the small hut, a Montagnard scanned the surrounding dried mud, paying close attention to the tree line fifty meters away. His name was Luong and his home was the village of Dac Sun.

Luong had returned to Dac Sun after helping a Special Forces squad clear a very active Delta sector of North Vietnamese Army and Viet Cong fighters. They'd been ruthless, spending weeks in the bush until anyone even remotely suggested as the enemy was killed. Luong was the lead scout, and much of the body count came from his knife or M-14. When he came back on leave, Dac Sun was empty, the village burned to the ground, only spirits of his loved ones remaining. Luong swore to the animal gods that should have protected Dac Sun that he would murder as many flatland Vietnamese as possible. Within a year, he was recruited by agents of the Phoenix Program, the CIA's name for those directing the secret assassination squads.

Luong was teamed with Morgan, and they became the most lethal and notorious pairing in the country, giving Luong the opportunity to murder or help eliminate even more *cut cho* Vietnamese. Dog shit.

On this starless night, a man appeared from the palm and jackfruit trees, moving slowly across the open area of the vil. He was followed immediately by a half dozen more black-pajama'ed fighters with their AK-47s covering every direction. Luong clucked his tongue lightly on the top of his mouth, the danger signal for Morgan, who was already moving toward the thatched door.

Something must have alerted the VC, who were already watchful. Instantly, the first man dropped to the dirt and began firing toward the hootch. Luong turned quickly and pushed Morgan back into the hut as bullets began to shred the bamboo walls. The night was lit by tracers and the crack of shattering reeds overwhelmed even the screams of the surviving family. Aiming at the back wall, Luong began to fire his M-14 into the bamboo, shoving Morgan through the hole. Morgan rushed outside, while Luong turned, letting loose burst from his assault with one hand while he pulled an M61 grenade from his belt with the other and tossed it at the VC. Bullets had nearly cut the hootch in half, chunks of wood filling the air. Luong dashed out the back as Morgan threw another M61 and ran toward the tree line, Luong close behind.

Before they made it to cover, Morgan stumbled in the dried mud from the impact of a 7.62 caliber Kalashnikov bullet in his calf. Luong hesitated only long enough to grab the back of Morgan's camo fatigue and pull him to his feet, pushing him into the trees as the bullets exploded all around them. Dropping to the ground and protected by the hardwoods, they turned back toward the rifle fire and began to pick off the remaining VC one by one, their M-14s on semi-auto. The mad minute was over in seconds, and Luong helped Morgan to his feet, guiding him through the jungle and back toward Can Tho.

As soon as he felt safe and hidden under the dense jungle roof, Luong stopped Morgan and cleaned the wound, wrapping it in gauze bandages. The round had just grazed Morgan, taking out a clean chunk the size of a stubby pencil. He was going to be OK, even if it was awhile before they reached base camp. During one rest break, Morgan stared into the darkness and began to question Luong, both their backs resting against a giant banyan, the trunk as wide as a VW bug was long.

"Why do you do this?" Morgan asked. "I think you'd have taken their scalps if we'd have had the time. At least an ear. Or a nose. I've never seen so much hatred in one man."

Luong was not one to talk much more than about basic needs and simple translations. And who or when to kill, especially a need-to-know when his hunger for dead Vietnamese would be satisfied. In fact, Morgan used to think he got more conversation out of one of the temple monkeys, who at least screeched for food. Even in the dark of a triple-canopy-jungle night, Morgan could see Luong was thinking, trying to decide what to say. Whatever it was, Morgan knew it would be short and packed with meaning.

"They kill all family," Luong said. "I fight with Green Berets. Come home to village. All dead. Women. Children. Old men. Everyone. Their souls must be free. The only way, kill Viets. Any Viets. All filthy Viets." He began to grip his M-14 as if he would snap it in half like a dried VC bone.

It was the only time Morgan heard the story. But it was not the last time he witnessed the loathing and revenge that consumed Luong. Over the next few months, Morgan had to pull Luong away from several slaughters that would have threatened both of them.

That was just the first chapter.

The Quickly Bang was fast becoming overwhelmed. All the Formica tables now held patrons studying the tea and juice choices. As usual, the level of conversation was at a decibel level to match the screeching cyclos on the street. It nearly drowned Nguyen's response to my tale. He put down his cup and glowered.

"I've heard this kind of *trau di tieu* before," Nguyen said. Buffalo shit. He didn't look me in the eye. It sounded like the words had been rehearsed. "These malicious tales are just lies spread by the western money mongers in order to disrupt our worker's utopia. We welcome all citizens of Vietnam with open arms into the community and family of socialism." He stopped with the platitudes and smiled like I imagined a bamboo snake would before the creature bit. "Even the box-faced mountain apes."

It was not the only time I'd laughed at the absurd jingoisms and intolerance that sprouted like rice shoots throughout the country. One thing the slogans had in common was they were fed by the *cac* coming from the mouths of our supposedly elected officials. I had to hold my fruit juice tight to keep it from spilling on the table that already held a half-dozen rust-colored weaver ants starving for more sugar.

As experienced as I was in poking the tiger in the rotting cage of Vietnamese politics, it was a guess how much Nguyen would tolerate without having me taken to the basement of Hung Dao Street for a long chat with an electric prod. As with our politburo members and politicians around the globe, "crows everywhere are equally black," and I sensed Nguyen understood this Chinese proverb more than he would admit. I pressed onward, not waiting for him to make the call requesting a squad car.

"You must know where my chronicle is going," I said. "Whether or not the rulers acknowledge their existence, the mountains are covered with a few million tribesmen who would fight to the death to burn any commissars or their lackeys alive." I took a short sip of my drink, watching a man pass outside the window behind Nguyen. The man was on a bicycle and covered completely by wicker baskets holding chickens. Feathers drifted in the wind, covering him in a white blanket. I turned back to Nguyen, who seemed to be at least tolerant of my rant. "Our job is to find out which one."

"Even if I believed a word of your mythical wanderings," Nguyen said, "you still haven't explained why anyone would be targeting our leaders in the politburo."

If I wanted to continue in this investigation, and I did, I would have to play my matching mahjong tile now. I reached in my pocket and took out the jungle picture, handing it to Nguyen with a smile that let him know how valuable I was.

Taking the photo in his hands, Nguyen stared down at the death scene. "Where did you get this?" he asked.

This time, I couldn't contain the grin.

"Coincidentally," I said, "at the home of a man named Nguyen. Maybe he was a relative of yours?"

"No."

"I think you recognize him. You were just at his house and followed me. That was a few minutes before you shot the woman."

"I'm tired of telling you I didn't shoot that woman."

"Oh, I forgot. You're as innocent as the men in the picture."

"Would you like to come down to headquarters now? Or tell me?"

"It was upstairs at the last victim's villa. Three of those smiling above the dead girls have been murdered recently. A snapshot nearly the same as this one was left on each victim. Certainly, they were younger then. I think you understand and are only tolerating me, a lowly Chinese detective, because I might be useful. I'm like injecting venom to save your life."

"And you recognize the smiling men?"

"Of course. You do too."

"Do you have copies?"

"No. I just found it a few minutes before we were introduced."

"This print is why you've been tiring me with your story of assassins? You're as dreadful as a hairless street mongrel with rabies."

"Well, they didn't promote you for being handsome. You can figure out a mystery just as fast as it took you to find out who was truly your mother."

"At least mine raised me. It would have taken questioning all the whores in District One to find your true mamasan. Every papasan in the neighborhood drank from her honey bags."

"No matter how much I enjoy the banter, you asked a serious question. I'll try to answer to your satisfaction, though that might give me as hard a time as it was for you to make your girlie-boy friend happy last night."

"Go ahead. I'm speechless with anticipation and hard as a rock."

"First, I'll start with a question. Who else is in the picture?"

"It looks like some dead hill people and some others behind them, three of whom have recently been murdered."

"Did you recognize the man on the far left?"

It was the real reason this dandy was tolerating my barbs. He knew the answer and had only been patient while he tried to figure out if I was aware the smiling man on the right was still alive and now was the most powerful man in the country, Nguyen Minh Triet, the President of Vietnam. Triet had risen to power by supposedly going after corruption, both in the government and private enterprise, especially the arrest of Truong Van Cam, better known as Nam Cam, the Orange Man, who was the leader of the city's secretive underworld. Most people on the streets of Ho Chi Minh City knew Triet differently and distrusted him as much as any other politician who hid behind walled bougainvillea-covered mansions and rode in armored black Mercedes limousines. If I didn't already realize it, I'd have to be careful this wouldn't be the last day I ate rice balls and *nuoc mam* fish sauce with my favorite ivory chopsticks. I just kept smiling and nodding like I was another stupid, subservient Chinese.

"Who do you think it is?" Nguyen asked.

"I believe he lives in the Presidential Palace in Hanoi," I said.

"How many more have seen the picture?"

"If you're thinking about eliminating them, let me suggest the ones who've seen the photo recently are not the threat. More likely, it's the ancestors of the dead innocents at Triet's feet in the picture." Now, I tried to add a little hot sauce to the discussion, suggesting I was important to the ongoing investigation. "And maybe their Night Snake friend."

"If what you say is true, how would you proceed?"

"Not by killing every old Montagnard mamasan on the street. That will only bring more gossip to the case."

"I didn't shoot her. I've said that before and won't again."

"And of course, that's why the officers from Sai Gon's finest did nothing more to find the killer. You must have thought she was going to do me harm. I'm more important now than any rag-wearing old cave woman."

We both knew who murdered the woman. She was what the western military called "collateral damage," even if she was somehow involved, most likely as a sentry. When the North Vietnamese rounded up suspected American sympathizers, even old women who didn't know anything about the round-eye invaders were tortured, expatriated, or killed. Those government lackeys just called it *xin loi*. Tough shit.

Nguyen shrugged and waved his hand, signifying that the death of the old woman was meaningless and unworthy of further investigation or discussion.

"Did you tell me that fable because you believe the Night Snake is back and working to avenge the supposed crimes against Luong's village and the girls?" Nguyen asked. Obviously, Nguyen knew more than he was letting on, his typically annoying style. I'd have to be careful with what I said, even more so now that I realized Nguyen had intel on Luong.

I stroked my chin, trying to look like the classic shrewd Chinese.

"Just throwing a carp on your plate to see if it still swims," I said, smiling. "There's much more to the legend," I said. "But only if you care to hear."

"Go on," Nguyen said. "I'm totally hypnotized by your eloquence."

I bowed again, this time, acknowledging the compliment, even if it was as hollow as Phan's head.

❦

The two small girls spoke little on the trek to the Highlands. Luong and Morgan had found the children cowering in a bedroom closet, the supposed property of the degenerate son of the president of South Vietnam. The youngsters weren't there just to cuddle. Morgan burned the villa to the ground, starting the fire with his trusty Zippo. Ky was left to die, along with a squad of dead thugs. Outside, Morgan wished the trembling children good health and Luong promised to take care of the girls. Now, they'd made it through the Delta, past Pleiku and Kon Tum, and into the jungled ravines of Luong's Montagnard tribe, the entire time knowing discovery by the Viet Cong or NVA would mean instant execution. The lack of conversation was OK for Luong, who wasn't much fond of talking anyway, especially in Vietnamese, the only language the girls knew. But they'd been quiet and followed him into the mountains, the journey mostly on foot, except when Luong could steal a cyclo. They existed on water, grubs, overripe bananas, bamboo shoots, and moldy rice. As the three refugees got within a few klicks of the destination, Luong began to feel the dread of what he might discover as if a coffin were closing around them. Besides, Luong had found something inside Ky's mansion that kept him focused on one thing.

On the last visit to Dac Sun, Luong had found the village burned to the ground and nearly three hundred butchered at the hands of the Viet Cong and NVA. Afterward, the few who'd made it to safety in the bush began rebuilding the vil with Luong's help. His work lasted only a few weeks. Then, he turned his energy into squeezing the blood out of every flatland

Vietnamese he could kill, torturing the unlucky few he encountered when he had a few extra minutes. Luong had no illusions about what might await him this time in Dac Sun. He didn't know where else to take the girls and wasn't about to abandon them with any lowland Vietnamese, who were all thieves, pedophiles, liars, rapists, and murderers. Leaving the girls cowering behind a banyan tree, he silently approached the clearing that was Dac Sun.

The houses were built on pine stilts, the roofs steep and thatched. Stairways led up to porches and open doors. Cooking pots and three-legged stools littered the verandas. Below the few homes, pigs were tethered and chickens pecked for crumbs and bugs. A few naked children chased each other with bamboo brooms, squealing in abandon. Dac Sun was not even a quarter the size it had been before the massacre, but it felt like the vil was about to reach adolescence, even if no men were in sight. Luong watched for nearly an hour, trying to sense danger. None came, and he went back to fetch the girls who were still cringing in the trees.

"*Den*," he said, come, and beckoned them to follow.

When Luong and the girls stepped into the open ground of the vil, the children stopped playing, standing stiffly and staring, obviously knowing to run away from a man with an M-14 would be useless and probably a death sentence. Luong and his charges slowly approached, the girls softly whimpering.

Seconds later, a grinning old woman with one yellow tooth, a long-sleeved white blouse, and a red rag wrapped around her head hurried down the stairs of the nearest hootch. Little barks of delight came from her mouth. Luong stopped and took off his bush hat, bowing. The woman picked up speed as she exited the steps. Holding up the hem of her ankle-length multi-colored skirt, she crossed the patch of earth in a few heartbeats. She stopped in front of Luong, grabbed his left hand, and stared at his face, tears filling her milky eyes.

Within minutes, the girls had been introduced to the village children and were led upstairs for an afternoon treat of pickled cabbage and dried deer meat. The two city girls were honored as if they were starving royalty from another planet, while the rest of the women came out and greeted Luong as the long-lost brother he was. No men. Luong hadn't expected any. If any adult or teen male survived the massacre, they wouldn't be hanging around in the daylight even years later. The war was still on and the low-landers continued their slaughter of the hill people, the justification for their extermination made easier in a battle zone.

Over the next few days, Luong told the women what he'd been doing as they nodded their toothless heads in approval, smiles crinkling their brown leathery cheeks. He'd never lose track of how many flatlanders he'd killed, and could recount every slaying to their satisfaction and glee. As the women wept, they became stronger, knowing there was someone avenging the souls of the innocent. Finally, Luong asked if any men had lived through the bloodbath. He was directed to a cave complex a few miles up the mountains, a site unapproachable without being spotted from a long way off. He left the girls the following morning and went higher into the cloud jungle.

No one stopped him, even though he felt eyes studying his movements with every step through the dwindling canopy. Besides, he wasn't trying to hide. The trails were easy to follow, and Luong had been on the numerous paths many times in his animal-hunting days. Now, he only stalked Vietnamese and didn't catch a glimpse of the feared laughing Nguoi Rung, the Central Highlands' Bigfoot, who roared with chuckles that resonated from his fat, hairy belly as he ate his prey.

After a few hours of climbing, Luong reached the entrance to the hidden compound and was hugged by several men not in the least surprised to see him. He was introduced to others he'd never known and teenagers who'd been naked toddlers the last time he'd been around them.

Again, he was required to spin tales of assassination, especially his partnership and adventures with the Night Snake, a man whose legend had even made it up the slopes of these ginseng-rich mountains and provided bloody, entertaining tales of ethnic-Vietnamese carnage. That night, the campfire sent its sparks high into the khasya pine trees, fueled by the hatred of a dozen Degar huddled close so they wouldn't miss a word of Luong's stories. Later, waking to the morning mist, Luong brushed off the dew and began his descent after a long good-bye to his Montagnard brothers.

This time, the NVA hadn't bothered to burn Dac Sun. When Luong entered the village, sobbing women surrounded dead bodies. Most of the murdered were young girls. Rice baskets, cooking pots, and the few possessions of the villagers were thrown around in the dirt. Chickens and pigs rooted through the debris, finding riches they'd never experienced. Luong walked slowly through the survivors, his M-14 switched to full auto. On a huge banyan tree that had once been the focal point of the vil, a pink scalp with long black hair hung nearly to the dirt. Someone had carved the words "*Su chet choc den ke phan boi,*" death to traitors, above the scalp.

One of the women ran toward him, weeping. She was short, no taller than most of the dead girls and dressed in a multicolored skirt, now soiled with mud. Gasping for breath between each cry, she struggled to stay upright. Luong could see she had the village female trait of only one yellow tooth in the front of her mouth. When she got close, the woman balled her fists and struck Luong on the chest. "*Ma quy. Ban giet ho.*" Devil. You killed them. Luong gently held her arms while she continued howling, her face turned down toward the ground and tears puddling below.

"*Mot nguoi nao do se tra tien, me,*" Luong said, softly squeezing her arms. Someone will pay, mother.

"*Ho da chup anh,*" the woman gasped. They took pictures. "*Va ho cuoi.*" And they laughed.

⁂

The street sounds were increasing, the tinny clatter and whiney honking. I watched Nguyen as I spoke the last words, sensing he was drifting into thoughts of his own as he finished his tea, staring down, his eyes almost crossing.

"It seems Luong has found copies of the photos," I said. "I don't know how or when, but it must have given birth to these killings." By now, there was no need to hide anything concerning Luong. Nguyen might have known even more about the Montagnard than me.

Nothing. Nguyen continued to study his nearly empty cup as if it held the teachings of the Great Buddha, a spirit our masters had just recently officially acknowledged might have existed.

It was hard to ignore that Nguyen was handsome. I wasn't one to visit the monthly Bitch Boy parties in District One that featured naked cowboys with pink scarves and fake holsters as their only clothing, but I did appreciate quality art. Nguyen could have modeled for the finest Tran Van Can portrait. Tran was the Vietnamese answer to Rembrandt, and his oil paintings hung in museums around the world, selling for more than most Sai Gon citizens made in a lifetime. I especially liked the brooding Nguyen, a pose he was keeping long enough to make me feel a little uncomfortable. Finally, he looked up, just as a raucous group of drunken young students pushed through the door chanting, "*Chung ta muon tra, chung ta muon tra.*" We want tea. We want tea.

Nguyen shook his head at the childish behavior and mumbled, "Too much TV." He looked at me, no smile on his lips.

"Did you hear about the murder of Vice President Ky's son?" asked Nguyen.

"The story didn't make the *Ho Chi Minh Globe*," I said. "But I did hear the rumors around headquarters. Sometimes, they forget I'm a spy for the People's Republic of China."

"We didn't publicize the killings," Nguyen said. "It was a massacre and had to have been carried out by foreign devils with the help of some Vietnamese traitors. The decision was made not to disturb the balance of our harmonious society." Not even Nguyen could keep from grinning at this absurdity.

"I don't have the details," I said. "Is there a connection to these homicides?"

"If the theory you've presented has merit, there may be."

"What would that be?"

"We believe an American and a Degar were responsible. They had to be highly trained assassins to breach Ky's villa and kill so quickly. It was a fortress. They must have had help from foreign spy agencies or organized crime. Or both."

"And you think it could be the Night Snake and Luong?"

"One guard survived. He saw only two men. One was certainly a Yankee devil. The other, he wasn't so sure about. But he did say he was 'ugly, like one of the mountain baboons.' We knew nothing about this 'Luong.' Now, your stories add up."

"Of course they do. Do you think I've spent twenty years without a promotion so I can recite fairy tales?"

"How did you come to know Luong? Maybe it is you I should be investigating."

"It's a common belief the Chinese are to blame for every dead dog on the highway, let alone murdered commissars. We are all still spying for Mao, even if he died nearly forty years ago."

"That is a well-known fact. You Chinese continue to hope you will conquer the Kinh people who are the ancestors of true and pure Vietnamese."

"Are those the same Kinh whose parents were a dragon and a fairy? A hundred children from one hundred eggs?"

"Yes. The Hungs and the Lacs. Every schoolchild knows the story."

"Even the lowly Chinese were made to learn these fables about our country's illustrious roots. I still don't understand if the Hungs were communist or capitalists."

"Careful, coolie."

"I see you are not above racial smears, esteemed master."

"Not when you insult the Party."

Often, my tongue had nearly caused my arrest for treason, and this time I was pushing the limit. Tough mangoes. The murders were too much for Nguyen. It was obvious he needed me or my balls would already be wired for an electric charge in a dank basement somewhere under the Security Service Building.

The problem was I had been trying to keep Nguyen occupied with my rudeness so I could decide who the two men across the street were studying so intently. While their attempt to look casual made them even more obvious as watchers, they might have been tailing the drunken students now arguing over who had the cutest kitty on the outside of their plastic cup. Not likely. It was either Nguyen. Or me. Their reflections in the mirror told me they were amateurs, not too comfortable with the crowds that shuffled past.

Since the Montagnard legend said they were on earth long before the lowlanders and not born to dragons and fairies, they tended to have faces that appeared older and squarer. Most had thicker bodies and longer arms, prompting the city-dwelling Vietnamese to often call them "*khi*." Monkey. The two men observing us were definitely mountain people and were as unmistakable as I was a Chinese half-breed. Nguyen would have called them "*moi*," savage, the most common ethnic Vietnamese slur for Montagnards. Surely the hill people had earned that name with their unrelenting hatred of the lowlanders as their people were being hunted to extinction, down from a population of three million to a few hundred thousand still paddy farming and gathering wood in the Central Highlands. If Nguyen hadn't noticed the stakeout, he should be demoted to directing cyclo traffic on De Tham Street. I moved aside, hoping that a bullet meant for Nguyen wouldn't go through his chest and into me.

The sirens prevented anything that might have happened. Echoing through the buildings that crowded the narrow street, two police Toyotas raced by, followed by an ambulance. When they were past, the watchers had melted into the pedestrian hordes. I moved back, while Nguyen smiled as if he knew what I'd just done.

"You've been very entertaining, Nguyen said. "Still, you haven't told me how you know about Luong and this Night Snake. I would like it if you tell me now and stopped playing mahjong in your pants. I'd hate to have to arrest you for withholding evidence. Your old, brittle bones might not survive the beatings."

Arrest. Detention. Prison. Repatriation. Re-education. Cleanse. All the same and Nguyen would never hear most of the story. No one would.

Sai Gon. 1976. I was only a teenager. Too bad I was a half-breed *Trung Quoc* boy. Chinese. All the yellow people, even if only part chink, were suspected of having aided the Yankee fascists who'd just been thrown out with their devil's tails between their legs. Now, it was time to teach us the superiority of communism and starvation.

It was early evening, well past the time for a normal fish ball dinner. That was a luxury my family hadn't shared in many months as the NVA approached, routing the ARVN along the way. We'd been forced to survive on whatever rice and grubs we could beg or salvage from the Cholon markets that were just beginning to reopen. No one knew what would happen next with the country now under the control of Northern barbarians.

They came through the door like it was made of paper. The police were after my father, but I was old enough to have been painted by the brush of capitalism. We were pushed into a covered truck with other hysterical prisoners and taken to security headquarters, soon to be on our way to the

Z30-D re-education camp. Unfortunately, we had not presented ourselves to the local cadre leaders. That meant we hadn't demonstrated genuine remorse for our misguided behavior. Instead, we had chosen to hide, not having supported either side in the recent people's victory over the running dog Americans. Those who had cooperated with the edict were promised they would be gone for a month at most, while our sentence was yet to be determined. Of course, the party defined what a "month" was and theirs didn't have thirty days. Altogether, 2.5 million were sent back to school in the jungle.

We rode through the night, bodies rubbing hard against one another at every bounce and turn. The driver seemed intent on hitting all the potholes in the dirt road. Breathing the moist air felt like I was wearing a soaking wet shirt tight over my head. The smell was of rotting fruit and water buffalo shit. There were no lights after we reached the farthest edge of the city and entered the forest canopy. No noise outside, either. Most everyone cried or prayed, the oldest clutching their hearts like the next jolt would be their last. The Montagnard beside me was named Luong, and he neither prayed nor wept, choosing to stare straight ahead as if he were intently planning to kill someone or escape very soon.

At daylight, the truck stopped in a small clearing, the vegetation barely cleared enough to allow light to reach the mud we stepped into. A few small bamboo huts dotted the edge of the camp, and we were pushed and prodded outside, the men toward one of the outbuildings, the women to another. Only a few of us could fit inside the abandoned hootch, the rest forced to stand at attention in the sun by guards who hit us with sticks if we didn't immediately obey their orders. Or if we did. Several times I had to grab Luong as he balled his fist and was about to strike one of our tormentors. "*Khong phai bay gio*," I said, pulling him back. Not now.

Within the next hour, three more trucks arrived. When they were unloaded, we were divided into groups of ten and shoved to small areas near the encroaching jungle. Screaming and shoving forced us to begin clearing, mainly using only our bare hands. Some of the crews gathered wood and were instructed to begin building more huts. An especially violent guard with an eye patch and a horrible jagged scar on his cheek took pleasure in beating whoever was closest for no reason whatsoever. His tool of choice was an oiled teak stick with dragons carved up and down its length. A blow would leave an impression of one of the beasts on the receiver's skin. Or skull. His name was Duc, and he would later die the night Luong escaped.

The system of informants began immediately. Guards were skilled at picking the weakest prisoners and forcing them to report even minor violations. Things like yawning during a lecture or eating a worm without sharing were punished by skin-breaking blows to the body. More severe breaches meant days in an airless hole with a foot of water at the bottom. Leeches, kraits, and rats were the only company. Of course, any real defiance, like escape attempts, meant death by a thousand whacks from sticks, shovels, and clubs in caves the failed fugitives were forced to dig themselves.

Supposedly, the purpose of the imprisonment was to teach the true path to those believed to have become social deviants through contact with the murdering Yankee invaders. This was done through constant repetition of political slogans, singing of patriotic songs, reading pamphlets and books, plays based on the superiority of peasant ways and labor, and nightly brainwashing talks both in large and small groups. The camps were a manifestation of Ho Chi Minh's principle that "fighting is less important then propaganda." Our brains were to be scrubbed clean through continual, forced re-education. This was promised to be accomplished in thirty days, including weekly visits from family. The average imprisonment was over five years, and I never had a guest.

At night, after work crews had built enough huts, we were jammed inside and made to sleep on the ground. During the monsoons, that meant floating on a river of water. In the winter, closeness was our only warmth. Luong was in my squad and usually slept beside me. Talking was not allowed. We were instructed to mentally review the day's teachings and absorb the superiority of a socialist society, totally adhering to rules like "I swear to engage in self-criticism, to be a model citizen of the revolution, and never to harm the Fatherland." In quiet moments, we were told to "seek truth in thought." Instead, after a few months, Luong and I figured out a way to whisper in each other's ears so that not even those on each side of us could hear. That was how I learned his story.

Because he was a "*ban thiu* Degar," filthy Montagnard, Luong was beaten relentlessly and forced to do the dirtiest jobs like burning shit and skinning rats and snakes. Since there was no such thing as clean clothes, he smelled worse than the rest of us. And that was enough to make even the guards gag. Never once did I see Luong kowtow to our captors. His favorite saying was "*chi co ca chet di voi dong.*" Only dead fish go with the stream. He never surrendered.

In the darkness, Luong murmured tales of the Night Snake and the massacres of his mountain tribe. Because of our bond, we were viewed, at best, as untrustworthy outcasts, at worst, *lo dit khi.* Asshole monkeys, now meant to include half-breeds too. Even though I was younger than Luong, he had befriended me as a fellow pariah and protected me from harm whenever he could. This meant diverting the insane rage of the guards toward himself. Then, one night, he was gone. His disappearance meant I was beaten several times a day until the soldiers got bored. Usually, the arrested escapees were paraded in front of us before they were killed. This time, not even a rumor of Luong's capture spread through Z30-D. Now, at the Quickly Bang, I could sense his presence in Ho Chi Minh City. And, the best way to protect him was to play along with this handsome fool Nguyen and his bosses, who would steal the gold from the teeth of dead Chinamen or any peasant who dared exhale in their presence.

The young people had finished their tea and left the Quickly Bang in search of cold 333 beer, yelling and pushing one another in mock karate battles as they went out to the still-busy street. Now, I was alone with Nguyen and the scowl on his face showed he wasn't content with my tales of re-education and broken ribs. Without a plan, my only strategy was to follow Sun Tzu's advice, "If you are far from the enemy, make him believe you are near."

The men who'd been watching from across the street hadn't returned. They might have been more my comrades than Nguyen would ever be. Regardless, it was puzzling why Montagnards would be following me unless it had to do with Luong and the murders. Their spots were now occupied by two women in skirts short enough I could see mounds of black pubic hair through their pink undies. They were chatting with a ragged man in a T-shirt who looked like he couldn't afford them and was old enough to be their *ong noi*, grandpa. But, I had been duped before by a neighborhood rag picker who died with a few million dong hidden in his rickety oxcart, the money found after he was killed by a runaway cyclo in the gray roar of a monsoon evening.

As Nguyen continued to study his manicured fingernails, my assistant, Phan, appeared on the sidewalk outside the open doors. His hands were stuck in the pockets of his black pants, and he looked sheepishly down at the line of cockroaches crawling by his loafers, trying hard to make sure I noticed how much his feelings had been hurt by my abandonment. I raised my hand and motioned him inside, the width of his body blocking the glittering neon that made the street shimmer like a sparkler at a funeral celebration.

When Phan stood next to our table, I pushed out a chair and told him "*ngoi.*" Sit. This made Nguyen look up and frown even more, mainly because Phan's head was nodding and he was smiling like a mentally challenged infant. I put my hand on Phan's arm and presented Nguyen with my most sincere face.

"This is Sergeant Phan," I said. "He has been given the job of watching over me so that I do not piss myself or on my superiors. Every day, he reports back to headquarters so they will know I haven't betrayed them or our socialist paradise, especially to our communist brothers across the northern border. He's also my chauffeur and bodyguard. I'm not honorable enough to be allowed a driver's license or a pistol, but they do let me out in public once in a while as long as I am spied upon at all times like the secret agent I've obviously become. I only wish they would tell me who I work for so I could get a new Sony TV from my foreign pay masters."

As I checked that the newly found revolver was still in my pocket, I watched Phan keep on wagging his head and staring at Nguyen, the grin getting bigger every second.

Nguyen wasn't impressed. It was obvious by the way he glowered and turned back to me.

"Is this your youngest son? His stupid smile is just like yours."

"No. He has been blessed with only Vietnamese blood."

"Again, you test my patience."

"I was only pointing out that he doesn't look at all like me. No slanted eyes and he favors the wide brow of someone whose seed came from along the Mekong."

"I don't care whose spawn he is. Tell him to go. Our business is about over."

Turning to Phan, I pointed to the door and said, "*Cho doi ben ngoai.*" Wait outside. He went, looking like a whipped street mutt.

Nothing seemed to faze Nguyen. At least none that I could tell by the impenetrable look on his poster-child face. He was staring at me in judgment, his black eyes clear and intense, and I thought I might soon be sorting slugs in the nearest farm collective, trying to occasionally chew one without being beaten bloody by an observant guard. Nguyen cleared his throat as if he was about to address the politburo.

"I will let this go for now," he said, leaning closer to make his point. "But, first I need to know everything about this American Night Snake you describe. I do not believe the Luong character could have done the things you claim without outside help. He has to be led by a capitalist agitator. As they say on *farang* TV, 'even your impressions will help.'"

Little by little, I was becoming more convinced my theory was true. Even if Nguyen wouldn't tell me everything he was aware of, unwilling to let a humble Chinaman in on the details, the Luong–Night Snake connection was more than plausible. The dilemma for me was trying to satisfy Nguyen while pursuing my own investigation, all without ending up having my finger- and toenails slowly removed as Nguyen watched while using a buffer and clear polish on his. While I agreed with Nguyen's conclusion, I knew nothing about the modern-day Night Snake and I was sure Nguyen could find out much more. And faster. Still, by remembering the descriptions and stories Luong whispered during our miraculous transformation into patriotic citizens facilitated by our compassionate leaders, I could guess the Montagnard was a player in the murders. Nothing I could tell Nguyen about the Night Snake was firsthand, only hushed conversations gathered between sessions of mud eating and beatings, while we felt our bodies leech slowly away.

It was difficult to be coy with this man. I would have to take advantage of the belief among Nguyen's kind that anyone tainted with Chinese blood, even if a half-breed, could never be truly understood. I made my face as blank as the waitress who sat behind the Formica counter, scrubbing flowered teacups with a brown towel she might have pulled from the gutter.

"I've told you everything," I said. "The rat will never understand the snake, even as he kicks his legs and slides down the krait's throat. He only knows he is being eaten."

"Spare me from the Buddhist *phan bo*," bullshit, Nguyen said. "I have no desire to be lectured on my karma making me come back as a cockroach or listen to your boring proverbs. Just give me some notion of the Night Snake from what you heard."

"That's like asking the monkey to tell you why the cow moos," I said. "I had no—what do they say—'point of reference.' The only white face I'd seen when I was thrown in the re-education camp with Luong was carrying an M16 and handing out cans of Spam to starving people in my village while the huts burning from his Zippo smoked behind us. I later was taught they were all *farang* devils and would eat my eyeballs if I didn't fight them. In that context, I knew only that the Night Snake was even more powerful and had more magic than the rest."

Nguyen wasn't one to smile, even if he meant it to be eerily threatening. Or seductive. As I once heard said about Vietnamese government officials, "smiles are expensive," and Nguyen must have been a beggar. He just stared, trying to make me feel like I was guilty of some unstated major offense, while he refused to blink and his eyes attempted to turn me to stone. Sorry, I was as good as him at this game, an old Chinese skill.

"You are testing my patience," Nguyen said. "I do not think your brain has been completely boiled by the opium you smoke most nights."

Uh-oh. This was something I needed to squelch. He must have read my file even before this supposed accidental meeting and was making it known he was aware of my vices. Blackmail would be a minor sin for Nguyen, and I smiled as if I were being tolerant of a grandchild who'd just pissed on my sandals.

"'Boiled'?" I asked. "I have allowed my thoughts and action to take me to the place most desired by the Buddha. That is to end my suffering and help those more in need than myself. I do not need the magic sap to keep me on the right path."

"Then why do I have an entire picture portfolio filled with photos of you going into Ma Jing's?"

"Strictly for police reasons. I am not at liberty to discuss an ongoing investigation."

"More *phan bo*. You even look guilty, while trying to not shit your pajamas, old one."

"I do not need the dream world for escape. There is too much work to be done on this earth to chase the dragon."

"Enough," Nguyen snapped, slamming his fist on the table and spilling what was left of his frothy tea. "I will not tolerate anymore of your lies. Tell me about the Night Snake or I will have boiling soybean oil poured down your treacherous throat."

My internal enemy, the bubble that started in the back of my head when I was about to smash someone or something, was building and about to burst like Nguyen's skull would if I squashed it between my calloused hands. This disrespectful mosquito's head was filled with sour blood and would splatter the walls of the Quickly Bang with brain matter if he didn't cease with the insults and demands. The anti-Buddha was about to run amok, and I would use the years of martial arts training to pinch his ears together and. . . .

I did nothing. Standing, I politely slid my chair into its resting place under the table and turned to leave before the red monster growing behind my eyes overwhelmed me and Nguyen's head was made into rice paste. My fingers brushed the pistol I'd stolen from the dead man's house, tempting me further. But I nodded and bowed, starting to leave without the requisite smile.

"*Ngoi fuck xuong*," Nguyen hissed. Sit the fuck down.

I didn't and started toward the honking horns and chaos on the neon-lit street where Phan was waiting, totally absorbed in defeating the anchovy assault on his SpongeBob cell phone game.

Fury. I had trouble with the Third Noble Truth. I had allowed the anger samsara to control my energy too often, and it was time to light a thousand joss sticks. Again. Beyond being a half-caste, my episodes of rage had assured a slow rise through the detective ranks and guaranteed I'd be a captain, or lower, for my earthly cycle. I took a step toward the bouncing fish on Phan's screen.

Nguyen grabbed my arm and tried to pull me back. I knew there was no chance I could fight without ending up a piece of charcoal floating on one of the funeral barges that passed on the Sai Gon River. Resistance was suicide, a slogan that my masters should have trumpeted around the country.

I pulled a quick Cuong Nhu serpent kata and had Nguyen's arm in a grip that would cause bones to snap if he fought back. Or moved.

Stalemate. He knew I wouldn't break his arm. It was obvious I hadn't reached the stage of enlightenment that allowed me to move on to the next level through an agonizing death. If I squeezed even a pound too hard, I'd soon be found rotting in a sewer on Le Loi alongside the cigarette butts and spider turds with no chance for nearing nirvana. Or he'd just shoot me in the face.

I shrugged and let him go, knowing I couldn't reach the pistol in my pocket before Nguyen got to his. Even if I shot him, his comrades in the intelligence branch would hunt me down, probably killing everyone they believed was part of my family just for amusement. Besides, I wasn't that angry. Or foolish. I hated these condescending, overbearing, righteous, superior *lo dits*. Assholes. They seemed to control my life and wanted my thoughts, too. Still, I wasn't prepared to die quite yet.

Nguyen was sending out sparks as he tried to melt me with his hollow black eyes. His hatred seemed even more embedded than mine. Here was a lowlife toad of a half-man challenging the authority of both him and the ruling class in our classless proletarian society.

This little Quickly Bang drama wasn't over yet. While I believed I'd been considerate and self-protective in releasing Nguyen's arm, he couldn't tolerate the insolence of my grip. Stepping closer, he slapped me, the *crack* of his hand on my cheek causing even Phan to look startled. I'd seen the blow coming. And let it happen, the film playing in slow motion. Nguyen, while handsome and fit, wasn't as quick as the lowliest white belt in my Cuong Nhu dojo. His arms seemed muscled, and he must have got his bulk from pumping iron or eating steroids like so many of the deviant Westerners who felt bursting biceps and pushing cement-filled tractor tires made them men. Turning my head slightly nearly canceled the impact to the point that I recited my mantra twice before the breeze settled from his swing.

We stood there glaring at each other for a few seconds, seemingly deciding who would take the lead in the next act. At least Nguyen knew. I was already floating away in a Black Pearl dream, a remnant of too many bowls the night before at Ma Jing's. Combined with the drone of my mantra, I was calming the devils, even if it killed me. Certainly attacking this apparatchik would be terminal disrespect.

The horrors wouldn't let me escape. My mind, while trying to blank out the pressures of a world entangled in gargoyles, drifted to another picture that had recently appeared on my desk. It was a composite photo of three journalists who'd been murdered the same night. At least the black lumps of charcoal could have once been humans. All three were doused with gasoline in their separate beds and lit on fire. Coincidentally, they had pooled information on an exposé of corruption inside the Communist Party of Vietnam that appeared in the *Ho Chi Minh City News*, the closest my countrymen could come to an anti-government publication. I'd been trying to place this man ever since he appeared. Now, I remembered Nguyen had been one of the officers pictured, standing beside a bed, looking truly shocked like all the others, one of whom probably supplied the matches. I slowly exhaled and turned away from Nguyen, moving toward the street, understanding it was time to show the man some deference.

Cliché. Or maybe it was too much TV. I lipped the words as they came out of Nguyen's mouth.

"*Ban se duroc nghe tu toi.*" You'll be hearing from me.

I waited for the "*chung toi dang theo doi bạn.*" We're watching you. But it didn't come.

It was apparent Nguyen valued his highly polished French leather shoes by the way they were shined to a black-mirror finish and the attempts he had made to keep from stepping near anything that might soil his treasures. He stepped over rotting mangoes, brown storm water puddles, and any other garbage that threatened at every step in Sai Gon. As I went past, I scuffed my filthy sandals against his imported shoes, making sure I left a deposit for Nguyen to deal with later.

"*Cuc,*" Nguyen barked. Shit. He stared down in horror as if there were a bamboo snake about to climb up his leg.

"I think you're right about that," I said, walking away.

Outside, the early-evening shift was transforming the street into its nighttime incarnation, food carts closing and packed up on their tall bicycle tires, the vendors pedaling off to huts close to the river or in the slums of Districts Four and Five. Steel doors enclosing the more permanent stalls slammed down and were bolted shut, using brand new "Made in the USA" padlocks. The volume of rock music went up as the bars tried desperately to attract those getting off work with bands playing Beatles and Stones music the listener would swear was the real deal. Tourists were tempted by the sound and light shows that made the road pulse with color, while the sweet smell of rotting fruit was overwhelmed by the exhaust fumes from the increased motor traffic that sounded like a thousand beehives had been overturned nearby. Women in groups and couples holding hands went past, single people squawking on cell phones, the faint scent of violet perfume trailing behind their giddy smiles. I took in the panorama, breathing slowly, having made the decision to fuck Nguyen and his kind with as sharp a stick as I could carve.

By the time I reached Phan, he'd shifted his concentration from the dolphin chirps of SpongeBob's world to shock of watching my behavior with one of the masters-of-the-universe category, rebellious actions no good patriotic Viet would dare take.

"Should I drive you to Ma Jing's?" Phan asked. "You look like you need to relax."

Out of the mouth of babes. Or something like that. I'd heard it said on TV by American actors and on infomercials. Or maybe it was one of those Christian psalms. Certainly not Buddhist or Chinese. Sometimes Phan amazed me with his childlike ability to reduce things to their lowest, most obvious element. While SpongeBob was his opiate, he could easily grasp my need for a bowl of the Golden Triangle's finest. The possibility made me smile and not worry that Nguyen or one of his lackeys would follow.

As we drove toward Cholon, the District Five Chinatown, I began to unwind, the dreamworld so close I could smell the clouds. Outside, advertising on the shops changed from the snakelike cursive of Vietnamese to the boxy writing of Chinese. The building fronts began to display the rounded tiles of Chinatowns I'd seen pictured around the world. Dragons and lions were everywhere in more colors and shades than I could ever describe.

Cooking rice, boiling chicken, and MSG smells replaced the decaying aroma of the rest of Sai Gon, and I knew we were getting close by the views of the river that appeared between the houses and businesses. My arms were the first to begin itching, then my head. I didn't bother to scratch, knowing full well we were minutes away from Ma Jing's.

The black Toyota with tinted windows behind us probably held at least two detectives who'd been ordered to keep track of my movements. They weren't there to enforce the strict laws against opium passed over a century ago to keep the scourge brought into the country by the Chinese devils out of the lungs and minds of Vietnamese. For now, I was useful and might help Nguyen solve the killings. Not tonight. I had earned a dragon ride at Ma Jing's, and political ambitions of others or the possibility of rescuing Luong weren't going to keep me from her door. It would take something along the lines of five megatons of high explosives.

Phan pulled to the side of Ngo Luo Street on a block fronting the Sai Gon River between a long row of ramshackle warehouses that appeared to be slowly sinking into the water. They'd looked that way for a hundred years. Only a fire or bomb would change their history. Ma Jing's didn't have a sign advertising "*Thuoc Phien Den*," opium den, nor a drawing of a pigtailed Chinese man sucking on a long pipe. What it did have was a blinking red Coca-Cola sign and no windows opening to the street, just a warped wooden door and a man who seemed to be asleep sitting on an old metal chair that was about to collapse at the same time as its occupant. I got out of the car and walked to him.

"Good evening, Jinhai," I said. He didn't open his mouth, only nodded toward the door. I knew the right hand in his soiled silk jacket pocket held a buzzer. Two pushes on the button would alert Ma Jing that a customer had arrived. Three would mean trouble, but Ma Jing had spent millions over the years to keep the district police smiling and not pestering her business or clientele. Besides, if they wanted to shut her down, she wasn't about to jump into the river and swim to safety, only hold out more dong.

Opening the door, I waved to Phan. The men in the Toyota parked across Ngo Luo in front of a fruit stand that seemed to specialize in bananas. Huge piles of them threatened to fall with the passing of a truck or one of the regular "Ring of Fire" earthquakes that rattled Vietnam.

Immediately, my world turned dark. I stood just inside, the door closed behind me, waiting for my eyes to adjust to the blackness and the sour smell of comatose men and smoke from the dream sticks. Ma Jing was at her station just to the right, acting like a ticket taker at the cinema. No warm smile of greeting. No words. No gestures. Nothing. Only patience while I got my mind and body ready to make a purchase of her imported magic.

Two hundred thousand dong, or about ten US dollars, and I'd have enough to enter the floating world for the next few hours. Five hundred thousand and I wouldn't wake up until tomorrow afternoon. I handed over two hundred thousand and got back two small balls of black tar, no pipe. I carried my own, now resting next to the pistol I'd confiscated. Ma Jing pointed down the hall, flicking her wrist and dismissing me like I was a smelly street beggar. Small talk wasn't allowed inside these tarred walls

The space was divided into dingy cubicles lit only by low-watt bulbs or candles that kept the rooms in near yellow darkness. As I wound my way down the narrow hall, I passed men lying on wooden beds, surrounded by ancient mahogany beams, most of the clients with unblinking eyes staring into the void. The only noise was the bubbling or hissing of pipes and an occasional moan. No one seemed to care at all that they were on display for anyone who walked by, their arms straight out and teeth reflecting the muted light. Everywhere, decades of smoke covered every surface as if they were the lungs of a seventy-year-old who'd smoked three packs a day for his entire adult life. It wasn't like Ma Jing would invest in the latest ventilation system on the market. The rows of unconscious men were her best advertisement and the quiet was a major part of the ambience she was selling. But, mostly it was about the opium.

The drug was first recorded in fifth century Greece, spreading east to where it had become a cash cow over centuries for numerous civilizations. Strangely enough, archaeologists have found evidence it was used for medicinal and religious purposes in the Stone Age. The British had built an empire on its trade and enslaved millions of Chinese while they built their Hong Kong fortress. Because it could be shipped in bulk over long distances, unlike most foodstuffs, opium became the currency of trade throughout the East, facilitated by Europeans who wanted to dominate the market routes. While Asian warlords still controlled much of the world's current production, Afghanistan was the leader in growing the plant, aided by the CIA. I didn't care, as long as Ma Jing sold me high-grade opium with over 16 percent morphine, the fog that sent me to a world far away and not the tobacco leaf and pig's feet oil most of her shoppers could afford.

The hallway twisted and turned like a dark maze lit by only the occasional flaring match and grime-covered bulbs. After a few turns, I found my favored spot in a dim alcove. I liked it there because I didn't have to climb over drugged men or worry about them doing the same. It was a rare individual recess and even gloomier than the rest. A wooden pillow was barely visible at the far end of the plank bed. The walls were slats of bamboo blackened from years of exhaled ecstasy. I crawled in, taking out my pipe, making sure not to overturn the opium lamp as I lay down.

As with most things in the netherworld, I wasn't about to put fire to the first tiny ball I placed gently in the bowl. My custom-made antique pipe didn't *danh tu,* burn, the opium. The silver and glass lamp provided the steady heat through its three-inch chimney to raise the temperature of the ball enough that it released the active alkaloids, primarily morphine, vaporizing the poppy milk and letting me draw in its enchantment. One of the few things I'd inherited from my grandfather was a long, ivory pipe stem with a fired earthenware bowl at the end that could be screwed off and cleaned, attached to the stalk by a metal fitting. I held the bowl over the Ma Jing–provided oil lamp. I was lying on my side, making sure the clouds were released properly and prodding the opium ball into the heat channel. Within seconds, the fumes were being sucked into my chest and I was entering floating heaven.

The release of dopamines in my brain was the furthest thing from my thoughts. Science was immaterial and meaningless. What I knew was that the first smoke inhalation raced to my head and quickly spread throughout my body, causing a slight grin to appear on my face and the warm fuzziness of a few shots of King Cobra Whiskey to tickle my arms and face. The next ball would take me away for two or three hours, and I needed only to stay sober enough to let the lamp do its wizardry. I fumbled the last ball into the bowl and held it over the chimney for a few slowed heartbeats. I sucked and collapsed to my wooden mattress, letting the spirits transport me to the land of endless dreams.

Time meant nothing. Calm was the best way to describe the next hours. A serene feeling of quiet. No more dead politburo members, two-faced detectives, Yankee devils, or vengeful Montagnards. I drifted above all the earthly madness, forgetting, for now, that I would awaken to the same trouble I'd just escaped. Nothing could possibly disturb my sense of calm.

From somewhere in the clouds I couldn't identify, I was being summoned.

"Captain," the voice whispered. Then, as I ignored the call, preferring to stay in a land of gold, jungle, and tranquility, the demand became louder and harsher, accompanied by someone shaking my shoulders.

"Captain, wake up," the voice demanded. "There's been another murder, and you're needed. Wake up. We must go."

Slowly, my eyes opened as if I'd used a screwdriver to pry the lids apart. I turned a head that weighed a thousand kilos toward the invading noise, trying to shake out the spiderwebs as I moved. It was Phan. And he looked desperate.

"If I don't bring you out," Phan said, "Nguyen will send in a squad." He looked at his iPhone. "We've got less than two minutes."

The most amazing observation was that Phan saw anything but Krabby Land and the Klown in his field of vision. I tried to sit up and all the muscles in my body felt like mud. Even raising my head in order to rest it on my palm was like trying to lift one of the Mekong elephants. I blinked, hoping this was just a bad dream caused by some undeserved karmic disaster.

Phan decided I needed help to get out of my cave and he began to pull at my legs, whispering, "*Day di,*" get up, as he gently steered me toward the plank floor. Under the influence of the Joy Plant, there was no fight in me and I let Phan be my guide back to the planet.

Fortunately, Phan already had gripped the best tool to awaken me steaming in his hand. A venti nonfat cappuccino from Starbucks, containing the caffeine blast that might chase the serpent away. He moved it back and forth in front of my nose, pulling me forward all the time but not letting me touch the container until I grunted to my feet, sitting back down on the edge of the wooden bed before I passed out. Phan pushed the coffee toward me and said, "We must go, Captain Fang."

I grabbed the lifeline contained in the cup and took a few long gulps. Thankfully, the liquid had cooled in the time it took Phan to make his delivery, and I savored both the flavor and the rush of caffeine I knew would soon sprint to my heart, kicking the dreamworld to the gutter. Phan clutched my elbow and pulled up again, steering me down the dark hallway toward the door.

On the nights when I was alone, the path to the front was hard enough to follow in the darkness. Now, still under the spell of *when shee*, I would never have made it by myself. Phan was my leader, and he made sure I didn't break my nose every time I crashed into a greasy wall or stumbled on a pair of slippers. No one said a word as we made our way through the web and into the light. Not even Ma Jing, who only scowled as Phan opened the door to the street.

Immediately, I was blind and had to stagger against Phan in order to keep from falling, making sure I didn't spill a drop of Buddha's blood from my cup. Phan had parked the Mitsubishi close to the exit, and he opened the back door, bundling me inside. As the seconds passed, I returned to low-level awareness, the jolt of a new drug streaming through my limbs. It took all my strength and concentration to sit up. I managed, cursing Phan with every twist.

"Where are we going?" I asked.

Phan was now in the driver's seat, pulling the SUV into the limited traffic.

"District Two," he said.

The rocket fuel in my cup was doing its magic, and I was fast coming awake, beginning to break through the cobwebs and realize the case was taking an even more sinister turn.

"Ah-ha," I said, trying to sound like I had recovered and had a newly minted PhD in life and investigation.

"Is that 'ah-ha' meant to tell me you have an opinion on murders in District Two?" Phan asked. "Or were you just clearing your throat?"

I scratched at my thinning hair, wondering if Ma Jing's was a vast breeding ground for lice or if it was just nerves giving birth in my head.

"If you paid attention to what's happening in this city rather than drowning in SpongeBob's adventures, you'd know of the vast investment our esteemed rulers have made in District Two."

"Oh, please enlighten me, master," Phan said. "I so much respect your knowledge and leadership, especially after I drag you nearly senseless from Ma Jing's."

This was the longest lecture I'd ever heard Phan make, and it made me giggle. Or maybe it was the *ah pen yen*, opium.

"Would you curse me going to the hospital?" I asked. "Or seeing the fortune-teller? I don't understand your dislike of Ma Jing. Furthermore, I don't care." I yawned and turned away. "Go back to smoking SpongeBob in your pipe or dreaming of slaying the sea monster like all the other ten-year-olds in this city."

It seemed I'd never learn. Phan seemed about to cry, his shoulders beginning to quiver with the first signs of bawling. I had to stop tormenting this wretched man, even if I knew this was his little act to make me feel guilty and stop. Just because he was a paid informant and a mole in my life didn't give me the right to terrorize him or taunt him about his massive deficiencies. I sighed, leaning back into the fake leather seat.

"Phan? Do you often wonder who your father is?"

"No, Captain. It is not my fate."

"During the war with the Yankee devils, many of our women were raped and contracted syphilis from the foreign criminals. I know your mother was so ugly she made the dogs bark and run to escape her face. Still, the Americans would fuck anything that didn't leave a slug trail and all of them had the clap. I think that's what ate your brain."

Quiet. That was what I craved. And another pipe full. I couldn't shake the fact that Phan, the seemingly harmless idiot, would put a bullet in my head from his .45 without hesitation. He knew who paid his cell phone bill and kept the latest SpongeBob updates coming. And it wasn't me.

Saigon was getting wound up for the night's action, bargirls outside every door where music blasted to the street. They wore skin-tight *ao dis*, the first modern designs created by Dung and Dung Tailors, with a slit up the side nearly to their hips and their breasts pushed high. Some were that stunning mix of French and Vietnamese, one of the most beautiful female combinations on earth, even if Chinese women were the finest. Behind the hostesses, lights in every imaginable color throbbed to the beat of the knockoff songs and drunken men fought with themselves about which door to go through. The few remaining food carts hawked fried chicken satay or some substitute species on a bamboo stick disguised to look like it. Everything seemed to be a shabby, worthless, overly bright copy. Or maybe it was just my mood.

Long before we arrived in District Two, I knew what we would find. I wouldn't have been summoned unless it was another Night Snake attack. Unfortunately, I believed I already knew one of the killers in real life and the other by his legend. Soon, I'd have to make a choice. Nguyen wouldn't let me stall much longer or I'd find myself the one with the blindfold on in the basement. It would be best for my soul and Luong's life to steer the investigation toward Frank Morgan and make his myth real.

The New District Two was the invention of our rulers, an attempt to create a thriving upscale neighborhood for the growing wealthy class. Thatch-roofed hootches had been burned or bulldozed to make space for modern high-rise apartments, roads, and houses. It was the home to many politburo members who didn't relish brushing shoulders with the unwashed masses and wasn't an area I hung out in or wanted to visit often. Everything that happened inside its boundaries seemed infected with crooked politics, and a half-breed like me was easily blamed for anything out of the ordinary.

Phan stopped the Toyota behind the barricades and police cars blocking Dang Giai Street. Uniformed officers milled about, smoking and chatting, on the alert for anything possibly suspicious. Near the front of a stand-alone modern house a block away, Nguyen stepped out the door, craning his head stiffly from side to side as if he were looking for something. Or someone. When his eyes found mine, he relaxed some and beckoned me with his latex-gloved right hand.

The street was lined with immature palm trees, lit by the corner lamps that cast shadows on the newly constructed villas. In the distance, the horizon was broken by the outline of several cranes and bats out for an evening feast. The noxious smell that seemed to coat every inch of the city was replaced by the dryness of construction dust, somehow having overcome the ever-present dripping humidity. I walked toward Nguyen, trying to brush the vermin from my head, knowing the next few minutes might determine if he started the interrogation by pulling out eyelids if I didn't tell him what he wanted to hear.

Smiling wasn't one of my skills. Usually, it meant I was being cynical, embracing mankind's follies and the absurdity of my countrymen. Like when I harassed the cretin Phan, rather than acknowledge the silly "Chinese" jokes my Vietnamese comrades loved to crack in my presence. One that actually made me laugh: "Chinese woman wearing G-string is high on crack." Or: "Chink who stands on toilet is high on pot." Nguyen didn't cause me to grin, only squeeze my sphincter, making me a real slopehead *chat che*, tight ass, in the slang of the pure breeds that commanded and surrounded me. I smiled anyway, acting like a long-gone brother coming home from battling the imperialists.

"*Nay e*," I said, stepping closer. Hi, friend. This casual greeting was a little presumptuous of me, since Nguyen would probably enjoy watching me spontaneously combust more than shaking my hand.

"*Ben trong*," Nguyen barked. Inside. "And"—nodding toward Phan—"leave your butt-boy outside."

It had taken Nguyen this long to start with the *người dong tính* name calling. Gay. At least he had shown some restraint. Now, standing only inches in front of me, I had to stop this line of slander before it became the main focus. I had to do it with some restraint, not "the last butt I shagged was your mother's, you spawn of a monkey" that was roaring in my head.

"Are you having PMS?" I asked. "Or is another dead body spoiling your martini date?"

"How do you know there's another corpse?"

"Surely I wouldn't be here if there wasn't. You'd have the expertise you need at your command. All those geniuses from the homicide squad who couldn't solve a murder if they did it themselves."

"Since you've got it all figured, who is it?"

"That's simple. It's soldier number four. Or should I say 'politburo member'?"

"Name?"

"You tell me. I haven't had time to do any further investigation."

"Ma Jing's?"

"Last time I saw you at the Quickly Bang, it didn't seem like I was needed right away. I told you what I thought." I stepped closer so no one else would hear. "A little relaxation makes me think better." I smiled and bowed, making sure to act like a whipped dog, ready to lick my master's hand. Nguyen's reference to Ma Jing's was a veiled threat, letting me know he could have me hooked to a cattle prod whenever he wanted.

"Come inside, slant eye," Nguyen said. "Now that you're relaxed, maybe you can help for once." He grabbed my arm and glared sternly into my eyes. "And this time, shut your rat-eating mouth unless I ask you a question." He squeezed hard before he let me go, and I got the message of how serious he was taking this investigation.

"Because your brain is tiny, does that mean your dick is too?" I asked. Or in Vietnamese. *"Boi vì bo nao cua ban la nho co nghia la dương vat cua ban la qua?"*

Either way, Nguyen wasn't happy and reached for something in his pocket. I expected a pair of handcuffs at the least. More likely a handgun. Instead, it was the picture of the murdered men smiling over the dead girls. He pointed to the soldier on the far right.

"It's him," Nguyen said. "I don't need you to identify the body. Come inside and get a feel for what happened. Tell me if there's anything new to this one. And stop with the buffalo shit." He stepped aside and nudged me toward the door.

"Name?" I asked, as we went into the mahogany-floored entry.

"Le Hong Sang," he said. "He is, was, the Minister of Public Security."

I knew Sang. Ultimately, he was my boss. Every policeman or intelligence agent in the country worked for Sang and news of his death would be celebrated with many a toast to his demise with clinking Tiger beers. I couldn't help grinning.

"One joy scatters a hundred griefs," I muttered. The old Chinese proverb seemed appropriate for the killing of someone as evil as Sang, known more for inventing new torture methods and chasing schoolgirls than catching criminals.

Nguyen chose not to hear and strode down the wide hallway, the passage surrounded by polished teak tables holding multicolored orchids. He strode rapidly toward the back of the house, where floor-to-ceiling windows opened onto a garden crammed with jungle flora, including massive bonsai plants shaped like dinosaurs and birds, peach bushes, Da Lat roses, miniature palms, lotus flowers, and more, all focused on a gigantic fountain where a *gweilo* winged nymph pissed into a marble pool.

Turning right, we entered what appeared to be a living room, not much different from the ones on American TV. Leather couches, hardwood floor, rugs, end tables, lamps, bookcase, large-screen television, massive sound system, and all the rest. The exception was the glass bamboo arrangements, jungle and temple tapestries, and statues of the Buddha. And the corpse.

Nguyen must have shooed everyone away, waiting for my impressions without others standing around. We were the only bodies still breathing in the room. Sang wasn't singing; he was lying motionless in a neat pool of blood beside his earless head. This time, the card was jammed into his mouth, the toy cobra next to it, both still easy to see.

I stood above the dead man, studying what was quick becoming stiff even in the sweltering house where someone must have turned off the air conditioning.

"First," I said, "it seems they're getting angry."

"Why do you say that," Nguyen asked.

"The others looked as if the killers were relatively fast and just did the deed and left."

"And how is this one different?"

"Notice the toy and the playing card have been shoved into Sang's mouth, not just lain on his chest."

"Yes. That's obvious. What else?"

"See that small mark just above his shirt? I'd guess when he's autopsied, you'll find other bruises. I think he's been tortured."

"Anything more?"

"The position of the body. The first three appeared to be sleeping. This one must have had a real nightmare, the way one leg is pinned under the other and his right arm hidden behind his back. I wouldn't be surprised if there are fractured bones too. Whoever did this wasn't being gentle. I'm only guessing until he's examined by that quack Dr. Ngo at the morgue. I'd suggest you be there before Ngo cuts him into pieces and makes his house special stew. Look for things like scratches or skin under his fingernails. Signs that might show he struggled with the killers. Maybe broken fingers or ripped clothing. I could go on, but you're the detective and you know all of this."

"So you think he fought?"

"You ask for my thoughts. Yes, it feels to me like there was more violence here than just a bullet to the back of the head and severed ears. I believe Sang was beaten first."

"Well, at least that's the end of it. Four in the photo and four murdered."

"No. There will be one more. That's why Sang was tortured."

"Are you still high on the poppy, Captain? Four in the picture. Four dead."

"And who held the camera? A Montagnard peasant who wouldn't know the difference between a camera and a space ship? Another soldier under the command of these butchers? Maybe one of the girl's sisters who was allowed to live and not raped and murdered? For once, try to have that coconut on your shoulders do something more than make Jell-O dessert."

Nguyen stiffened as if he'd gotten a vicious cramp in his lower back. Surely, it was my words and the realization there would be at least one more killing on his watch. It didn't make him joyful and accepting.

"If I didn't think you could be of some value in this investigation," Nguyen said, "I'd have you and your mother hanging by your toes in the cellar of Nunh Do Street."

"Yes, and you'd still have your finger up your ass. That's about as close as you'd ever get to finding who did this." I nodded down toward Sang.

The sound of muffled chuckling came from the hallway behind us. While this kind of sparring and insults took the place of iPads and all the modern conveniences of the West, Nguyen couldn't tolerate the rumors that would soon spread like napalm through the Sai Gon police. He pushed me toward an open sliding glass door and into the garden, shutting it behind him.

Outside, the humidity was even worse, only lessened by a slight breeze that made the banana trees sway gently. There was a delicate spray from the fountain that did little to cool either Nguyen or the temperature. He pushed me under a palm, gripping my forearm like I was about to bolt.

"You are getting to be worse than a leech in my groin," Nguyen said. "I can no longer tolerate your insolence. It has become a distraction and sidetracks me and my men from solving these crimes. I order you to stop. From now on, all communication between you and me will be about the case. Nothing more." He shook me to make his point clear.

Now, it was time to become a true detective captain. A pillar of the Vietnamese police. A hero of the revolution. Push my ego to the back and show this struggling man the true path before I was sunk in a tiger cage in the Sai Gon River.

"If you opened your eyes to more than the girly-boy dancers at the 61 Club," I said, "maybe you could keep from getting your *duong vat* (dick) in a fish ball grinder."

Suicide. Vietnam didn't report its numbers. That wouldn't compliment this worker's Shangri-La, the total most likely ranking the Republic somewhere in the top ten. Being a homicide detective, I knew the reality. My task was to decide if a murder was worse than a suicide. Which of the two would be more damaging to the profile of this perfect society. In other words, we led the world in the rate of "accidental deaths," the preferable alternative. Now, I was close to becoming a statistic caused by the pistol that bulged from under Nguyen's armpit.

Instead of pulling his gun, he shook his head from side to side, making a *tsk, tsk* sound like I was the babysan who'd just shit on the teak floor. It was a constant source of amazement how many insults the average Vietnamese could tolerate. It was as if they had grown another layer of scales in their skin that deflected anything painful, embarrassing, or to the point. Maybe it was Buddha's stricture that "better than a thousand hollow words is one word that brings peace." Or it could be that Nguyen wasn't going anywhere in his search without me and he knew it.

He finished the nodding with a sigh and released my arm.

"I would like to call a truce," Nguyen said, bowing slightly. "We can work together, or I can have you assigned to monitoring the garbage scows on the river. What is your decision?"

It was getting warmer in the garden, the afternoon sun now overhead even if I couldn't see it through the typical cement gray sky of Southeast Asia. I scratched the few remaining hairs on my head and thought over the alternatives.

"I can imagine the pressure you're under," I said. "Those beetle dungs in the politburo have to be scurrying for safety, while they piss their pajamas in fear they may be next. You've already killed an unarmed woman, so there doesn't seem to be an atrocity you're not ready to commit."

It was my turn to sigh. I did, and the weight of this battle fled my body like stomach gas from a corpse. Nguyen didn't even bother to deny any of my accusations.

"I'll cooperate," I said. "But I can't promise I'll stop getting testy when you irritate me. As Chairman Minh said, 'I do not suffer fools well.' Or maybe that was W. C. Fields."

This got a smile from Nguyen. It wasn't that funny, and I took it as a peace offering. I grinned back, admiring the sparkling whiteness of his teeth compared to the yellow-brown opium color of mine.

"All right, uncle," Nguyen said, trying even harder to be endearing. "Can we review what we know?"

"Go ahead," I said. "Dazzle me."

Nguyen stiffened and cleared his throat like he was about to give a speech at the police academy.

"I'll start with the most recent events," he said. "Because of the photo, we had Sang under surveillance. He was found dead this morning. That means someone clever and skilled enough to avoid detection killed him during the night. We have an arrest warrant out for this Luong person you told me about, but we don't have any pictures of him. Because of your theory that he is being aided by the Yankee Night Snake, all Americans are being watched. We are trying now to get more information on him. You were right and we believe his name is Frank Morgan. No one with that name has entered the country in some time. That doesn't prove anything. False passports can be bought in this city for less than a buffalo steak. To make it short, we need to find out who took the picture of Sang and the others."

"That might be difficult, since they're all dead," I said.

"We have also been attempting to learn which military unit the victims were attached to during the American incursion. When we find out, we'll begin questioning anyone identified."

A clattering sound came from the house. We looked toward the windows and saw Ngo struggling to his feet, shards from a newly broken lamp surrounding his feet.

"We'd better get inside before he does more damage," I said.

Opening the door, I stared at Ngo, again wondering how anyone so ugly was allowed to continue breathing. He was sight pollution at its worst and made all the more ghastly because he had such a nasty personality.

"*Chao ong*, Jell-O face," I said. Hello. "Did you find anything useful before you destroyed the crime scene?"

The rolls of putty on Ngo's face sagged even more, hiding his bad eye. With his good one, he studied me like I was on his dissection table.

"It's you, *du ma*," he said. Motherfucker. "And I thought you'd be out drinking kitten blood and playing with your tiny noodle dick. Or executed for your foul mouth." He was on his feet now, bent over, the hump on his back higher than his head. He was a perfect Quasimodo, but even more hideous.

"No," I said. "I'm still alive and would look better than you even if I was the carcass of a dead shrew."

Seeing Ngo stagger just a bit, I stepped closer and let him slump against me. I could smell the *bia hoa* on his breath and remembered Ngo liked to start drinking beer before he ate breakfast. He tried to push me away, but I stayed near. For some reason, I liked this man who'd almost given his life for his country and would have been luckier if he had, rather than end up looking like a handful of stale dough balls. He was panting from the exertion of standing, and I let him settle down.

"Give us your first impressions, Dr. Ngo," I said. "First, how long do you think he's been dead?"

Ngo poked at the body with the toe of his slippers.

"Well, he's in full rigor mortis and hasn't started softening," Ngo said. "So that would make it sometime in the middle of last night. Probably not long after midnight."

"And what do you think killed him?" Nguyen asked.

Ngo looked up. If he could somehow contort the globules into a frown, he would have. His voice was enough to show his contempt.

"Maybe he drowned," Ngo said. "Or choked on a peace of dim sum. Or on his ears. That bullet hole in the back of his head could be just for decoration. A kind of permanent piercing. You see a lot of that in the street punks nowadays."

"What about the bruises on his neck and the way his legs and arms are twisted?" I asked.

"Car accident?" Ngo said. "Plane crash? Some kind of sicko sex game using a collar and a cricket bat?"

"Have you noticed anything else?" Nguyen asked.

"I was about to roll him onto his side when somebody knocked over that lamp. Now, I think I'll wait until we have him at the morgue."

"Compared to the other three," I said, "is there anything unusual?"

"Like the fact that he seems to have tried to eat the picture and the cobra, his legs and arms are clearly broken, and I'd guess he's been beaten by the marks around his neck. I'll also go out on a limb and speculate there will be a lot more bruises when I get his clothes off. Maybe even some cigarette burns and fractured fingers. Basic torture when you don't have time and tools like Nguyen and his comrades store in the basement of Hung Dao Street."

"Do you have any idea why this one might be unlike the others, esteemed doctor?" Nguyen said. "I'm just asking for opinions, not facts. We don't have hours or days to wait for more data."

Now Ngo was in his element. Playing Sherlock Holmes. Or Dr. Moriarty. Getting the deference no one would give him after they'd seen his gnarled face and camel back if they hadn't already bolted in horror.

"So this repulsive gimp can be of some use, eh?" Ngo said. He chuckled and the noise sounded like a pig with indigestion. "I think the killers are running out of time. They must know there's a massive manhunt going on. Whatever they're after, they have to find it soon." He looked down on Sang's body. "That's why this one was tortured. Also, they're telling us things are about to get ugly and personal with the picture and toy jammed in his mouth." Ngo turned to me. "What do you think, son of a chink whore?"

"I agree with you, uncle," I said, not taking the bait. "This is the second murder in twenty-four hours. And the most violent. But why do you say 'they'?"

"First, I'm not the 'uncle' of a yellow bastard like you. Still, I appreciate that you have a brain unlike the other apes in your race." Ngo pointed a crooked finger toward Sang's face. "There are no marks there. Nothing to show he was gagged or taped. No signs of restraint that I can see. That means he was held by one person while the other administered the pain. It's impossible to torture someone without the victim being tied down. Or held. Probably carried out by soldiers or spies. It was professionally done. And with hatred."

Ngo was confirming everything I believed. Two men. Both with experience in killing and torture. Ex-military or intelligence. Relentless and seeking revenge. I glanced at Nguyen, wondering if he had gained anything new.

"Thank you, uncle," Nguyen said. "Please have Sang's body taken to the morgue and give it a thorough autopsy. I will await your report. In the meantime, we will continue to look for the killers."

"I'm booked solid today, detective," Ngo said. "I have a tee time at two this afternoon at Long Thanh. It's the Men's Club Tournament, and I'm the defending champion."

Nguyen looked at me, his brow curled in a question mark.

Ngo and I started to laugh at the same time. To think for even a heartbeat this gnome was able to swing a five iron was ridiculous. He might as well have said he had a modeling job with *Ringier*, the leading Vietnamese fashion magazine.

It didn't take long for Nguyen to recover. He scowled and pushed his hands in the pockets of his pressed suit pants.

"Well," he said, "when you're finished with your round, please make your way quickly back to the morgue to mingle with the people you're more comfortable with. Dead ones."

Ngo tried to come to attention and gave a sloppy salute to Nguyen that made him look like a troll in some beastly alien army.

"Always at your command, General," he said. Turning away, he yelled toward the men waiting with a gurney to transport the body.

"What are you idiots waiting for?" he yelled. "Your brains to explode with a useful thought? Maggots to hatch on your mother's pubes? Take this man to the office. I have work to do for the master class, heh, heh." He loped away, swinging his arms like he was Dr. Frankenstein's assistant.

Both Nguyen and I shook our heads in amazement that such a being still walked on the earth, realizing he was as close to a genius as our stunted society could tolerate. He would come up with more answers, using the prehistoric equipment at his disposal.

Ngo's discoveries weren't of much interest to me. Four murdered and the pace was accelerating. If there was to be an end, we had to find the fifth man. Or the killers. Nguyen had already shown he was capable of murder himself by the killing of the Montagnard woman, even if he continued to deny the slaying. He wouldn't hesitate to fire if either Luong or Morgan came into his sights. I walked outside, searching for Phan among the group of policemen smoking and swapping stories on the street. I wanted to talk to Luong or Morgan before they were killed.

Many of the Montagnards had become Catholics, and those who lived in Sai Gon tended to camp out in the Bhinh Thanh District that sat on a peninsula in the river. Since they were still hunted and persecuted, it was nearly impossible for Montagnards to find work anywhere in Vietnam outside the Central Highlands. Still, a few stubbornly remained, mostly in cardboard or tin shacks by the river and could be seen begging in the more wealthy areas of the city along Le Loi Street. If there was anyplace I could go to hunt Luong, it was the area of ramshackle huts where the mountain people camped.

As I went toward the Toyota, Nguyen yelled at me to stop and caught up before I could open the car door.

"Where are you going?" he asked.

"There's nothing more to see here," I said. "I want to check out a few things."

By now, Phan was in the driver's seat and I put my fingers on the door handle.

"What 'things'?" Nguyen asked.

"They're not fully developed in my mind yet," I said. I stooped to get into the back seat, but Nguyen held my arm.

"Don't be holding back on me," he said. "I can find you anytime and make sure you have an unpleasant evening."

Closing the door, I said, "You can always reach me on Phan's cell. That's if he's not too absorbed in Sponge Land."

Phan pulled away. Within blocks we'd passed the police barricades and immediately melted into the chaos of Sai Gon.

"Where to?" Phan asked.

"Not Trang Long Street in Bhinh Thanh," I said. "Close to the river." For once, I was too deep in thought to remember the dumpling stuffed into his head.

At every intersection, we were surrounded by motorcycles and bikes, with the occasional oxcart. It looked like many of the people were carrying everything they owned piled on their heads and their burdens teetered with every step. Horns *meep, meeped*, and the fumes from the engines cast a blue cloud over every scene. The cloying smell of ripe fruit and simmering garbage overcame my sense of smell. It was a perfect moment, cloaked in this madness, to try to figure out my next step. There wasn't much time.

For thirty years, I'd let the ruling powers control my life. I'd risen as high, or even higher, in the ranks than ever expected by me or anyone else. Chinese were so inferior they were held in less regard by the Vietnamese than the cockroaches that filled every gutter on Sai Gon's streets. And hated more. I would go no further and always have hacks like Nguyen questioning my every move and being spied on by morons like Phan. My only defense, and often attack, was words. I tried to make the government zombies I encountered at least a little ill at ease with my caustic remarks. There wasn't another way to vent I could see that wouldn't put me in the eternal re-education camp meant for dead traitors. With Nguyen, I'd pushed it to the limit. But that wasn't what was itching at my brain like head lice. It was Luong. He was the most honest and forthright man I'd ever met. While he was simple in his needs and wants, he had been forced to become a killing machine because of the slaughter of his people. I wasn't going to let Nguyen and his kind execute him. At least, not without speaking to him first.

The problem was keeping my findings from Nguyen. I'd have to make sure Phan was planted firmly in a place where he would be so engaged with Bubble Trouble he wouldn't care if I was about to assassinate the Premier.

There weren't more than a few kilometers to drive. It still took nearly an hour before I could see the river in on our right through the gaps between the cement block buildings. Wires were strung like cobwebs and were almost thick enough to block the view. Ahead, struggling palm trees marked a break in the ragged construction.

Women in bright headdresses and long, full skirts squatted by the road, hands out. Behind them, shabby lean-tos filled the narrow space between the street and the Tu Thiem Bridge. Nearly naked small children raced between the women, chasing one another in some kind of a tag game. I told Phan to pull over and got out, instructing him to "spend some time having a cup of tea at the Treedome." Phan grinned and took out his cell, fingers blazing across the screen.

The woman had milky eyes. She nursed an infant, and her smile showed only a few stumped yellow teeth. Brown wrinkles creased her leathery face.

The scarf wound around her head was checked with reds, greens, blues, and blacks. Cross-legged, her flowing dress was brown with dirt and nearly covered her calloused feet. The babysan slept, and black hair poked out of a threadbare blanket that covered everything but its face. Beside the woman, an open cloth basket held pots and pans, small bags of rice, cans of Nestlé milk, and a few pieces of what had to be clothing. If a tourist had to guess the woman's age, they would probably say 70. But I knew she was less than thirty. I approached slowly, knowing she'd most likely been warned that Chinese were devil spawn. I held out a few dong and bowed.

"Mamasan," I said. "I honor you and your child." I bowed lower and handed her the money that disappeared into a fold in her blouse faster than I could follow. "I'd like to ask you a few questions. First, may I know your name?"

She nodded slowly and said, "Hacmon."

I squatted beside Hacmon and tried to seem even smaller than I was. The traffic noise made it hard to hear, and the children playing added to the noise. I pressed closer.

"Do you know a man named Luong, Hacmon?" I asked. "I am his friend. I know he's from Dac Sun. We spent many years together in the camps, mamasan. I know he would like to see me again."

No hesitation. She bored into my skull with those tapioca eyes and held up four crooked fingers.

"You come back," she said. "Four hour. Bring many more dong."

From behind the woman and the shadows of the palms, I could feel I was being watched. It was just a slight rustling of the dead fronds and movement in the darkness of the hootches. It reminded me this was a place where only hill tribesmen were welcome and it was easy to be disappeared in the brown water of the Sai Gon. I bowed again and said, "*Cam on,* mamasan." Thank you.

At the Toyota, I had to slam the door to pull Phan's eyes away from Bob's adventures. He started the engine and turned back to me with his regular "where to, boss?" He'd been watching too many of the *Hawaii Five-O* reruns on VCTV. The stupid grin on his face reminded me it was correct in our socialist society to be kind to those less fortunate than ourselves.

"To the coroner's," I said. "Maybe Ngo will have some scraps for you to eat."

Phan nodded in anticipation and pulled into the traffic.

Within a few blocks, I was wondering if there was time for a detour to Ma Jing's for an afternoon delight. Trembling with the fantasy, I decided I wouldn't be able to leave the dreamland and still make it back to meet Hacmon.

Ngo's office and facilities were located in District Five at Cho Ray Hospital, the biggest in Vietnam and one that claimed to "meet all global standards." I'm sure this was true if it were being compared to worldwide butcher shops or beauty salons. It was a standing joke in Sai Gon that, when sick, it was better to see the neighborhood barber or bartender, the historical caregivers and dentists in Vietnam. The place had a dozen floors and 1,200 beds. Ngo's morgue was in the basement, just like it was a real hospital.

There was no trouble finding a parking spot, since Phan ignored all the signs except the ones that read "Reserved for Government Vehicles." Usually, that meant an army Jeep or a politician's Mercedes. When he pulled in near the door, I looked around as if I'd be able to see if anyone had tailed us. I didn't think we'd been followed to Bhinh Thanh, but I was certainly no expert and would be surprised if Nguyen let me roam free. I sat forward and patted Phan on the shoulder.

"Wait for me here, nephew," I said. "I'll be back. Maybe I'll find some chicken satay for you to chew on at Ngo's."

"Excuse me, uncle," Phan said. "I've been ordered not to let you out of my sight. I have to come with you."

There was no use arguing. Anyway, Phan was easy to distract if there was something I didn't want him to see or hear.

"*Em,*" I said. OK.

Inside, I walked downstairs and past Ngo's secretary, ignoring her calls to "*dung lai.*" Stop. I just waved and let Phan deal with any problems as I went through the swinging doors into a frigid hell.

At the end of the darkened hallway, Ngo's theater opened up into a large room lined with steel doors about one meter square. The middle of the space was covered with metal tables and trolleys filled with instruments on white cloths. The lights were muted, but lamps hung from the ceiling if more illumination was needed to find a bullet wound or intestinal worm. The smell was like the 150 proof snake wine, a favorite with the tourists in District One bars, mostly because the snake was still in the bottle and had been distilled along with the rice. Straight alcohol. Ngo was hunched over a table in the middle of the space, the hump higher than his head making him look like a camel slurping at the oasis.

Without looking up, Ngo said, "Just in time, Captain. I was about to check his *cac* for any signs of recent sexual activity. I don't think that's relevant in this case, but it's procedure. Besides, I figure you'd enjoy getting an eyeful."

"Have fun," I said, walking slowly toward Ngo, praying to the Enlightened One that he'd finish soon.

As I got closer, the putrid reek filled my nostrils. I half expected flies to be circling in hordes as would be the case with most decaying bodies in this part of the world. We were inside, and I was immediately able to identify the smell of insecticide mixed with the alcohol and rotting flesh odor. No flies. Gore only. And I wanted to run.

I slowed and reminded myself of my Buddhist beliefs. We were all meat, and a time came for every one of us to feed the living and move forward to another incarnation. I should be happy for this dissected body who I assumed was Sang's, the fourth victim. The only thing I was sure of was that I had a handkerchief in my pocket in case the scene of a dismembered body caused the bile to rise from my stomach. I squeezed it and moved beside the bent-over Ngo.

The naked corpse was still mostly intact, and the bruises that covered the upper part of Sang's body and neck were dark blue and sunken. There were a few cuts across his chest that had been cleaned of blood and his *cac* was in Ngo's fingers.

"You want to give me a hand?" Ngo asked, chuckling and not looking up. "I don't need much. It's tiny even for a Vietnamese."

"Not my thing," I said, trying to stop from gagging.

Ngo dropped Sang's *cac* and moved up his body, pointing to the contusions.

"It appears someone thought Sang was their wife," Ngo said. "Or a punching bag." He waved his hand over Sang's chest, stopping at his forearms and pointing. "As I suspected, they used a lighter or cigarette to fire him up." He probed one of the burn marks with a forceps. "Ouch. That must have hurt."

Too much more of this, and I'd certainly hurl the morning's fish balls on the tiled floor. There wasn't a lot I needed to know, now that I saw this cadaver had been treated harsher than the other three victims.

Moving his hand like a baton, Ngo placed the forceps next to Sang's ghost left ear.

"Notice the tear marks here," he said. "The wounds are ragged. Unlike the other three where the ears were sliced off cleanly with something very sharp. This time, it seems like someone strong just jerked them off, so to speak. Shows some rage. Or the need to act quickly."

"Could one person do this?" I asked.

"Not likely. I don't see any evidence of restraints. Ropes, handcuffs, plastic. Nothing. That means someone must have held Sang down while the other one played inquisitor. If you want to wait for the fun part, I'm about to split him from chin to groin. If we get lucky, they'll be worms crawling around in there. As you know, nearly 15 percent of all our comrades are infested with the grubs."

I'd seen enough and had no interest in worms. Whoever was committing the murders, their behavior was escalating, showing some kind of desperation. They needed to locate the fifth man before we found them, and they must know a nationwide dragnet was already in place. I had to find Luong before Nguyen and his death squad.

"Thank you, esteemed uncle," I said, wiping my mouth. "I need to get going."

"If you need a barf bag," Ngo said, "clean up after yourself. I hate the smell." He shook his doughboy head. "You amateurs need to get a stronger stomach. Or stay away."

I kowtowed, not bothering to answer, and staggered toward the hallway, wondering if the Buddha had ever watched an autopsy. If so, he might not have gotten so fat.

Walking down the dim passage, I knew my opinion that things were ratcheting up had been confirmed by Ngo's findings. I still had a few hours before meeting Hacmon and decided I should spend them doing a little research down at the station. Outside, Phan was waiting. No surprise. His head was down and an elephant herd wouldn't distract him from Krabby Land. I nudged him with a slippered toe.

"Back to the station, Sergeant," I said. "You can call Nguyen and tell him what we thought was true. The killers are getting anxious." My stomach was rolling like a sampan in a typhoon, and I was in no mood to harass Phan.

"No Ma Jing's?" Phan asked. "You look like you could use some medicine, Captain."

"Just go," I said, grabbing my belly and groaning, visions of slime-ridden worms crawling out of Sang's discolored body playing on my eyelids.

"Are you sure I can't get you some rice porridge and ginger?" Phan asked. "You're starting to turn white, and I don't want you mistaken for a *gweilo*." He chuckled.

"If you don't start the motor in the next two seconds," I said, "I'll be forced to tell your mother about the sex change you're saving for."

Phan gasped. "That's not true and you know it, Captain."

"Yes, but your mother doesn't. *Den bay gio.*" Go now.

As we drove through the smog of Sai Gon toward police headquarters in District One, the blue fumes and ever-present fester of decay made me even queasier. But it was the daymare in my head that was most unsettling, sparked by the memory of a recent news story that appeared in the *Saigon Times*. It seemed a thirty-four-month-old child, Tran Van Dat, had gotten seriously ill. When he was examined at the Ministry of Health Clinic at the Tam Tra commune in the Nui Thanh District, he was diagnosed with ileus, or intestinal obstruction, caused by two pounds of worms. Pictures of the heaving mass accompanied the story, and it had put me off bowls of pho noodles ever since, even the ones with Mekong duck and saffron, my favorite. I could tolerate black and blue marks, knife wounds, bullet holes, and even the red puckered circles from cigarette burns. But the thought of what might be slithering around in my abdomen made me want to blow my rice ball breakfast.

The traffic assured the two-kilometer trip back took nearly fifty minutes. By the time we arrived, I would only have a moment to check in before we had to head back to Binh Thanh. That would give the denizens inside enough opportunity to make sure I knew how much I was hated. I told Phan to park in a *Du Tru* space. Reserved.

My office was a windowless room on the top floor that used to be the janitor's storage area for cleaning supplies. It still smelled like Lix Floor

Liquid, the most popular washing brand in Vietnam. The aroma had seeped into the walls and reminded me of the chemical plants that spewed their poison into the atmosphere and were clustered around the toxic city of Phu My. My workplace was high in the building, a location that assured it would be constantly airless and sweltering. I ran the gauntlet and made my way to the stairs, since the lift rarely worked.

I half expected to hear the normal "fuck the eighteen generations of your ancestors," the most common and supposedly hurtful insult to lay on a Chinese. I'd grown the thick scales of an iguana against that one, but still didn't like the words of the uniformed officer who hissed, "You wear a green hat, chink." Loosely translated, that meant I was a man-whore who was the offspring of another man-whore and only fucked other man-whores. I ignored the *mong*, asshole, not wanting him to know that one stung.

As usual, headquarters was crowded and frenzied. That made it a little safer to climb the stairs without too many verbal assaults. I wouldn't have to wait for Phan. He'd show his face after he'd made his report on my activities to Nguyen or whoever else was my unknown minder. The reason for the visit was to try to search the computerized files on the old Sony desktop, the outside of which should have been scrapped years ago. The inside held a few surprises. I had stolen the password that allowed me to get into the "*bi gioi han*," restricted archives that might give me a lead on how to identify the Night Snake, Frank Morgan.

Turning the corner from the stairs toward my workplace, another officer, this time with gold epaulets on his shoulders, passed, accompanied by his squad of slaves.

"*Cho yade*," he said in Mandarin greeting. Simply put, he'd just called me a "stinking Chinese slut." I guessed he was confused about my sex, but I wasn't about to correct him.

Inside the relative safety of my baking office, I turned the Sony on, sat in the plastic chair, and took out a bottle of Sanawa water. This Van Phat Company's alleged crystal clear water had yet to be confiscated like most of the other brands in Sai Gon because they contained *Pseudomonas aerugionosa* bacteria, which can cause infections and sepsis in humans. I drank the warm liquid and tried to relax, reciting my mantra and rubbing my belly while the computer whirred and crackled, sounds I'd programmed the machine to make.

There was no way Nguyen or any of his lackeys would cooperate with me. While I was expected to tell them absolutely everything I found or guessed, they wouldn't share intelligence with a half-caste Chinese dog muncher. For one thing, I might solve the murders before them and that would be intolerable. Thankfully, I could access the daily reports and, more importantly, the still-secret and inflammatory records from the American war.

With a *pop* and a few Windows notes, the Sony signaled me it was ready. I put my hopefully-germ-free water down and decided there was not time to read the daily reports. I headed back in history to the "Top Secret" intel from the late 1960s and searched for "Frank Morgan." There was plenty to read.

In the days before dong made its reappearance, piaster was the name given to South Vietnamese currency. During the late 1960s and early 70s, Frank Morgan, aka the Night Snake, had a bounty on his head of one million piasters or ten thousand American dollars, a fortune even today for the average Viet. It was known then that Morgan was a CIA-trained and CIA-controlled assassin, probably the deadliest hired gun of all time, and was run out of the Rand computer base. Rumors like this were the breakfast of US Military and spy intelligence. The Phoenix Program was his boss. They were mandated to murder anyone who met certain profiles or smiled at the wrong person at the wrong time or breathed the same humid air as Westmoreland. It didn't take much since "one dead gook was as good as another."

Morgan was suspected of killing well over one hundred Vietnamese, including women and children. His usual method was a silenced bullet to the back of the head from his .22 caliber Hush Puppy in the middle of the night. The pistol was named that because it was often used to quiet barking dogs who might sound an alert. The legend was he could sneak up on anyone anywhere in the dark, thus the nickname "the Night Snake." He was rumored to have an unidentified Montagnard sidekick for a native guide. There was a shadowed picture supposedly of him walking into the Phoenix Program sector of a base outside Chu Lai, but there wasn't much of value in the photo. Another unverified story said he'd been involved in the murder of his commander and had fled the country after helping a number of AWOL soldiers escape to Sweden via Cambodia.

After Morgan left Vietnam, the An Ninh lost track of him, but his myth continued. Mamasans across the country scared their babysans into better behavior with the threat the "Night Snake visited bad children in the dark." Supposedly, Morgan had gone to work full-time for the CIA, traveling the world as a paid killer. Nothing more was known about his Montagnard buddy, whom I recognized as Luong.

Something was niggling at my brain. Even though I was barely more tolerated in the Chinese community than Vietnamese, I did have contacts there and was even occasionally invited for a mooncake, boiled carp eyes, fried eel tails with spicy prawns, and gallons of *bia*. Not long ago, at one of these feasts, someone had told me a story of an American who had come to Sai Gon with a beautiful woman, staying in Cholon under the protection of one of the District One Mandarins. During their short visit, the son of a former South Vietnamese president was killed well after midnight at his villa near the botanical gardens along with a few bodyguards and dogs. Nothing was proven, but it was whispered throughout Cholon that the Night Snake was back and had gotten his revenge. Most of the details were sketchy or hidden by the ruling authorities, not wanting to upset the population. At the time, the case wasn't assigned to me, being as politically charged as it could have been. I was too unreliable to be involved and listened to the saga without making connections. Now, I wondered how I could have been so clueless.

None of this would help me find Morgan. With the snake hunt that had to be going on across the city, he wouldn't be able to stay undercover for long. No paleface American could. For one thing, even walking on the streets of Sai Gon, he towered above the locals, let alone the blinding way the sun would reflect off his white skin. My only real hope was to get to Luong before Nguyen.

Motivation. Mine. Not the killer's. Keeping secrets from Nguyen wouldn't enhance my career path and, more likely, would shorten my life expectancy to that of a moth around a bonfire. If it was a question of my career, it didn't matter much. It was impossible I'd ever rise beyond captain. I could always work in a noodle shop or learn to be a hairdresser, if they let me live. I'd been sacrificing my ethnic identity to the great god of advancement and safety for too long. Even Buddha was disgusted. Sometimes I even wondered if the pipe would ignite for such a useless creature. This could be a chance for redemption. At least in my mind, if not the universe.

Still, it wasn't just about me. Luong had told me the story, and now, I'd seen the picture. The smiling perpetrators of that atrocity needed to die. It was justice, and I would do anything I could to shield both Luong and Morgan from capture so vengeance could be carried out. I moved the cursor to where a *click* shut the computer down and stepped to the door, knowing Phan would be lurking somewhere nearby.

The hallway was crowded with civilians and police, all sweating in the heat of a nearly airless and stifling third floor. As expected, Phan leaned against the wall, legs crossed and nose almost a part of the cell phone he held within an inch of his face. I'd seen him in this posture enough times to realize he was still aware of my presence no matter how absorbed he appeared to be. He wouldn't acknowledge me until I spoke to him or walked away. Then, he'd follow. I nodded and we moved toward the stairs, trying to jockey through the throng.

"Filthy Vink," someone spat. I'd always liked that one, an English language hybrid slur of chink and Vietnamese. Showed more creativity than *du ma*. I kept moving, not slowing so that someone might catch and trip me, a common occurrence around headquarters. Phan, thirty years younger, had no trouble staying close and protecting my backside. We made it out the door and into the blinding sunlight without further incident or insult.

At least Phan had wheedled a vehicle with air conditioning out of his superiors. If it were up to them, I'd be riding an old one-speed bicycle. We got in and Phan began to back up, while I mouthed his next words.

"Where to, boss?" he asked.

"Bhinh Thanh," I said. "Chop, chop."

We had an hour to make it to the rendezvous with Hacmon and, in the motorized bedlam of Sai Gon, we'd be lucky to drive the few kilometers in that amount of time. I sat in the backseat and tried to dredge up more memories of my years with Luong, time spent learning to become a part of the new socialist society. If I could get to him first, there might be something to help both of us when we finally met again.

The meanderings wouldn't take me away from the specter of the dead Montagnard woman I was convinced Nguyen had shot. Something about her was familiar, and I couldn't quite put my finger on why Nguyen had done the killing unless he had more information about Luong than he told me. If, in fact, he did know there were Montagnards exterminating politburo members, mountain people in his sights would be open targets, especially if it appeared they might be threatening someone engaged in the investigation. There must be a connection between the woman and Luong, or she wouldn't have been watching the house where the third body was found. It cost the woman her life.

"Yada, yada," as they said in Vietnamese. My mind was spinning like a fox on a tether. But Luong's words from decades ago echoed in my skull.

"A woman who survived the massacre at Dac Sun," he had said, "was the one-toothed hag. She had been mostly responsible for the girls. She had a giant mole on her chin with hairs as long as my fingers, but she made everyone laugh when she twisted them in her fingers, crooning, '*Em be cua tii*.'" My babies.

A siren began its klaxon honk, and I wondered if the officers inside the car were after me. They weren't, and they roared by as fast as the traffic jam allowed, almost knocking down several bicyclists who tried to nudge in. One of the policemen even nodded and smiled, as if he wanted to send a message that he'd be seeing me soon.

Maybe it was too many nights at Ma Jing's. Or, lately, the lack of the snake soup that definitely made my mind sharper. It was now past a day before I grasped that the woman Nguyen had killed was the one Luong spoke about from Dac Sun. It seemed there were more villagers included in the politburo killings than Luong. I didn't understand how Luong contacted Morgan, but I did get why. The Night Snake had returned. It was payback.

The city passed slowly in the early-evening rush hour, making the gridlock only slightly worse, and the usual serenade of jammed cars and motorbikes sang the endless song of Sai Gon. Neon lights were flickering on and rats ran across the sky, getting ready for their nocturnal feeding and balanced on the robin's nest of electrical wires that dangled and sparked overhead. As we got closer to Bhinh Thanh, I became more convinced that I needed to save myself. Not from the Vietnamese masters or my job. It might be my last chance to do something really good, justified, and important. By the time Phan pulled the Toyota to the side of the sprawl, I was ready to be Lei Kun, the Chinese God of Thunder, a spirit that punished criminals whose offenses had gone undetected.

Hacmon sat cross-legged in the same spot where I'd seen her last. This time, there was no baby at her breast. She was in the shadow of a palm tree, the river visible through the rundown hovels behind her. It was quiet. Too quiet for this time of the evening when there should have been children playing and mamasans rushing to cook whatever food they had gathered to add to the night's rice meal. The only smell wasn't of frying fish, boiling oil, and spices. It was of raw sewage, much of it floating by on the Sai Gon. Tonight, the whole community seemed to be on hold. I understood that it was all about me. I told Phan to wait and he nodded, taking out his phone.

For some reason, I started to sweat. I was wearing my plainclothes detective uniform of black slacks and short-sleeved white shirt. Now, the armpits were getting dark, not in the least usual for me. I rarely even sweated. I believed my glands had ruptured with the torrent that flowed during my years of eating grubs and lice at the camps. I stepped around a pile of moldering garbage, not wanting to get the non-uniform slippers I always wore covered in the goo that oozed from the pile. Hacmon watched with a neutral expression on her craggy face, and I could feel the sentry's unseen eyes on me from the shadows.

Beside the old woman, I crouched.

"*Xin chào*, mamasan," I said. Good evening. I bowed.

"*Chao cau*," she said. Hello, young man.

"Have you had your evening meal?" I asked.

"No. And you?"

"I would be happy for a bowl of chicken fried rice and *bia*."

"No chicken today. Maybe dog. All taste same-same."

"I'm trying to quit."

This could go on for awhile. It was the normal polite talk that was required before business. I was about to ask her about her family and ancestors when she cut me off.

"Many eyes are on you, *chau trai*," she said. Nephew. "You only walk upright because Luong has made it so. You must tell me what you want, or you will be floating in the river like any other dead fish."

This was unusual. A straightforward conversation with a Vietnamese without the normal ritual avoidance and approval ballet. I bowed, respecting her wishes and nervous about my answers. If they weren't exactly what she wanted to hear, I figured it would only take a slight hand sign and I'd be flayed alive until I told them who I worked for and what I really wanted. Or what they expected. As the Great Buddha said, "There are two mistakes one can make along the road to truth . . . not going all the way, and not starting." I started.

"Luong is my brother. We spent many nights whispering our stories to each other in the camps. I know about Dac Sun. I know about the girls. I know these things only because Luong told me. I even know about you, Hacmon." I bowed respectfully again.

"*Tiep tuc*," she said. Go on.

I glanced at Phan, hoping he was still consumed by a cartoon world. Silly me. Of course he was. When he was this absorbed, I could have been dragged away kicking without him noticing. I turned back to Hacmon, praying to Buddha he was right that "when words are both true and kind, they can change your world." It seemed I was now fixated on the Buddha. It must have something to do with my own thoughts and fears about my imminent move to the next cycle of life. Or death. Whatever was more fitting. I tried to cleanse my thoughts and focus on the now and hoped my voice wasn't quivering like a guitar string.

"I believe Luong has returned to Sai Gon," I said. "I also think he has something to do with the killings of several powerful men. There is an extensive pursuit going on, and it's just a matter of time before they come here looking. Even though I work for the police, I want to speak to Luong. I will not betray him."

There it was. It would be up to her whether I ever ate another fried scorpion at Bo Tung Xeo restaurant on Li Tu Trong Street, one of my favorite places because of the way the cooked arachnids crunched like popcorn. She waited, studying me like she was deciding how many hard-earned noodles to put on my plate. Finally, she raised her right hand without taking her stare away from me.

Within seconds, the Toyota was surrounded by ragged beggars, apparitions from a Hollywood zombie movie shot in the slums of Sai Gon. They didn't threaten, just stood glaring at Phan like he was dinner. Blocking the doors, the wraiths put their hands on the windows and stopped him from getting out. Hopefully, he wouldn't pull his pistol and start blasting away.

He looked at me, and I dipped my head, trying to signal him I was OK and he wasn't about to be transformed into a flesh eater.

Hacmon struggled to her feet, pushing herself up with the help of the palm tree. She brushed off her long skirt, cinched her blouse, and adjusted her colorful headdress.

"*Di theo toi*, Captain Fang," she said. Follow me. Ouch. It seemed everyone knew me and I knew no one. More proof this woman was involved in whatever plot was being carried out.

Within a few steps, we entered another world. This slum wasn't at all like the ghost town behind the Kay Dim Market that sprung up in the old French cemetery. That was a sprawling mass of mud for poor Vietnamese and a breeding ground for some of the most ruthless and violent youth gangs in the city. It was a brutal area, rife with tuberculosis and other diseases, including the highest concentration of HIV/AIDS in the country. The path Hacmon led me down was well swept and dry, as if the inhabitants had put in a drainage system, until it ended in a kind of rickety boardwalk, a half-meter wide and hanging over the edge of the river. There was little garbage and all of the tin or cardboard hootches seemed tidy. As we wound our way down the narrow walkway, only a few old women were in sight. In the distance, someone was listening to My Tam sing "Bleeding Love," one of her biggest hits. The sound was tinny and nearly overwhelmed by the noise coming from the river as we moved along, swaying with the current and waves. The Montagnards must have cared about how they lived, because this wasn't the usual ghetto or river rat squalor.

One more sharp turn and Hacmon stopped. She gestured me to stay where I was and disappeared into a hut that leaned toward the river as if it was about to topple. She'd gone through a thin blanket that covered the entrance without a word, and I tried to keep from trembling, knowing it wasn't up to me whether I got out of here alive.

A voice from behind the curtain. One I would never forget.

"*Di vao anh trai.*" Come in, brother, Luong said.

I shoved the blanket aside and stepped into the gloom, the space lit only by a small kerosene lamp. It was stifling, but the man across from me squatting like a mamasan doing the wash wasn't sweating. I was about to drown in my own juices. It was easy to recognize my old friend, and I wondered if we might hug, an action becoming more common with the onslaught of Western TV, but I knew touching another man wouldn't be in Luong's repertoire unless it was with a garrote or a knife.

Before I could offer a greeting, someone from behind pushed me to the rug-covered floor and pulled my hands back. Immediately, fingers began to search my clothes in a thorough frisk, while my head was rammed into the mat. It was surprisingly clean and smelled like cleaning fluid and toe jam. The Sig Sauer was lifted from my pocket, but the dong was left where it was. Luong only watched as the person finished and vanished. Obviously, I'd passed this test even if I'd showed up packing a gun.

No apologies. Luong must have known we were both professionals and this kind of behavior was routine. I might have done the same to him no matter how many hours we'd spent murmuring our life stories.

"*Ngoi*," sit, Luong said, nodding toward a crooked folding chair someone must have salvaged from the Dong Thanh dump. I stood, brushed myself off, and sat, putting my arms on my thighs in the most unthreatening posture I could take. I was smiling, actually joyful and excited that I'd found my long-lost friend. Luong didn't return the grin. He'd always been of the opinion that smiles were costly, and he was without a dong.

"Why are you trying to find me?" Luong asked.

The shadows flickered around the small room, revealing wall hangings of tropical mountain scenes and pictures of Degars in American clothes, laughing in front of SUVs in what had to be the United States. It was probably in the state of North Carolina, where most of the Montagnard expats had emigrated.

"I think you know," I said. "If you haven't guessed, Hacmon must have told you."

There would be no customary waltz of asking about relatives and ancestors. No pleasantries masking the real intent. Luong always went straight to the meat and ignored the rice.

"Tell me anyway," Luong said.

"First," I said, "you must understand I'm a captain in the Security Forces. Really, I'm a homicide detective responsible for cases in all of Sai Gon. Or Ho Chi Minh City if you prefer." I waited to see if a pistol would emerge from the folds of Luong's shirt. Or a knife. Either one would mean the end for me. He didn't show any change in posture or facial expression.

"Go ahead," he said. "Enlighten me with something I don't already understand."

I bowed and went ahead, intending to give Luong the condensed version.

"Then you will know about the dead politburo members," I said. "All murdered in the last week and an old picture of them smirking above some dead young girls left on their bodies, their ears cut off, and a toy cobra on their chests as well. All were shot in the back of the head. The last one, Comrade Sang, was tortured before he died."

I stopped, waiting for Luong to confirm or deny. He wouldn't say anything, but I hoped his body language would give me a hint. Not a chance. He was like a statue of a truly stoic but thin Buddha.

Not the typical inscrutable Chinese, in these tense situations, I tended to want the silence broken. Luong could be still and quiet forever, a trait I believed he groomed to perfection when he was in the jungle waiting to ambush more lowland Vietnamese.

"The police and An Ninh are already looking for you," I said. "And a ghost Yankee named Morgan. The clues you left were too obvious. That's the part I don't understand. You could have killed them discreetly, and no one would have suspected you or a roundeye. But you left a trail even the morons in my department could follow."

"Do you remember the stories I told you of the girls the Night Snake, Frank Morgan, and I saved?" Luong asked. "On the nights you and I had enough strength even to talk. Maybe you'd found a beetle or a fly and shared it with me. I was never good at hunting anything but gooks. If you recall, those girls were rescued from the closet of the son of the former president of South Vietnam, Nguyen Cao Ky, before we thought we killed him. Morgan entrusted the girls to me, and I took them to Dac Sun while Morgan was shipped back to America." He cleared his throat and spat on the floor. "I snuck them to the mountains, and the men in the picture slaughtered the girls along with many more of my tribesmen. I told you all this thirty years ago. I want you to understand what is happening now."

"How could I ever forget? You were so filled with hatred it coated you more than the mud. But why now?"

"I never knew who murdered the girls other than they were Viet Cong forces. Then, Morgan came back to Sai Gon, and I was contacted. Being part of the police, you must have heard about the deaths at Ky's mansion a while back?"

"Yes, but it was kept out of the papers and very low-key."

"I will tell you only that, during that period, I came into possession of a picture showing four men grinning above the bodies of the girls. Since then, my mission has been to identify all of them. I did. Except the one who took the photo. Morgan has gotten his revenge with me. We're still looking for the last man."

"So Morgan helped you?"

"Yes."

"You know a man like him is very hard to hide in Sai Gon. Most all foreigners are followed after they enter the country, if only for a short time. Particularly Americans of his age."

"Yes. And I won't tell even you where he is. Morgan will evaporate in the wind when this over."

"How do you contact him?"

"Mutual friends. Some even in Cholon with the other Mao lovers."

"Did you ask him to come here?"

"Of course. And he didn't hesitate."

"So you know I'm trying to hunt you down too?"

"Certainly. Now you've found me. What are you going to do?"

"I was thinking about using my Cuong Nhu skills to tie you up in knots like a noodle ball."

There it was. He almost cracked at my absurdity. The corners of his mouth tried desperately to turn up in a smile, but the weight of his heart pushed them back. He did blink, another reflex he had totally under control, signaling me I would live a little while longer.

We'd gotten through the basics. I'd already made up my mind the path I would take, no matter if it led me into darkness. In this moment, he was the judge, and I had to convince him I was on his side or I'd never be soaring on the dragon's wings at Ma Jing's again.

The only sounds came from the hiss of the kerosene lamp and sampans on the river, the worn-out boats coming home with the day's catch of one of the species of swamp eels or 1,200 varieties of fish that inhabited the Sai Gon. Luong continued to focus intently on my every movement, mostly my face. If he was trying to wait me out, he was the winner.

"What about the woman who was shot on Hoa Da Street?" I asked. "Was she with you?"

"Yes," Luong said. "She was there to find out who was leading the investigation. She was killed for that, and her slaughter will be avenged too. She was called H'Khar. She was from my village and helped with the girls. She was out gathering tangerines when the soldiers came."

"You know who shot her?"

"Yes."

"Who?"

He hesitated, his impenetrable face giving no tells. After a few seconds, he answered.

"His name is Nguyen. He works for the An Ninh. He will be punished."

"Are you planning to kill everyone who is trying to find you?"

"No."

"So, there is an end point?"

"Yes."

"I thought so. I have a copy of the picture that seems to have started all of this. As you stated, you and Morgan have killed four, and now you are looking for the fifth man, the one who took the photo. I believe I can help."

"Why?"

The big question. Just because I'd been called "squint" and "slant" and much worse for fifty years, mostly when I was working as a policeman and by my own comrades. Just because most of them would shit on my head before they shared a bowl of rice with me. Discriminated in housing, cars, guns, promotion, and every other aspect of life while I found the killers who don't exist in our utopian society. None of those reasons gave me the right to become a traitor to the worker's paradise of the Republic of Vietnam. Of course it did. I'd never joined.

"Do you remember that night at the camp when the monsoons were so heavy we thought we'd be able to paddle to freedom right from our sleeping mats? When the scorpions became so heavy with water they dropped from the thatched roofs, and we devoured them in a feeding frenzy like they were duck eggs? When even the ants couldn't dig deep enough to keep dry and we gorged on their crispy bodies?"

"I remember."

"And what did you do when the guards came and began to beat us for 'eating what belonged to the people without permission'?"

No response. It wasn't in Luong's makeup to take credit for anything valuable or promote himself. He would never be one of those Vietnamese soccer players who danced after they scored a goal, pointing to their chests. He waited for me to finish the story without comment.

"You told them I was innocent, standing up in front of me and taking the blows from their batons until they knocked you into the mud. You said I had tried to stop you and I gathered the bugs for tomorrow's soup to share with all of our socialist brothers, but you took them from me. You said you were the one who needed more rehabilitation. For that, you were thrown in a tiger cage in the swamp, tied down so only your head was above the water. You almost drowned. When you were released back into the camp, your legs were shriveled like you had polio and your face was bulging like a giant red chile from mosquito bites."

"What is your point?"

"It's simple. That was only once. There were many others. You saved my life. For some reason, you were my guardian. Now, it's time for me to settle the score."

"How?"

"I won't kill anybody. What I will do is try to keep Nguyen and the others from finding you. I'll also help you locate the fifth man."

"We already know who he is."

"Did Sang tell you?"

"Yes. But it took more than one cigarette."

"Please tell me more about Morgan."

"I think that would be unwise. You know he's in Vietnam. That's enough."

"Will you tell me your plans?"

"Again, unwise."

"I might be able to point them in the wrong direction if I knew which way to go."

"All I will say is this one will be more difficult. Then, we will have to give our greetings to Nguyen."

"Is there anything in particular you think I should be doing?"

"Just remembering what it would mean if you betray us."

"That is not why I'm willing to help."

The threadbare blanket that covered the door was pushed aside, and a white man stepped in. He was under two meters, but still taller than most Vietnamese—other than Nguyen—and had to duck to keep from hitting his full head of hair on the wooden struts of the tin roof. The white shirt he wore was untucked and hung over the waist of his khaki shorts, not disguising the pistol at his waist. His grossly hairy legs ended at leather sandals. He was a typical Yankee devil tourist, probably a vet coming back to mend a soul blackened by the imperialist invasion. He would easily blend in with the legions like him seeking forgiveness. Unlike Luong, he was smiling.

"I've heard much about you, Captain Fang," he said, holding out his hand. "I'm Frank Morgan."

I stood and shook, bowing.

"By the way," he said, "I love that name. Sounds like a breakfast cereal. Or maybe a new species of snake."

I had no idea what he meant and just shrugged.

After the hand clasp, he moved past me to stand by the still-squatting Luong. For sure, it was now two against one, though I doubted either of them needed any help if they wanted to restrain me by themselves.

"I think you have a driver out there who's getting quite nervous," Morgan said. "One of Luong's cousins had to take his phone away before he called in the cavalry."

Sitting down again, I tried to look relaxed.

"He's probably more upset he's being kept from SpongeBob SquarePants than worried about me," I said.

"Oh, I love that game," Morgan said. "But I like Angry Birds better. Death to the nasty little piggies."

There couldn't be anyone more opposite than Luong than this man, and he was nothing like the cold-blooded killer Luong had described all those many years ago. In fact, he seemed more like a buffoon in a Cheo play at the National Theater.

Eyes. As the light danced on the walls, I got a better look at his eyes. They weren't laughing. Years of interaction with criminals and sociopaths had exposed me to the black, bottomless void that served for eyes among many of the crooks and murderers I'd encountered. I'd also seen this phenomenon among high-level politicians and military commanders. While they often could joke and hoot like jesters, no one could ever find a sign of life in their eyes. Maybe it was the shadows or my imagination, but I couldn't find anything reflected in Morgan's. They just sucked everything in like black holes. He continued to stare, a slight grin curving his mouth.

"So, Captain," Morgan said. "Are you here to arrest me? Take me to the basement at Nguyen Du Street and play doctor with my balls while I confess to murdering Buddha, Uncle Ho. Or anything else you tell me to." He chuckled and shook his head from side to side.

Then, he stopped. Something had passed over him like a specter of evil, and he was no longer in a comedy. It was a deadly drama. His face lost any joy and was now a mask that made it clear he was serious.

"I must tell you," Morgan said, "I am here not only to help my friend, but to rid your country of monsters that should have been exterminated years ago. Nothing will stop us short of our deaths. If you try, I won't hesitate to use this."

I didn't even see his hands move. Before I could blink, he was behind me and there was a garrote around my neck. He pulled me back into his chest and moved around so his mouth was beside my left ear.

"You can still hear," Morgan hissed. "The others can't. You'll join them if you speak of us to your comrades or in any way betray our whereabouts."

The Night Snake tightened the steel wire, and I was sure blood was beginning to drip on my collar. I did know from Luong that Morgan was an expert with the garrote, his second choice for assassination. He probably knew exactly how many pounds per square inch of pressure he could exert before drawing blood or decapitating his victim. Morgan waited a few seconds and then decreased the pressure, his lips still next to my head.

"Who knows you're here?" he asked.

If I shook my head for emphasis to my answer, it might end up in my lap. I didn't move anything but my lips.

"No one but my driver, Phan," I said. "We might have been followed. I don't think so, but I'm not trusted. Also, Phan reports back to our superiors about my movements and activities. Don't let him use his cell."

"Who would he report to?"

"His name is Nguyen. I believe he's with the An Ninh, not the police. No one relies on a lizard like me since all Chinese evolved from that species and have forked tongues and slippery skin even if half my blood is Vietnamese. Have you heard of Nguyen? It seems Luong has."

It always seemed important to me that I keep the perps talking, just like in the detective novels I read and those that aired on VCTV. At least it resulted in breathing a little longer. Besides, the criminals always spilled their guts before the end of the book or show so everyone would understand the entire story, even if that was rarely the case in the real world.

Luong hadn't moved, barely letting his eyes follow Morgan. He was a Montagnard statue, ready to spring to life if needed.

"Nguyen?" Morgan said. "You might as well ask me if I know someone named 'Smith' in Salt Lake City. All you gooks are named 'Nguyen.'"

"I'm no 'gook,'" I said. "I'm what they also call a 'forty-fiver,' among another thousand more slurs. They say that's because my eyes are supposedly on a forty-five-degree angle to my face. And my ancestors weren't named 'Nguyen.'"

"Thanks for the education on Vietnamese racism," Morgan said. "I'll stick with 'gook.' It has so much history for me." I couldn't see him, but I knew he wasn't beaming any longer. "Where do I find this 'Nguyen'? I think I heard you tell Luong there was a 'Nguyen' who shot H'Khar. If so, it's just another reason for a visit to his bedroom in the wee hours. Do you know where he lives?"

"I've never seen the man before yesterday," I said. "And lowly McChink's like me don't get invited over for boiled shrimp and wine."

"That could be one of your first assignments. Finding out."

"Oh. I'm part of your crew now?"

He'd let a centimeter of slack loosen the garrote. Morgan twisted the handles again.

"You want to *di di*? Take a nap at Ma Jing's?"

"How do you know about that?"

"You've been followed ever since you left Danh Nguyen's. You must not be much of a detective if you didn't spot the tail. But we did make sure the others who were following you had an accident."

"You believe I'm willing to abandon everything I've built for decades to join a conspiracy against the rulers of the country?"

"Yes. I don't know you have a choice."

"I'll have to . . ."

The shots sounded like Chinese New Year's firecrackers lit off across the river. Everyone in the room was too familiar with the crack of a K-50M Vietnamese submachine gun, the weapon of choice in the Saigon Security Services, to mistake it for a bunch of street kids having fun. Morgan released the steel wire, and we all looked toward the noise, realizing together it came from the direction of the street.

Luong was on his feet first, pushing Morgan and me through the thin curtain that served for a door.

"*Nhanh, nhanh*," Luong said. Quick, quick.

They must have practiced an escape. Morgan didn't head back in the direction we came once we reached the river only a few meters away. Instead, he turned down the rickety boardwalk. The planks swayed gently with the rhythm of the river as we hurried east, toward the Tu Thiem Bridge. Both Luong and Morgan were in better shape than me and seemed to move with the grace of much younger men. I struggled to keep the pace, since my free time was spent mostly at Ma Jing's rather than exercising.

On the river, sampans, Ghe Nang three masters, and trawlers criss-crossed the water, and a few dugout canoes loaded with fruits and vegetables battled the wake from the bigger boats. The wooden walkway was bordered by tin shanties on one side and the water on the other. Shrubs and a few straggly palm trees fought for life wherever a few inches of earth opened up. Bougainvillea wound its way around the older huts and the flowers filled the air with their honeysuckle smell, fighting a losing battle with the small streams of sewage that leeched from under every shack. No faces peeked at us, preferring not to get involved with a Chinaman, Montagnard, and roundeye scuttling from something that couldn't be good.

Behind me, I could feel Morgan had stopped. I turned around and watched as he pulled out a few planks and flipped them in the river. It only took him a second, and he was up and following, motioning me to get moving. Now, no one could tail from this side.

A bend in the river meant the walkway made a sharp turn. It ended on a dirt path that wound through palm trees, plastic bags, Coca-Cola bottles, melon rinds, and disintegrating furniture. Within a hundred yards, we reached the boundary, a dock with a small boat tied up to rotting timbers. Luong didn't hesitate to jump in the dinghy once we'd skipped over the gaps in the wood. He beckoned me to leap next, trying to steady the wannabe craft against a piling. Boats were something I'd never felt comfortable with, especially ones as wobbly and decayed as this one. Besides, what did a mountain tribesman like Luong know about steering this death trap with the 150 horsepower Evinrude hanging from the stern by a few nails and a bungee cord. There were none of those orange life preservers I'd seen in pictures. A couple inches of brown water swished around the bottom as Morgan leaped on and headed toward the back, pushing me down onto a slatted seat as he passed.

Luong was in the rear, watching as Morgan pulled the starter cord. I'd been right. Luong appeared to be viewing a hadron collider, his face in a frown of total befuddlement. The motor started with just a couple pulls, and Morgan signaled me to unloose the mooring line. By the time the rope was inside, Morgan had hit the throttle and the bow shot up. Within seconds, we were in the main channel heading toward the bridge. There would be no chance of conversation until Morgan eased up on the gas.

Since I'd entered Luong's hootch, I'd not seen another face other than Morgan's. Except on the boats. The riverside Bhinh Thanh community was obviously controlled by Luong and his clan. They must have been told to stay inside and keep their eyes closed. None followed us as we sped away.

I had no idea what had happened to Phan or why the shooting had started. I could only guess that someone from the An Ninh had found me and their pursuit had been foiled by Luong's people. If it was Phan who'd alerted them, it might save his life. Now, it seemed I was part of the gang whether I wanted to be or not. At least I was with people who wouldn't call me "MSG" or "Kung Fu" or one of a thousand insults.

"Hey, panface," Morgan yelled. "Move to the middle so you don't capsize us with all the spring rolls in your belly."

At least he was smiling, apparently happy with our escape and the thrill of steering the boat through the river traffic. The wind in his longish salt-and-pepper hair blowing in the breeze, the khaki shorts, and the grin made him look like a modern-day white devil pirate. I slid a few inches to the center and stared at Luong, who seemed as tortured as me.

Luong was crouched just ahead of Morgan, his hands held out to the rails on both sides, rolling with each sway of the boat. I thought I saw his lips moving in a silent prayer, but couldn't believe this man was frightened by anything other than a grenade. The only thing that distinguished him as a Degar was his face. His features were much less cramped, his cheekbones fuller, and his eyes were not nearly as angled as a lowlander. His dress was one of a Vietnamized hill person, not a tribesman attempting to hold on to his regular mountain outfit. To me, it was a clear attempt to blend in with his collared shirt and black pants. What did give him away were the leather sandals. They were thick brown and strapped tight to his ankles.

Within minutes, we'd bisected the river and were in Phuong 28, the district mostly famous for its transvestite bars, like Creme of Sum Yung Gy's. Morgan piloted the small boat to shore next to a dock that bordered a few industrial warehouses that were open to the air and covered with metal roofs on thick hardwood poles. Workers scurried between piles of bananas, eggplants, lotus roots, opo squash, and hundreds of other Southeast Asian fruits and vegetables. Many of the mostly men struggled under huge loads in baskets balanced on their heads. Normally, this wholesale market would be jammed with screaming buyers disembarking in small dugouts and clients arriving on the street side in their carts, mopeds, and Japanese trucks. It was now late enough in the day that the chaos was decreasing and preparations were being made for tomorrow morning's commerce. Soon, the evening deliveries would begin. Morgan nodded at me to tie us up to the pier. He shut down the Evinrude, and we climbed onto the dock. No one paid us any attention, and Luong led us through the overflowing piles and wooden containers toward Tran Nao, the main thoroughfare in the neighborhood.

On Tran Nao, we waited for a taxi. Without Phan, I didn't think it would be easy to hail a ride. We were quite a threesome and not a real Viet-namese among us, since Montagnards were a sub-race and didn't count. I was even lower on the racist pole than him, almost a nonhuman. Morgan was just plain scary, over six feet tall and a reminder of napalm and Operation Arc Light bombing raids from fifty thousand feet. If we didn't find one soon, a passing police car would surely notice us and the day would end with us strapped to a chair in different cells.

It didn't take more than a minute or two. I should have known this part of the escape would have already been arranged. A white Nissan van with blacked-out windows and a Vinasun sign on top pulled up in front of us. The rear door slid open before it had completely stopped. Luong pushed me inside and followed, Morgan right behind. The driver sped away before my butt hit the cloth-covered seat. I glanced at Morgan, and he was grinning as if he were on the roller coaster at Dam Sen Park.

This was not the man Luong had described in detail to me at the camp while we tried to keep the leeches from sucking us dry. That one was focused and stern, humor not part of his makeup, totally absorbed in carrying out his deadly missions. Maybe he was exhilarated by being back in the game. At Luong's hootch, he'd already made a joke, and here he was smiling like a teenager getting his first hand job. But, I didn't get the impression Morgan had ever retired. This kind of adventure was what he lived for, and he might as well enjoy the ride. I'd soon find out what kept the smile on his face.

Luong was babbling Degar gibberish to our chauffeur and touching him gently on the shoulder. It sounded like he was trying to slow the man down so we wouldn't get stopped for speeding or in an accident. In Sai Gon, fender benders often ended up in brawls that included knifings and lots of butchery. It seemed like a new video of a street fight aired on YouTube daily. One of the recent battles on Hoa Da Street had ended up with two dead, both bleeding out on the pavement, and one survivor who'd never use chopsticks again. Over ten thousand people per year died in car accidents in our small country, almost as many as went to the next world from AIDS.

We were on our way back across the river, using the Thu Thiem Bridge to end up in District One. The cab slowed on Dong Khoi Street, next to a crumbling four-story building close to the Municipal Theater. I immediately recognized it as one of the festering slum dwellings that were popping up across Sai Gon. These abandoned or condemned structures are ruled by the Viet-Ching, an offshoot of the American Vietnamese street gang. Inside, a refugee from the paddies could find a place to sleep for about sixty cents a night. For that, a renter was able to sleep two hundred to a room, stacked like cordwood on top of one another, separated only by a slab of plywood on wooden struts. A working bathroom was a dream. The best that could be hoped for was that the dormitory from hell didn't burn down during the night. There were hundreds of these structures in the city, and I had seen enough of them in my career as a homicide detective. Murders were a nearly daily occurrence, mostly ignored by my superiors since they saw it as just another lizard squashed. There was no doorman, only a massive Japanese ex-sumo wrestler, obviously on loan from the Yakuza, who collected money and threw out the dead at daybreak. Luong bowed as we hurried past this giant gatekeeper and up the stairs, pushing our way through the hordes of men smoking and chatting in the hallways. No one paid us much attention.

At the end of the fourth-floor hall, a doorway opened onto the stairwell that led to the roof. We climbed up, and Luong pushed a square metal hatch aside, exposing us to the sunlight. He immediately started walking toward a two-by-four thatch-roofed hootch at the far side of the space. Chickens and pigeons pecked on the gravelly surface, while a few hens sat on eggs in wire cages. Odds and ends of rusting furniture were spread around in front of a thin canvas flap at the front of the shack. At each corner of the roof, a man sat on a stool, watching. They had the wide, stern faces of Montagnards and barely glanced at us before returning their gazes to the streets below. Luong pushed inside the hut, and we were met by the most beautiful women I'd ever seen.

In the West, I'd heard there was a belief that Eur-Asian women were the loveliest on the planet, particularly the offspring of French-Indochinese, the result of racial interbreeding during the French occupation of Vietnam. Of course, Chinese and Japanese wouldn't consider any woman who wasn't from their pure strain, since everyone else was a heathen and below contempt. Blacks didn't count, especially in Asian eyes, since they were all "apes." Me, I was now convinced the best-looking women on earth came from whatever planet this woman was spawned. She was grinning, her eyes settling on Morgan with a smile that could have made me light a joss stick and drop to my knees in adoration. He went to her and pecked her on the cheek, followed by a long hug, her green eyes closed.

Luong took out a cell and punched in a number. Again, he was speaking Degar and I couldn't understand a word he said, but it seemed clipped and commanding. After he finished, he went back outside, leaving me alone to watch the couple whisper and hold each other. Now, I knew why Morgan was such a happy soul. After a few minutes, the woman looked to me and gestured I sit on the end of a cot by the near wall. I did without taking my eyes off her.

"*Nin hao,*" she said in Chinese. Hello. "My name is Hatati. I'm a very good friend of Mr. Morgan here and also, Luong, who you know. I've heard good things about you and hope we, too, can be allies." Without waiting for my answer, she turned back to Morgan, and they renewed their hushed conversation.

It was a simple request. I already knew I'd probably learn to use Twitter, dance naked in Lam Son Square, abandon the Buddha, or do anything ridiculous Hatati asked just for a chance to get to spend more time with her. I had found rapture. And it wasn't at the bottom of a bowl.

While I watched Morgan and Hatati talk in voices too low to hear, I wondered about my relationships with women. Or lack of. Sure, there was the one most lasting and dreamlike. That was Ma Jing, though my love was never consummated. There had been a few that lasted more than a night and only cost a couple duck eggs and a bowl of scorpion soup to impress her. Those were rare and always ended with the siren's call to the dragon world. Lately, I'd been seeing a shopkeeper who sold umbrellas and used tires. But we spent more time fighting than fucking, and even Buddha knew it was doomed. Generally, the dealings I had with ladies were commercial-only and I spent my time covering my back as I slowly climbed the police ladder and relaxed moments with the long pipe. If I'd met a female like Hatati, I may have switched vices.

She had a dimple in her tanned cheek and a cocoa face that probably wouldn't whiten even in Hanoi. Her skin seemed like it was as delicate as a Ming Dynasty urn. Thick black hair hung straight to her slim shoulders and there was a suggestion of the weight room in the bulge of her biceps. Lush, heavy lips covered teeth white as coconut meat. Still, it was the eyes that drew me. No hint of contact lenses. They were emerald green, a rarity in Asian women, maybe even a birth defect, one that could make her Miss

Universe. She wore sensible shoes, real Nikes, loose jeans, and a white blouse that showed only slight curves. Her outfit was nothing special, but she would look breathtaking in a garbage bag. Morgan was a truly lucky albino.

Voices from outside. Urgent. In Degar, although it was clear something was happening, even if sounded more like warthog grunts than a language I recognized. Morgan and Hatati were on their feet, dashing toward the door before I could even look away.

On the roof, an evening mist was promising a deluge. Maybe it was global warming. Every year, the typical afternoon rain torrent had been moving to later in the day. Three of the guards in the corners had moved in the direction of the door and were pointing .22 caliber handguns at the opening. They must have been disciples of Morgan with their choice of weapons. Luong pushed us away toward the fourth sentry who was muscling a long plank over the edge of the roof. Luong and Morgan instantly began to help the man, while Hatati and I swiveled our heads between the hatch door and the men steering the long board into space.

The first man to appear had a white helmet on his head, the kind Vietnamese policemen wore with the narrow beak. None of the lookouts hesitated, firing enough rounds to force him back into the darkness of the stairwell. In the meantime, Luong, Morgan and the other guard had wrestled the plank so it provided a fifteen-meter skyway to an open window in the adjoining building. This surely had been planned and was meant to be our escape hatch. Nothing high-tech here. Jason Bourne wasn't part of this scene, and I wondered if I'd make it across without a swan dive to the pavement below. I much preferred to stay on the ground and wasn't a fan of elevators, airplanes, or mountains.

Morgan was the first to cross. He disappeared through the window. Back in seconds, he motioned Hatati to follow and I watched her run like a sika deer over to the other side, her firm buttocks pressed hard against her jeans. The sight prompted me to go next. I glanced backward and saw that someone had pulled a basket of sand over the hatch, making it nearly impossible to open from the stairwell. Luong flipped his wrist, gesturing I should *di di mau*. I did, trying to follow the age-old tenet to not look down. Unfortunately, after the first few steps, the plank began to sway. I figured that's why Hatati had gone so quickly. I needed to get it over with before the fear froze me.

Mistake. I peeked down. Below was a tangle of electric wires, some sparking in the twilight like firecracker tails. Neon lights from Dong Khoi Street cast shadows down the passageway, giving some color to the gray concrete walls. The narrow alley was deserted except for the rats and few ulcerous dogs that raced between piles of rotting trash. A solitary gigantic cat sitting on the windowsill watched the rodents fighting over a slab of decaying fish guts, waiting to strike when the dogs slunk away. I took this all in with a trained detective's eye in a heartbeat, convinced I'd better get moving or I'd soon be the main course for the denizens below. Wobbly legs and all, I dashed toward the window and Morgan yanked me inside. Luong was right behind, followed by the sentries. When the last one jumped through the window, all of the men except me grabbed the board and pulled it into the long room, closing the opening without any hesitation.

Morgan and Luong took pistols from the men and went to the door of the room. I noticed the guns were Browning .22 Buck Marks, made of aluminum and highly reliable. They held ten rounds, and while they weren't much good outside twenty-five yards, they would certainly make anyone trailing us think twice.

Morgan opened the thin wooden door a few inches and peered outside. After a few seconds, he stepped into the hallway, signaling us to follow. It was easy to figure out we'd have to get out of here quickly before the entire neighborhood was blocked off. Someone must have noticed us getting out of the taxi and called in the troops. There had to be a city-wide alert in affect, those in power positions at the Communist Party in horror that any of the lower class would dare threaten their control, especially since they were worried they might be murdered next.

Elevator. Maybe I'd get to confront all my fears before this day ended. A man stood beside the lift door, holding it open. Maybe it was one of the cell phone calls Luong had made, but I was getting more impressed with the planning of this op as the minutes passed. We went inside and Luong pushed the "G" sign, a worldwide Otis standard I assumed meant "Garage," even in gookinese, as Morgan might call it. No one said anything as we went downward, pressed close together in the small metal-lined space. Now I remembered I had claustrophobia that was usually only treated by a pipe full of Ma Jing's finest or the memory of its calming cloud. For a substitute, I used the sight of Hatati to slow the devils. The door opened before the panic attack could take a firm hold and I began quivering like a bowl of Che Dau Trang, the delicious Vietnamese white bean, sticky rice, and coconut milk dessert I usually ordered after a superb pho dinner.

In the basement, we hurried to a late-model white Mitsubishi DX minivan parked close to the exit with its engine already running. Luong took the wheel, and I wondered where he learned to drive any kind of vehicle other than a water buffalo cart in the highlands. By the time we'd slid the door closed, Luong was accelerating up the ramp and onto Hai Ba Trung, the street behind Dong Khoi, where the police would have already been marshalling to storm the building.

"Stay down," Luong barked. "We've got a few kilometers to go before we get to Cholon. The police are scanning traffic." He put a chauffeur's billed cap on his head, along with a pair of black-rimmed sunglasses, while the rest of us squeezed lower to get below the windows.

The sirens wailed, and no one stopped the van. Within a few blocks, the howling decreased and we were headed home, District Five, the place where I was born and now lived.

From the seat behind me, I could hear Hatati whispering. Morgan and this stunner were having a lark, it seemed. I supposed it was because he hadn't shot anyone in a few hours. Morgan peeked up.

"You want me to call Mr. Liu now?" Morgan asked Luong.

"*Co*," Luong said. Yes.

Cholon and Mr. Liu. This couldn't be a mere coincidence. The past few days had been filled with mysterious symmetry that made perfect sense when I was able to be rational and thoughtful. Of course these foreigners and mountain people would be involved with the most notorious Mandarin in all of Vietnam. They needed help to battle the entrenched power elite. No one better than the leader of the Chui Chao Triad. He was always referred to only as Mr. Liu or the "Dragon Head." That is if you didn't want to be treated to the Five Pains, the classic Chinese execution that starts with a very sharp blade and the amputation of the nose, followed by one hand, then one foot, and finally ends with castration and cutting the body in half at the waist.

While I moved more pieces around the Go board in my brain, we drove to District Five, Cholon. The Chinese had settled this District as they migrated southward and taken up residence in Cholon at the time of the founding of Sai Gon in the eighteenth century. The area was still controlled mostly by its Chinese populace rather than the laws of any country, including Vietnam's. The rulers of China held more sway in Cholon's alleys and sweat shops than any ranking political hack or police officer of the Socialist Republic of Vietnam. Herbal shops, restaurants, food stalls, and tiny markets selling everything from cat meat to rubies lined the narrow streets. The population dressed more like they were in Shanghai than Sai Gon. Beside the crumbling multistoried buildings, temples appeared on most blocks, again wearing the hats of the maze of electric wires that seemed to crown Sai Gon. I knew the traffic would move even slower when we reached the main street, Nguyen Trai. There would be barely enough room for two cars, let alone the rickshaws, cyclos, and carts that still covered the neighborhood.

Just by watching the skyline out the window from my prone position, I could tell Luong had turned onto Lao Tu Street and, after a block, into a dingy alley. I sat up, knowing we were safe. Morgan and Hatati were already glancing out the windows. In this confined, dark passage, there was only one lane, and the street was compacted from bicycles leaning against the walls on both sides. The alley was in eternal twilight, surrounded by old, crumbling buildings three stories high. Wash hung on frayed telephone lines that crossed over the street from balconies outlined in wrought iron, and the shutters to the sides of most of the windows had only a few crooked slats remaining. The walls were blackened by years of soot, dripping tiles, and boiling grease. When we passed, any pedestrian had to press his back against the filthy walls or be crushed. There were none, but I could feel many eyes watching. Luong stopped at a wooden door with cracks that showed blackness on the other side. He stepped out and slid the side door open for his passengers, leaving the engine of the Mitsubishi running. Before we entered the building, a man emerged from the gloom and drove the van away.

Within seconds, we were standing close together inside a tomblike space. The others didn't wait and began to climb splintered steps that groaned and wheezed with every footfall.

"Follow us," Luong said.

"And don't touch anything," Morgan said. "Spiders."

"*Cuc*," I hissed. Shit. I hated the furry bastards. Living just a few blocks away, I knew the District was infested with hairy jumping spiders, the kind that could sense movement and reacted by hopping onto exposed skin they could somehow sense and biting. They seemed to have created a synergy with the ticks that lived alongside them, comfortable homes in the dark and decay. It was yet to be determined how many spider punctures were fatal. Even one was quite painful, feeling like being poked by a sharpened chop-stick. They had a white strip down their backs and a round head that held two bulbous brown eyes. The crawling monsters loved the gloom. I made sure not to rub against the walls and slowly trailed the chatting Morgan and Hatati who seemed to be at home in the blackness and unconcerned about the evils that surrounded us.

Suddenly, a muted lightbulb fizzed on above us and I could see the outline of a man at the top of the stairs. Greetings were given as Morgan, Hatati, and Luong went past the man and into an open door.

"*Wanshang hao*, Captain," good evening, Captain, in Mandarin, the man said, bowing as I went by. I stepped into the astonishingly bright room, followed at once by the distinguished-looking man with the white hair and beard.

The tall, thin gentleman wore a black skull cap and a delightful smile, a grin that could have been curling the face of a local child offered a spicy honey squid candy. His outfit was black silk with flecks of gold, cut perfectly to conform to his body. His feet were encased in gold slippers and his fingers glossy with a fresh manicure. The beam on his unwrinkled face made me feel welcome and terrified at the same time.

Mr. Liu motioned me to sit on a long satin-covered couch that already held Morgan and Hatati. Luong had walked over to the far wall and was admiring a collection of ancient Chinese war helmets that seemed to be from the Ming Dynasty because of the many dragons painted in gold around the sides and the blunted spike poking from the top. Everyone was as relaxed as if they were in their own living room. I sat and marveled at this strange family, none from the same ethnic background and at least three of them stone killers.

"Tea, Captain?" Mr. Liu asked, sitting in a padded wooden chair with intricate flower scrolls cut into the armrests and back. "I've just brewed some Monkey King Tea that arrived this week from Anhui Province. It smells like orchid blossoms and leaves a sharp, sweet aftertaste."

"I would be honored," I said.

He turned to Morgan and Hatati and said, "I know you would like a cup. I'm quite sure Mr. Luong would not. I don't think his stomach will rest until his soul is healed."

Dancing. Nothing would happen until the ritual was complete. We would discuss the lateness of the monsoons, the recent mysterious die-off of ten thousand buffalo in the northern mountains of Cao Bang, the health of elders, and the astonishingly high price of pork dumplings. Nothing of any significance would pass between us until everyone had a chance to sort out their strategy and position based upon body language, speech patterns, comfort, nerves, tics, and anything that might give someone the upper hand. Or surrender. This was a tradition in which I was well-versed and usually calmed me, especially after sipping some of the excellent Monkey King Tea that was as crisp as it was sweet. I put down my porcelain cup and sat back on the couch, waiting for the waltz to begin.

"You have been kind enough to pay us a visit in my humble home, esteemed Captain Fang," Mr. Liu said. "I would like your patience while I explain a few things." He bowed slowly, and I knew absolutely he would kill me where I sat if I didn't play my role precisely as he had written the script.

Luong had taken up a position behind Liu. Hatati and Morgan were still to my right and had been quiet during most of the conversation that had taken place in the last few minutes. The atmosphere had changed like the drop in barometric pressure before a typhoon.

There were no rumors of Liu's power. Only facts. Not even the security forces of the Vietnamese government threatened this man's empire. No one who crossed him suffered less than the loss of a few fingers. The unlucky ones were cremated alive where they slept without their family having to pay for the service in dong. No one got to scatter the ashes. His control of District Five was total. As long as we were his guests, there wouldn't be any threat to our safety his army couldn't defeat, unless the invaders drove tanks. Even then, Liu probably had an arsenal of M136

AT4 Light Anti-Armor weapons stolen from US military bases that would stop the tanks in their tracks and incinerate those inside. Besides, he most likely owned a fleet of helicopters to whisk us to Cambodia or some safe house. Liu was a major arms dealer, as well as heroin smuggler, gambling and prostitution boss, money changer, extortionist, and orphanage owner. Regardless, he was as polite as if he'd learned his manners from loving parents and his genteel demeanor said he wasn't the sleeping bamboo snake I knew him to be. He had made the offer of kindness, tea, and information. There was no way I could refuse if I wanted to have a second cup of the flavorful hot drink. Or breathe. I nodded, indicating Liu had my permission to continue, a gesture as unnecessary as signaling the executioner to pull the switch.

"I must assume you know who these people are, as well as myself," he said. A statement, not a question.

"*Yao*," I said. Yes. "Except the young lady."

"She is Miss Hatati," Liu said. "My niece."

I didn't know if he was speaking metaphorically or if Hatati was truly related. She only had a hint of Chinese in her face and I was sure she was some kind of extraordinarily beautiful Asian hybrid. No matter. Liu would tell me if it was crucial.

"Of course," I said. "But I have no idea how she fits into all of this."

"Please," Liu said, "it will all become clear soon."

"*Mei shi*," I said. OK.

"I will begin with Luong," Liu said. "You may interrupt at any time if you get confused. I want you to understand and I am not offended by questions." He bowed. "Sometimes, I assume too much. It is my burden."

I nodded agreement.

"This story begins in the Ming Dynasty," he said, "when my Han ancestors rebuilt the Great Wall and constructed much of the Forbidden City."

I almost groaned, knowing there might not be enough time in my lowly life to hear the rest of the tale, but I remained quiet, not suicidal.

Liu grinned and slapped his knee with an "I gotcha" grin.

"Don't worry, nephew," he said. "I'll skip ahead a few centuries to what is important now." This was all so bizarre. No one seemed to be taking seriously that there was a manhunt going on across the city or the murders of some of its highest-ranking officials.

"*Qing ni,*" I said. Please do.

"I am going to speak for Mr. Luong, Mr. Morgan, and Miss Hatati now," he said. "If I am in error, I am sure they will correct me."

"Please proceed," I said.

"Before Mr. Luong met you," Liu said, "he was a close comrade of Mr. Morgan. That was during the American offensive. You know this, but may not know they rekindled their friendship very recently. The reuniting ended with the death of one of the true villains of our beautiful country, who had lived well beyond when his black spirit should have been condemned to eternal life alone with only despised ancestors to join."

Liu didn't name names, but this confirmed what I had heard and I knew he was talking about Ky, the evil egg of the former president and whore for the United States. It had often needled me that this vile creature had lived and prospered after the communists reunited the country. Even the rumor of his death had gladdened me, and now I was being told it was real. My mood was already lightening, and I could feel a few of the mice scurry from my head. I bowed in approval.

"I will let Luong tell the next chapter," Liu said. "That will have the added advantage that he doesn't enjoy hearing his own voice as much as I take pleasure in mine. We will be finished before the Monkey King gets cold." He smiled and the bowing continued.

Luong was standing and it was evident he didn't relish speaking in Vietnamese, only killing them. Before he started, the hatred oozed from his brown skin like mud between our toes during the rainy season in the camps. He stared trancelike straight ahead.

"As you will remember from our nights together," Luong said, standing stiff as marble, only his lips moving, "when Morgan and I first went to Ky's villa many years ago, we found two young girls hiding behind a curtain. They had been raped by Ky. I took them to the mountains with me. They were slaughtered while I was away and I have never forgiven myself for that error. You know this, but I am attempting to keep the story straight."

"Thank you, Luong," I said. "Please go on."

"Not too long ago," Luong said, "I was contacted by a mutual friend who told me Morgan was back in Vietnam and wanted to see me. Of course, I agreed, and together with Mr. Liu, Miss Hatati, and a few others, we went back to visit Ky. This time, he didn't live. During our short time at Ky's, I took a diary from beside his bed. Inside was the picture I'm sure you've seen lying on the bodies that have been found in the last few days. Now, there is only one man left. He was the one who took the photo and was harder to find."

"Who is he?"

"First, we must know where you stand."

"A few more questions, please."

"Go ahead. But I may not answer."

"Background. Where have you been and what have you been doing since I last saw you boarding the truck to leave camp wearing that ripped T-shirt and not much else? And does that have something to do with the 'mutual friend'?"

An attempt at a smile. Unfortunately, Luong's effort was even scarier than I recalled. It looked as if he were gut shot and had succeeded holding his intestines in with his fingers.

"After my escape, I've had a number of jobs. Some here and some outside the country. I'm not at liberty to discuss my career except to tell you Mr. Liu has been involved. Even Morgan sometimes. Any queries about 'mutual friends' will need to be addressed by Mr. Liu."

"So, that just told me nearly nothing."

"You'll have to make up your mind with the information I've given you. Otherwise, ask Mr. Liu."

"You do speak good King's English. Almost as if you went to Oxford."

"I will say I've been there, old chap." The rigor mortis smile again, the words and accent from *Downton Abbey*.

"And you drive a car? Last time I saw you, you thought they were 'steel oxen farting blue flames.'"

"Yes. I've even leaned how to pull the chain on an indoor toilet and use paper to wipe instead of dried banana leaves." He stopped the grimace and looked at a space a thousand yards over my head. "But joking is not why we're here. You must make up your mind so we can decide what to do with you. *Nhanh*." Quickly.

Silence. The kind that comes just before the judge reads the jury's findings. Morgan and Hatati sat beside each other, not touching or moving. I could sense that either of them would strangle me with a garrote if Mr. Liu dipped his head. Luong wouldn't be nearly as subtle.

From somewhere, Chopin's Nocturne Opus 9 Number 2, performed by Yundi Li, my favorite pianist, was softly playing in the background. The roar in my head had masked the sound before. Now, it crashed like thunder while I tried to decide how to continue smelling the orchids that adorned some of the polished antique tables. The room had white-washed walls, decorated with a few ancient tapestries. Their cost could have paid several decades of my salary. And Phan's. More lacquered end tables from the Qing Dynasty held lamps and a few books. Liu must have enjoyed the smell of lavender, because the incense burning in the corner gave just the slightest flower smell that mixed well with the flowers' scent. I cleared my throat, trying to stall. Or maybe just to let them know I was really going to speak sometime soon.

Saved by the ringtone. An old black cordless phone was beside the chair where Liu sat. The handset was like one of the first bulky mobiles that had hit the market close to twenty-five years ago. The sound was more of a buzz than a Nha Imperial Court melody, the most popular sound on Vietnamese cells. It must have been a direct satellite phone, not hooked into the Vina-phone network. Liu reached over and picked up the receiver, putting it to his ear, his face a Shamanic mask showing nothing.

"*Ni hao*," Liu said. Hello.

For the next few minutes, Liu listened, only occasionally making a short response that did give me some indication of what he was talking about only because of the lack of the words "yes" and "no" in Mandarin. Chinese speaking that dialect tended to respond to a question with repetition. For instance, if I asked you, "*Ni tou nee ma?*" the question being, "Do you fuck your mother?" you might answer, "*Xihuan ni tou nee ma.*" "I do like to fuck my mother." So, when Liu said things like, "I know that four have been eliminated," I could deduce he was talking about the four who had been murdered.

After awhile, Liu handed Morgan the phone.

"Having a late-night spot of brandy, Nutley?" Morgan asked by way of greeting.

This "mutual friend" must have been a Brit and everyone seemed to know him but me. "Nutley" was apparently in the game too. Maybe at a decision-making level. Minimally, he was most likely a minder for some spy agency. For the English, that would be MI6.

Morgan was much more outgoing than Liu and peppered his conversation with insults like, "Brits will fight till the last American" and, after a long series of growls and sputters, "Are you going to attend your parents' wedding, old boy?" These two must have been extremely close by the way they abused each other. There was one I wanted to remember to use on Phan if I ever saw him again. "Are you really that stupid or is this a play?" A little highbrow for a SpongeBob addict. More likely, I'd get to say it in front of a firing squad.

When Morgan finished, he handed the phone back to Liu and looked at Hatati.

"The old guy sends his 'cheerios' and said he's saving one of his best Cuban's for you," Morgan said. "I hope he meant cigars."

Hatati smiled, but there was something in the green of her eyes that made me aware that Big-Eyed Whip Snake also had emerald eyes. And his bite was poison. She slowly brought her head around so she was staring at me and I knew the waltz was over.

This was getting bizarre and frightening. All the openness wasn't a part of my country or heritage. Usually, I had to try to wade through layers of innuendo, lies, obfuscation, and feints. These people didn't seem to be hiding anything. That could mean only one thing. I was on their team. Or dead. As Confucius said, "It is more shameful to distrust our friends than to be deceived by them." Luong was my oldest ally, and I would rather take the side of right than continue to kiss the arse of the illegitimate bosses who would never let me into their club. Decision made.

Taking the safest path, I bowed, facing Liu.

"I would be honored to be part of your planning," I said. "I do not know what you want of me, but I will do my best."

No one gasped in relief or even smiled. They looked at one another and nodded. Liu was the first to speak.

"We are pleased to have you with us," Liu said. "I will make this as brief as possible because there is work to be done. Quickly. We need you to keep the investigation away from us while we find where the last of the killers is located. If you can give us any help in finding him, it would be quite useful."

"I still do not know who the fifth man is."

It was Luong's turn. He stepped beside Liu's chair and crossed his arms on his chest.

"Tran Dai Quang." He didn't need to say more.

The Minister of Public Security. In other words, the head spy, policeman, torturer, executioner, and communist puppet in charge of keeping every Vietnamese citizen in his or her place by whatever ruthless means he chose. Demanding we all adhere to the communist party line and worship at its temple. "No mercy" was his rule of thumb. He probably pulled out a few fingernails every morning before his first cup of lotus tea. In many ways, he was my boss, and I had heard his point of view and suffered his scorn too many times. Certainly, he would be leading the hunt for the people in this room. Nothing would be too distasteful to Quang in finding the killers. The number of innocents killed and their guilt was immaterial to him. In the meantime, he would be in hiding, protected by a regiment of guards, Quang screaming and demanding results. He wouldn't hesitate to call all his sycophants "*do ngu*," stupid, or something more descriptive like "*lo dit*," asshole. Whatever expletive he used, the message would always be clear. "Find these *lo dits* or you're a *do cho chet*." Fucking dead dog. If I were more prone to sweating, beads would have exploded on my forehead. Quang was absolutely the worst enemy anyone could have in our socialist kingdom. As Confucius said, not Buddha, "Wherever you go, there you are." I was here and three pairs of eyes were studying me like I was the crunchy rat tail in their shrimp paste. A detective, I still needed more data and I tried to be unreadable. Keep them talking is always a good investigative strategy.

"How do you know it's Quang?" I asked.

"Are you still with us?" Luong asked. "You know exactly who he is. And how dangerous the next few days will be."

"I would like more information," I said.

"No," Luong said. "We don't have time." He glared at me with the look I'd seen before he strangled the one-toothed informer who had betrayed several prisoners in the camp. The man was responsible for numerous executions by hanging, the victim's bodies left dangling on display from banyans for weeks until the flies and crows left only the bones. Luong didn't hesitate to break the traitor's neck. It was time to stop the ballet.

"Just one more question," I asked and didn't wait for the pistols to come out. "Do I get to help squeeze the blood from Quang's black heart?"

No hugs. Luong moved to an empty old chair that was probably worth more dong than it would take to buy the entire building and every person inside. By the recently passed Decree on Property Ownership, the People's Committee had allowed foreigners limited rights to own apartments, not land or houses. No one could buy a building in Cholon. Of course, the Chinese inhabitants didn't bother to ask permission and the market was always open if you had the right contacts and enough dollars, since dong didn't factor into high-end transactions in this neighborhood.

Morgan took the lead, edging forward on the couch where he was sitting close to Hatati.

"I don't think it wise to tell you everything now," Morgan said. "Kind of a 'need to know' that protects all of us. I will fill you in on what I believe is important. The rest you'll have to figure out on your own. That's if you survive." No smile. He was dead serious. "We'll also expect complete honesty from you. There are things in your head we need to know." Now, he did grin. "That's if all the black tar you inhale hasn't coated your brain like creosote."

It seemed everybody was aware of my habit. Did they also know I used my right hand rather than my left to *su thu dam*, masturbate, in the rare moments when I went to sleep without riding the magic cloud? The practice of manual stimulation was totally acceptable in Vietnamese society, though I did understand the word and behavior was taboo in the Christian hypocritical West that believed dropping napalm on blameless peasants was more acceptable than pleasuring oneself. If it was so uncivilized, why did these heathens invent the Internet?

Whenever I crossed the border from Vietnam into the China of Cholon, I drifted away from the Buddha into the arms of Confucius. I could feel a strange transference that was physical as well as theological. I couldn't stop listening to the great man's advice that "a man with head up his ass can't see shit." I didn't want to appear stupid to these killers, so I wanted to heed the profound Confucian guidance that "looking at small advantages prevents great affairs from being accomplished." At least for awhile, I would cooperate and not try any tricks that we half-breeds were famous for. I put on my stern face and tried to look the cagey contemplative Chinaman.

"Some of the few delights allowed in our socialist paradise are the western movies that are copied and available on the Binh Tay black market," I said. "Some time ago, I confiscated a box of these pirated DVDs from the criminal gangs who distribute the fakes. Before I turned them into to the Electronic Fraud Department at headquarters, I felt I had to review the films for obedience to communist thought. I think I've heard James Bond say 'need to know.' Or maybe it was Jason Bourne. Does this mean I'm a spy now?"

Everyone smiled. Except Luong who continued to believe that smiles weren't to be casually squandered. Maybe I'd broken the tension. Or they were ready to move on with or without me. Whatever, Liu was the first to cross-examine me. He stroked the arm of his silk robe and watched me like I was the mahjong honor tile he didn't need to fill his meld.

"Tell us about your investigation," Liu said. "Who is involved and what they know."

Trying to seem as straightforward and guiltless as a child, I told them about my findings and, in a limited way, the involvement of Nguyen. I stressed how easy it would be to guess the motive behind the murders, even if the investigators knew nothing about Luong. The pictures and the toy cobra couldn't have been bigger clues to general identities. With names and months to canvass the entire Central Highland Montagnard community, an impossibility in a region where flatlanders were as welcome as malaria, they would be hard-pressed in fingering a specific suspect. I was certain even the highest levels of the security service wouldn't have access to American military or CIA files and wouldn't be able to track Morgan. The wild card that might mean my being thrown to the hogs was Nguyen. It was obvious I'd shared too much with him and it could jeopardize the lives of us all. Dancing around this question would take all my skills. Morgan was the first to make me hop.

"You know Nguyen is aware of me and Luong?" Morgan asked. "And you were the one who told him?"

"Yes," I said. "But that was before I met you, Hatati, and Mr. Liu. I was being a detective and didn't understand what was truly happening. It would have been extremely suspicious if I didn't have some opinions."

"Do they trust you?"

"About as much as you believe in the communist revolution. Half-breeds are famous for being weasels, not patriots."

"Will they let you continue?"

"We'll have to invent a good explanation for the hours I've spent with you and how I escaped the raid on the river."

"What do you think would work?"

"Well, I was pursuing a lead. It took me across the river and away from Phan. I had no idea what went on with him. By the time I was able to get away from this useless pursuit, hours had passed and now I was back at the office to report."

"Sounds kind of lame to me."

"You don't know the dynamic between a Chink-Vietnamese and the Security Services. While they hate me, they're terrified I know more than them. And I might have some magic powers the Chinese have possessed for centuries. It's a very useful attitude. I'm a master at using my standing to humiliate them. Usually, they are too moronic to notice."

"You really think you can stroll back to your desk and they won't arrest you?"

"As the great Sun Tzu wrote, 'In war, the right way is to avoid what is strong and to strike at what is weak.' Their weakness is their desperation. The pressure coming from Quang and his puppets must be extreme. There is no indication you will stop killing. More likely, you will be coming for Quang soon. They do not have enough time to torture everyone in the country, a dream they have had for decades. I'm their best chance at finding you."

"And you can keep quiet even when they burn you with a hot iron? Shove a chopstick up your dick and wiggle it around like they're trying to hold on to a greasy noodle?"

"How colorful! But my bosses aren't so wasteful. They pick up used plastic bags on the road. True environmentalists. They tie the bags over the prisoner's head until suffocation is the only future. Not so complicated as water boarding. Just as efficient. I think I could make it a few rounds before I give your children up. Mine too, if I had any."

"Could be that honesty isn't the best strategy here. You might try to convince us you'd never rat out your allies and suffer through whatever they invented to brutalize you."

"As I've been told, 'we don't have time.' I agree with that."

"So we let you go, and you just saunter back to your desk? We did already take your pistol, and I'm not quite ready to give it back."

"That wasn't mine. I found it in a drawer at Danh Nguyen's villa. I'm prohibited from carrying a weapon unless one falls into my pocket."

"Convenient, but not convincing."

"Again, quoting my master, the Great Sun Tzu, 'speed is the essence of war' and I can be of great value in keeping the mongoose from the Night Snake's throat in the short time we have before Sai Gon is under a blanket curfew."

"Are you sure you can help us find Quang? And Nguyen?"

"Nguyen will be easy. Quang, not so much. I believe I can do it. I will have to be subtle."

These kinds of rambling discussions were normal in a culture that was just learning to use their iPods and appreciate that the people behind the TV screens weren't supernatural demons. Montagnards hadn't reached that level of incarnation yet. Luong was getting nervous as the wall clock ticked off another minute. He was beginning to sway back and forth and smack his lips.

"We let him go," Luong said. "We won't be here much longer, and the security forces wouldn't dare raid Cholon anyway. He's already given them enough information about us, if they didn't get there by themselves. We do need his help to find Quang if Nutley isn't successful."

Morgan looked toward Hatati. She nodded, and he turned to Mr. Liu. He waited just long enough to add a touch of drama and then nodded too.

For the next few minutes, we outlined a plan that mostly covered how I was to contact them. My job was simple. Find Quang. Then Nguyen. Their job. Kill them both.

At the door, Mr. Liu bowed, his hands tucked inside the loose sleeves of his silk robe. There was no need for threats. It was a common understanding between all of us that, if I betrayed them, there would be no further generations of offspring from my loins or anyone I had ever befriended.

As Mr. Liu closed the door, I could already hear Luong, Morgan, and Hatati urgently planning. I smiled, knowing, for the first time in even my vast fantasyland, I had the resources of MI6, the CIA, and the Triads cloaking me in their veil. This was something new for a humble squint detective raised in a slum and taught lessons in a re-education camp.

Down the dimly lit stairs and out into the night, I wondered if I had a few minutes to stop at Ma Jing's on the way to headquarters. Not a chance. A Honda Civic and driver were waiting for me on the street, and the chauffeur was programmed to ignore any of my instructions. Within fifteen minutes, we were parked in front of the Sai Gon police control center on Tran Hung Dao Boulevard. The trip had been uneventful and rather boring, as the city reacted to the massive hunt and stayed inside more than normal, worried they could be pulled into the security cordons.

My feet were barely on the pavement when I was grabbed by two men in the normal plain-clothes detective uniform of short-sleeved white shirt, brogues, black slacks, and sunglasses even though it was well after sunset. They both might have been on the department power lifting team because they had little trouble raising me off the ground and carrying me into the building with a hand in each of my armpits. I didn't bother to resist. It would've been useless and I'd get to the same place with broken bones rather than unharmed.

That place was downstairs. The Vault. They didn't use the lift, but I was elevated below, my feet dangling six inches from the wooden staircase. Two flights and we reached a steel door. It was quiet, except the constant drip of aged water pipes and the scurrying of rats in the walls and screeching as they fought over a toe morsel. Not even screams. I knew there was another door just beyond this one that contained most of the noise behind its bulk. That was a relatively modern remodel. Prior rulers hadn't been as sensitive about the public's attitude toward people pleading for mercy or respite from the nipple clamps.

The man on my left knocked with his free hand, staring straight ahead and not even glancing at me. He actually held me a few inches away from his body as if I were a simmering bag of turds. Or pus-ball Chinese-Viet mongrel. I think he would have used a third hand to pinch his nose tight. The distinction he held was a harelip that curved from the top of his mouth to his left nostril. He "humpphed" with each wheeze, his breathing obviously impaired by the disfigurement.

Moi sut. Harelip. Cleft lip. Agent Orange. No matter how much this man found me repellant, the abuse he must suffer everyday was almost beyond my appreciation. While I might be mocked as the "offspring of a lice-ridden whore," this man was ridiculed for having a slime worm on his lip by everyone brave enough to insult him. No wonder he was a bodybuilder. It was no fault of his that his genes had been scrambled by a miniscule fraction of the millions of gallons of defoliant sprayed in Operation Ranch Hand and other quaintly named American bombing raids. The dimethylsulphoxide, diquat, and tordon chemicals supplied by Dow made a nice addition to the company's bottom line. My captor might have been a lucky one. Other innocents had been born with kidneys outside their bodies, legs where eyes should be, no nose, or other deformities that left them as good as dead the moment they were bred. Many more had learning and mental disabilities not as noticeable as the physical affects. I couldn't help but think of Phan. And it was a plague that continued to follow the generations of those who lived through the bombing with more harelips per square kilometer in Sai Gon than any city in the world. We waited for the door to open and I studied the man's defect.

"You really should go see Operation Smile," I said. "They repair over two thousand harelips per year. It's free and it doesn't matter that you're older than most of the patients. They'll have you looking like Lee Byung Hun in just a few hours." Hun was one of our most popular movie stars, and this man wouldn't look like him with a complete face lift. Little harm in trying.

No comment. Only a snort that was hard to distinguish from his other restricted noises. And there was that tightening on my biceps that felt like my arm was being crushed between two armored tanks. It didn't seem my advice was well-received.

The door opened and we were ushered into an enclosed space by a woman outfitted in a tan blouse and skirt and sensible black shoes that could have been worn by the Queen of England. I'd heard they were popular now and called Doc Martens, but I was far from a fashionista, a descriptive word I found fascinating when I'd first read it on the cover of *Cosmopolitan Vietnam*. She was no model, short even for a race closer to dwarves than Watusis, and a face that sported a permanent scowl creasing her mouth and turning her eyes farther downward. Maybe a little makeup would have brightened up skin that didn't appear to have seen sunlight in many months.

The man on my left must have been a friend. He moved closer and whispered, *"Rat vui duoc gap ban, Mi."* Nice to see you, Mi. He touched her elbow and smiled. She returned the look and struggled to ignore him, making it clear she was trying too hard.

I hadn't paid much attention to this one. He was too normal and the only unique thing was his voice. He sounded more like he was in the middle of his treatments for a sex change and the hormones hadn't completely heightened the tone of his voice.

Survival. The next few hours would determine if I walked out of the building on my legs or in a bucket of ashes from the furnace where most of the bodies ended their time in this incarnation. I knew I was trying to shift my focus to these underlings in order to avoid the pain I understood was coming. Somehow, it was working and by the time the next door opened, I was able to stand by myself without fainting.

We were greeted by screams. The regular employees of this part of the building would be on overtime, asking pointed questions of anyone even vaguely suspected of participation in the slayings of politburo members, an unheard-of and heinous crime in our worker's Eden where democracy was a title rather than a truth. Again, words and thoughts were there for me to hide behind until the first blow broke a tooth. I was steered down a dimly lit hallway, past closed doors that emitted babbling and shrieks, no light. Eventually, I was led into a small room with only a metal armchair bolted to the floor and a drain below.

The two men pushed me inside and made me sit, stepping back and crossing their arms on their chests. The woman left, her shoes tapping on the cement. Above me, the light flickered like we were about to have a power outage. It was time to prepare as best as I could for what was about to happen and hope for mercy.

"Did the two of you come from the same syphilitic mother?" I asked, looking from one to the other. "Or did her vagina bring forth maggots rather than healthy babies?"

Neither one made a move toward me. They must have had strict orders to ensure I was unharmed until the masters appeared. Both developed tics above their eyes, and I could see the muscles in their arms strain their shirts as they tried to keep all the testosterone in check without imploding.

In the upper corner, I could see where the camera was hidden. It would take someone who knew it was there to identify the small hole for what it meant. These two guards would be aware that everything was being recorded or else they probably would have begun the beatings themselves. My country was attempting to join the twenty-first century or the twenty-sixth, since it was year 2555 in many Buddhist calendars. Technology was arriving by the boatload, and the security forces got first choice.

No knock. The door pushed open with a slight squeal of rusty metal hinges and Nguyen walked into the room. He was wearing the same clothes and still looked freshly groomed and pressed like the rock star he tried his hardest to be. He gestured with his hand for the two minders to leave, holding the door open for them.

"Boys, tell your mother penicillin is the answer," I said. They left without a look back.

Nguyen wasn't in the least entertained. He glared and leaned against the wall, quickly moving away and brushing something grizzly off his shoulder.

"*Cuc,*" he hissed. Shit.

"Too high on the wall for that," I said. "I think it's probably brain matter. Or puke."

"You can't stop yourself," Nguyen said. "Your insubordination has become more boring as time goes on. You somehow believe your remarks are humorous and a diversion. Neither idea is correct."

"And if I bowed to your every wish, it would be more fun?"

"Healthier."

"Are you planning to beat me to death? Or be more sophisticated? Nails in the end of the bat? Brass knuckles? Steel toes?"

"It all depends on you, Captain Fang. Tell me what I want to know and you can walk out of here. Being able to walk at all will be a victory."

Not yet bound, I waved a hand in dismissal and smiled.

"Ask away. I would like nothing more than to cooperate with my superiors in our socialist democracy. It is my duty as a law-abiding citizen."

"Where did you go this afternoon?"

"Bhinh Thanh.*"*

"Why?"

"Following a lead. I am a captain of detectives."

"How did you come onto this 'lead'?"

"A confidential source."

"There is no such person for you. Tell me who directed you to Bhinh Thanh."

"If you had listened during our last conversation, rather than admire yourself in the mirrors, you would remember I told you a story about a Degar and our time together in the camps. Where do the Montagnards gather? Could it possibly be Bhinh Thanh?"

"I recall every word and insult. But why did you disappear? You must be aware there was a shootout not long after you entered the slum."

"I was led away supposedly to meet someone who might know about what was going on."

"And who did you meet?"

"No one. My escort heard the shooting and told me to follow him. I had no choice. Another man pushed me down a path, threatening me with a knife. I was frightened they would think I was behind whatever was happening. Were you behind it?"

"Where did they take you?"

"Across the river. They held me for a while, then let me go, telling me I was very lucky to still have my *duong vat* still attached." Penis.

Nguyen began to chuckle. It started with just a grin and a sound like he was clearing his throat of phlegm, increasing rapidly to guffaws that threatened to develop into a fit. I had to admit, he was quite attractive when he wasn't trying to be cool, serious, and aloof.

"*Di an cuc,*" Nguyen said. Go eat shit, a common phrase when a Vietnamese felt they were being fed that bodily discharge. "That is the funniest thing you've said since I met you. I never thought we'd get anywhere near the truth without taking more profound measures." He turned toward the door. "I'll be back soon with someone you wouldn't want to meet in your worst nightmare." He walked out, leaving me alone to my terror.

A pleasant thought. Recently, Human Rights Watch, one of those heathen groups that tried to cast my country as a bunch of cavemen who didn't differentiate justice and liberty from being tortured to death for spitting on the sidewalk, had published a report on the extent of "police brutality" in

Vietnam. For instance, one man had been beaten into a coma with rocks by policemen for supporting Gai Li and not Sai F. C. in the Vietnamese V-League, the country's highest professional soccer union. Another man was reported a victim of suicide after a dispute with his daughter, the wife of a policeman. The officials told his family he had committed suicide by hanging. His relatives expressed doubts that suicide was the cause of death. They said the man was found dead sitting down, with a leather belt around his neck and no marks on his throat. It seemed, from reading a restricted report I happened to find on a comrade's desk, that being given a traffic ticket could no longer just result in the loss of your dong, but your life. Numerous speeding offenders had been "beaten to death" by cops for such heinous crimes as not signaling a right turn or blowing through a red light. The statistics pointed to an epidemic of cruelty in the thousands, not the few aberrations found in any civilized country. Outside of the traitorous Human Rights Watch Report, I knew the fatality rate of those taken to this dungeon was "eyes only" data. It was close to 100 percent. I sighed, realizing the next few breaths should be savored. I closed my eyes and attempted to let my mantra settle the goblins threatening to overwhelm my soul.

The usual tactic was to leave the prisoner alone for an extended period, allowing the captive time to dwell on his devils and soak up the fear, softening his resistance like a mango about to explode with too much distilled sugar. I knew this strategy as well as the "good guy, bad guy" method I was sure would come soon. I had already made up my mind about whose side I was on. The challenge was to get out of here alive and able to help Luong finish his mission.

It might have been minutes. Or hours. I had succeeded in slowing my heartbeat and breathing to the point I could have been mistaken as dead. Far from it. I was composed and rested when the man entered the room, carrying a large metal briefcase. It was Tran, the in-house torturer and reputed executioner when the time came to finish things. The stories of his barbarism circulated through the building, especially late at night when it was dark and quiet, time for the ghosts to roam the halls. No one knew his name or dared get close enough to ask. They called him "*Lat*," a shortening for "slicer," but never to his face. The reputed contents of the briefcase that rarely left his hand helped make his myth and name appropriate.

Lat was mostly distinguished by his total physical anonymity. He was the classic master spy who could blend in anywhere because he was so ordinary. Average height, not too thin or fat, black hair and eyes, nondescript clothing, no scars, nothing that would make him stand out. Until you made eye contact. It was as if his pupils sucked in the energy around him. A black hole that absorbed all into the vortex anyone could sense was ultimate pure bottomless evil. He had never been known to smile, and he didn't now as he stepped near, setting the case on the floor and moving behind me. Not gently, he pulled my arms back and cuffed them together in back, fastening me tight to the metal slats in the chair with plastic restraints. Within seconds, all the mellowness vanished and I began to breathe shallowly. I knew this would be a battle of wits and no one wanted me dead. Yet.

The legend, more than his bland presence, was what terrified me. During the war with the Americans, a famous female Viet Cong sniper and torturer code named "Apache" became famous for tormenting US prisoners close enough to a firebase that everyone could hear the screams and the blow-by-blow narrative she gave of what she was doing to her captive. Apache operated mostly in the Delta and did the majority of her work in the night where the VC was King. In her case, Queen. She hung the captured soldier naked on a bamboo rack and started by pulling out all of his fingernails, then bending the fingers backward until they broke. From the fingers, she moved on to strategic carving all over the body, taking a lot of time on the eyeballs. While she worked, she chewed betel nut and cooed to her prisoner, occasionally spitting juice into his eyes, reminding him of all the "pussy" they got back home and would never see or feel again. The final act was always the same. She grabbed the naked man's cock and balls in her hand, shrieked in delight, and cut them off. Not satisfied yet, she released the terminally wounded man and told him to run for it. No one made it more than a few steps with blood spurting everywhere and the horror overcoming even the pain. When the man dropped to the ground, she stuffed his genitals into his mouth and left him strung up in a tree to be found by his fellow GIs. The rumor was Lat was her apprentice and now was more talented than Apache ever was.

Today's show began with the slow ritual opening of the briefcase, a serenade of love featuring "oohs" and "ahhs" as Lat fondled his treasures. Inside, each in a separate foam compartment, were a variety of pliers, knives, scalpels, tweezers, hammers, drills, clamps, and spray cans. Nothing looked friendly and I couldn't help but laugh.

"You must be used to making house calls," I said. "Everything the door-to-door Marquis de Sade needs in one small case."

Just a sense. It didn't seem Lat was a man prone to conversation. Most likely, he'd been given a few questions to ask and he wouldn't waste any energy on chitchat. Surely, they wouldn't want him to start on my face or anywhere that could be spotted if I was going to see the smog of Sai Gon again. A mangled man stumbling around the city brought too much attention. That didn't mean a few broken fingers and cuts that would be covered by clothing were banned.

Mother. At times like these, the moments when we sit bound to a chair, watching a devil sharpen his tools, planning which part of the body to slice first, we tend to think about *me*, mom. At least I did. The *dee chaw*, bitch, hadn't been able to keep her legs closed for the Chinese merchant who came to the door and offered her an old Flying Pigeon bicycle for the use of her vagina. A few years later, I inherited the antique. It was my first bike and I was reminded of my father's origin every day of my adult life with the barrage of "*vang moog.*" Yellow ass. And much worse. My mother did love me enough to tell people in my early years that my name was *Xau Xi Coc*, Hideous Toad, since there is a cultural belief that giving a child the name of something rotten, ugly, or useless will keep the evil spirits away. Not even the demons would want such a pathetic creature as me, and the people I worked with agreed with that to this day. Still, in my heart I had nothing but fondness for the woman who'd nursed and fed me even when a bowl of rice was a feast. We ate after the bottles of snake wine were dry. She preferred the jugs with the floating reptiles still in the glass, fangs exposed like white fish hooks. Trying to regain some of the contentment I'd experienced a few seconds before, I focused on the memory of her decomposed body being dug up a year after her death, the final installment of the year-long mourning ritual. The chopsticks were still between her teeth, the rice gone from her mouth, but the coins still jingling where her tongue used to be. She had successfully reached the next circle and the worms were well fed, assuring her ascendance. I breathed easier, comforted by the warm reminiscence. At least I felt secure for a *ksana*, or one-seventy-fifth of a second in Buddhist time. Lat was turning toward me, a pair of needle-nosed pliers in his hand.

"I'm going to skip to the most important questions," Lat said. "I don't care about your name, birth date, or address. Or who is your whore of a mother. I want to know what you were doing this afternoon in Binh Thanh."

"How did you know my mother was a whore? Who told you?" I was outraged.

Lat sighed, resigned to another tedious day at the office. He moved behind me, binding my ankles to the chair before he cut the plastic cuffs on my hands, guiding my arms forward and refastening them on my lap. I didn't resist, knowing it was about as futile as yelling at a mongrel mutt to stop barking at the moon. I needed a rock to throw at Lat. Or a pistol. I slumped forward, trying to void my mind.

"Again, what were you doing in Binh Thanh?" Lat asked.

"I was following a lead," I said.

"What lead?"

"From a confidential informer."

"There is no 'confidential' in this room."

"I have groomed many sources in my years as a detective."

"I want a name."

"She is dead. Her name is Hacmon. She was a Montagnard."

The game was always to give up as little as possible based on some grain of truth in order to sacrifice the minimum of fingers. And blood. There was no longer a definition or concept of "lie" in these kinds of interrogations. It was all about survival and keeping secrets without losing an eyeball. At least until the final surrender. They would never find Hacmon in the warren of hootches that made up the Binh Thanh slum and had no idea if she had passed on. Anyone the authorities questioned in that neighborhood would look dumbfounded and reply, "*Ai?*" Who. The real challenge would be to shield Luong and Morgan. I stared into Lat's eyes, trying to transmit how totally sincere and forthcoming I was.

"Did she take you to Luong?"

Uh-oh. Nguyen must have prepped him well and he wasn't going to waste any time. He most likely had other patients to chop into mouse food.

"She tried. He was no longer there."

"Why did you disappear?"

"I was trying to find him and got lost. That place is a real rat warren."

"Did you hear the shooting?"

"What shooting? I went across the river and took a taxi back here."

"And you never saw or spoke to Luong?"

"No."

"I know you are lying."

He held the pliers in front of his face, twisting them around as if he were inspecting it for ticks and fleas. Next, he began to open and close the pinching end like he was flexing.

"There's an old saying in the West that 'this is going to hurt me more than you'. That's not true in this case. I will enjoy slowly pulling out all your fingernails, you half-breed. I even have a jar of salt and a bottle of sulphuric acid to spice up your life. After I get done with the nails, we'll move on to other areas." He reached for my left hand, holding it by the thumb.

"Oops," he said. "Almost forgot."

He dropped my hand and turned to his briefcase where he took out a wide web belt. Moving behind me again, he wrapped the belt around my chest and the back of the chair, securing it tightly.

"There," he said, "now you won't hurt yourself jerking around from the excruciating pain you're about to experience."

He stepped in front of me and grabbed my left hand, this time gripping my index finger so only the tip showed. No matter how calming the visions of Mother were, I began to shake, trying to pull my hand back as the pliers got closer to their prey.

"That won't do you any good," Lat said. "I'll just have to tie you to the arms of the chair. If that doesn't work, there're two guys you called mutant names a few minutes ago who would be happy to help."

He moved the pliers closer and watched me quiver.

"Last chance," Lat said. "And when we get started, please try not to shit yourself. I hate the smell. I think you've already pissed." He nodded toward my stomach.

I glanced down and saw the spreading darkness on the crotch of my pants, not even realizing I'd let go, the warmth now making it obvious.

"I told you the truth," I gasped, finding it hard to make the words come out. "Hacmon said she could take me to Luong. When I got there, another woman told me Hacmon was dead. Then, I tried to find Luong alone. I left Phan to watch the car. He can verify much of this."

Without comment, Lat pulled my finger closer and tightened the nose of the pliers on my nail. In one smooth motion, he jerked out the nail like he was pulling a tooth. For added pain, he squeezed the open wound with his fingers, rubbing them together.

No blood. Just a fireball of pain that shot through my arm and into my head, making me dizzy with the intensity. My entire body reacted to the force of the violation. I did try to tighten my sphincter so I wouldn't be sitting in my own dung. Or maybe it was only a reflex. I opened my mouth, a scream building like a tsunami in my throat. Before it could birth, Lat slapped me. Over and over.

"No yelling," he said. "Save it for later."

Within seconds, my head slumped to my chest and I closed my eyes, trying to think of anything except the throbbing that was shooting up my arm, threatening to explode my head like a rickshaw on a ripe melon. I couldn't see Lat and figured he was getting set for the next finger. I'd know soon enough.

"I've got to *di dai*," Lat said. Take a piss. "You just relax. I'll be back soon." With that, he stood, taking a small shaker out of his pocket. He doused the wound with salt and walked away, leaving me wailing and shaking uncontrollably. It took what felt like a dynasty for the howling to end. It was more likely minutes, but I continued to quiver like I was naked inside the walk-in freezer at Ngo's morgue.

After the door opened and closed, I was alone, apart from the camera. And a shiny speckled green gecko that had magically appeared on the wall. I knew Lat was using basic interrogation methods. Allowing me to unwind and think about the pain that had just been inflicted and, more importantly, the depth of what was to come. At least it seemed they didn't want me mutilated. Not yet. I stared at the gecko and forced my mind to wander anyplace other than the ache in my finger and the bubbling of its juices in the brine, fear lodged like a fish ball in my throat.

There were over a thousand varieties of geckos in the world. Vietnam was the home to many hundreds, ranging in size from less than an inch to nearly a foot long. The most often seen in my country was the common house gecko, just like the one I was watching as he sat motionless, waiting for an insect. Below the ground, this one must have enjoyed the flies that mysteriously appeared on a lifeless body or piece of meat within minutes, depositing larvae that would soon become adults. The haunted place of horror had seen thousands of corpses and it would be an easy source of food for a silent, stealthy gecko.

Green with red spots, my new friend clung to the wall as if he had glue on his feet. He didn't. I knew it because I used to collect the little lizards. It was his toes and not some kind of adhesive liquid squirted out that kept him attached. The explanation was called the van der Waals force, named after some Dutch scientist who had nothing better to do than watch geckos and create mathematical equations. One of the observations was that gecko's toes bent in the opposite direction of humans' and that trait allowed them to grip on nearly any surface whether upside down or level. Along with the many ridges on their feet, geckos could stay unmoving for hours until a meal showed up. At least I had this trivia to try to distract the crashing in my head as my hand began to swell and stink. I attempted to keep from focusing on my misery and what terror was to come. That was as easy as becoming the next premier of China.

Before I could witness if my gecko comrade was going to find a succulent fly to dine on, the door opened and Lat strode into the room, his chest pumped up like he was competing in the Mr. Vietnam contest. He evidently loved his job. Without hesitating, he swaggered over to me and grabbed another finger. I began to shriek immediately, even before he could rip out one more nail. When he did, the tears began to flow down my cheeks. Lat stepped back and put on a pair of leather gloves. Not wasting any time to tell me to quiet, he slugged me on the right ear, then the left. Now, my head was filled with the sound of my own screams and crashing of a thousand cymbals. Lat shook me until I opened my eyes.

"You were telling me a fairy tale about a woman named Hacmon," Lat said. "I want the real story. More importantly, I want to hear where Luong is hiding."

At times, when I became dehydrated at Ma Jing's after hours of riding the waves, a burning sensation would overwhelm my esophagus, the acid rising from my stomach and emptying the sludge in my mouth. It tasted like battery acid and felt the same. Now, a river began to flow up my throat, and I retched, trying to get as many of the toxins as possible on Lat as I spit it out. He was too experienced and moved away as soon as he saw what was about to happen. All I succeeded in doing was dripping the scum on my chest. I closed my eyes and tried not to hyperventilate.

The next thing I saw was Lat picking up different size scalpels in his briefcase, scrutinizing each one as if he were about to make a momentous decision. I could only imagine. Eventually, he seemed satisfied and turned back to me, holding a surgeon's tool that was so sharp it seemed to be cutting the air. The blade was little more than a centimeter wide. Steel handle and all, it was about the length of a chopstick, and there was little doubt Lat knew how to use it. He came close and began to cut off the buttons on my shirt, popping them like they were sesame seeds on a hot plate. When my chest was exposed, he held the blade against my left nipple.

"Anymore," he said, "I tire of the fingernail method. I find it much more rewarding to begin cutting. I tend to start with a nipple."

The room really did begin to spin and my breathing had the rhythm of an AK-47 firing on automatic.

Before Lat could begin the nipplectomy, the door opened and Nguyen walked inside, flanked by the two syphilitic guards.

"That's enough, Lat," Nguyen said. "We have more urgent plans for the captain. You'll surely get to finish later. For now, I need him."

Lat scowled, but didn't object. He moved aside.

Love. My life had been mostly barren until this moment. If I could have gotten out of the chair, I would have kissed Nguyen and become his sex slave like any of the harlots on Tu Doa Street. I began to cry, the tears of joy mixing with the drops caused by the pain and flowing freely down my face.

Nguyen nodded to the men and they cut off the bindings, helping me to my feet.

"You reek," Nguyen said. "We'll stop by the bathroom before we go upstairs."

I waved good-bye to the gecko, who seemed completely unimpressed by all the drama, and we went into the hallway. I was about to break out in a Chinese Wushu dance, feigning the use of throwing knives and martial arts moves, steps recently made popular at Cholon nightclubs. In the moment, it seemed more advisable to act meek and thankful.

"Did your mother's clap cause the rot between your ears?" I asked the man holding my right arm. "And your brother's too? I think I can see the pus for brains leaking out your nose." I looked at the one on my left. "No, that's snot. Your brains got flushed." Immediately, the pressure on my biceps increased to that of a boa constrictor squeezing the life out of a baby alligator, a video I'd seen recently on YouTube. I smiled. I was alive, reminiscing, and insulting. Life couldn't get peachier.

At the end of the hall, Nguyen opened a door and my handlers pushed me inside. It was a big room, completely empty other than a drain hole in the middle of the sloping floor.

"*Dai*," Nguyen barked. Strip.

"What?" I asked.

"*Dai*," he said even louder.

"You want to see my *buoi*?" I asked in total amazement.

One of the guards pushed me in the room. From behind the door, the other one brought out a fire hose and began turning a bulky black faucet.

"Your choice," Nguyen said. "You can shower in your clothes and be soaked for hours or take them off. I really don't want you dripping all over the building. Still, this country has freedom of choice."

Gagging with laughter at this absurd political comment, I began to undress. Abruptly, I stopped, smelling the odor from my pants as I bent over. I stood up, spreading my arms.

"Go ahead," I said. "Shoot me."

"Good choice," Nguyen said. "Your clothes are as rank as your mother's pussy."

The first blast almost knocked me to my feet, pushing me back against the far wall. After only a few seconds, I couldn't stand any longer and dropped to my knees, hugging my chest and trying to keep my head down, eyes closed.

The strength of the water felt like thousands of darts penetrating my body simultaneously. It wasn't all that unpleasant, except I worried the force might break an arm or leg. I knew the guards wouldn't mind in the least if they had to carry me out screaming, making sure to pinch any fractures with glee.

When I was suitably cleansed, Nguyen motioned for the man to stop. I shook like a wet dog and began to tremble in the cold.

"We'll just wait a moment," Nguyen said. "Press your clothes with your hands. Get as much of that water out as you can before we go. I'd hate it if you leave slug trails."

I did as I was told, sheepishly feeling like one of the dead giant rats floating down the drain every morning before the market on Chau Van Diep Street opened. They were infamous and as big as the hairless street mongrels. Before they ate the Aminopterin poison, the huge rodents had been even fiercer than the freakish dogs who roamed the neighborhood in packs, carrying off unattended babies and licking the entrails. I pressed my pants and shirt as best as I could, the water dripping into the drain, and looked up, still completely soaked and feeling moistly vulnerable. Now would be the time to give them a hangdog look and attitude. I bent toward Nguyen, shivering.

"If your breed sprang from apes," I said, "you didn't jump far enough."

"You're as dumb as a river carp," Nguyen said. "Just shut up and follow me. Your escorts will make sure you don't get lost."

We shuffled out, climbing flights of stairs until we reached the fourth floor. At no time was I able to walk without my two minders holding on and steering me. Every once in a while, I tried to make a right turn when Nguyen went left. Not a chance, but I relished the cretins' scramble to keep me on the straight and narrow. A few times, I acted as if I were about to faint, relaxing all my muscles and slumping. The men were forced to prop me up. After a few minutes, we walked down the top floor corridor and ended up in what I assumed was Nguyen's office.

"Leave him," Nguyen said. "Wait outside."

The two morons left and I staggered quickly to a chair in front of the desk, not waiting for Nguyen's direction. Sitting, I cradled my throbbing hand close to my chest, wondering if Nguyen had a bandage anywhere near. Or some Queen Morpheus.

The office was utilitarian, probably quite different in luxury from the mansions his level of bureaucrats went home to with their swimming pools,

Laotian slaves, and chandeliers. Even the walls were painted gray to match the gunmetal desk and unpadded chairs. The required picture of Uncle Ho hung just behind Nguyen's head when he sat, and he adjusted a few papers in front of him, making sure they were perfectly square.

"Anal, eh," I said. "No piece of paper out of harmony and no half-breed left with all his traitorous fingernails."

"The 'anal' part comes later when you're alone with your so-called syphilitic guards," Nguyen said. "For now, I want you to keep silent until I tell you differently."

"I wouldn't dare open my mouth around someone with your obsession."

"That's the last words I want to hear. I don't care how valuable some think you might be. If you disobey, I'll just let your new best friends outside share some special time with you. And Lat."

I nodded, Lat's name the clincher.

"I heard what you said in the interrogation room. While some if it was likely true, most of it was pure lies, dishonesty a talent you chinks have made an art form. You're almost as untrustworthy as a Cambodian. Or a cobra."

No response required. He stopped and looked at the papers on his desk with a blank stare, while I tried to plan the next moves in the lethal Xiangqi game that had just opened with his first move. I couldn't let Nguyen capture my General with his army.

Since I'd just had a shower, it wasn't me that stank so badly. The smell was a combination of sweat, wheezing air conditioners, fear, and prawns with *nuoc mam* fish sauce, the spicy kind made with garlic, vinegar, and hot Thai peppers, a paste no Vietnamese could live without for long. Life without *nuoc mam* was survival without blood. But there was another ingredient in this building that had more to do with decay than life. Years of body fluids drained, chunks of flesh severed, and bodies dragged limp to the incinerator, had coated all the walls with the stench of pain, agony, and death. I tried pinching my nostrils shut, waiting for Nguyen to push another pawn forward.

For the next half hour, Nguyen questioned me, and I stuck to my story, adding very little. It was becoming clear he and his bosses wanted more from me than my bumblings. I parried, waiting for Nguyen to get to the point. He didn't get ruffled in the least, finally winding down and pushing his chair back.

"First," Nguyen said, "we'll get those fingers treated. Then, you're going to go back to Binh Thanh or wherever you think you can find Luong. We want you to make contact and find out who's helping him. As normal, Phan will accompany you. We will assume they know how you operate." He sat up straight, fiddling with the buttons on his starched shirt. "If you cooperate, we will forget all the criminal revisionism you have demonstrated. Agreed?"

It didn't take me long to answer. I wanted out of this stinking building. Fast.

"I would be honored to join the revolution and our eternal class struggle, comrade," I said. "Simply give me my marching orders and I'll goose step into the worker's state."

Nguyen studied me like he had discovered a tumor, but couldn't decide if it was malignant. He nodded, unconvinced, but not wanting to spread the cancer.

"I will call for a nurse," Nguyen said, reaching for an old black rotary dial phone on his desk.

Within minutes, a stunning beauty in a white uniform appeared at the door. My taste in women tended more toward my Chinese side, but this striking Vietnamese female might make me change my appetite like Hatati had. Nguyen snapped instructions to her, ignoring the massive *bac mas*, tits. She silently raised my fingers and applied cream, wrapping them in a thin covering. It seemed she was used to the kinds of wounds I exhibited. Maybe because of her immense cleavage or the analgesic swab, the pain rapidly diminished.

Watching Nguyen and making sure my elbow made as much contact as possible with the remarkable nurse's *bac mas*, I wondered why Nguyen and most Vietnamese men didn't appreciate the artistry of a pair of gigantic *vus*. Breasts. Often, I'd heard big boobs linked to water buffaloes rather than exquisite females. The tendency in this country was to idolize *vus* the size of lemons rather than bitter melons. For one, I was, grateful to fondle a pair of pillowy *bac mas* and transport myself to the days when my tramp of a mother held me to her *vus*. Because of our cultural bias, most breast augmentation procedures performed in Vietnam were on "tit tourists," foreigners looking for cheap surgery. As my voluptuous nurse bent over, I turned toward her, accidentally getting my nose between those Michelangelos.

As in everything spectacular in life, it all ended too soon. She dropped my hand back into my lap and walked out, not having uttered a word. Nguyen was ready for my discharge and only waited for the door to close.

"I'll expect a report by morning," he said.

"The focus of this investigation is to find Luong and anyone who could be helping him?" I asked. "That's assuming he's the killer."

"Yes."

"Are you willing to tell me who the next victim may be?"

"No."

"You must believe there is one?"

"Possibly."

"Like the man who took the picture that's been left on the other target's chests?"

"No comment."

"I'll have to spend some time on my computer. I believe there is intel there that will help me reach Luong."

"You have an hour. Then I want you on the street."

"Yes, comrade."

The subservience always rankled me, and I made sure I underlined this with a bow. Apparatchiks like Nguyen rarely read the cynicism and that was true now. He waved me away.

"*Di di*," he said. Go

My fingers began to burn and ache again. That was nothing compared to the joy of getting away from Nguyen and heading toward my office on the third floor.

Upstairs, Phan was waiting outside my office. For once, he wasn't on his cell, battling with Sheldon J. Plankton. In fact, he was staring down at his scuffed shoes, looking like he'd just soiled his trousers. Having just experienced such an event, I knew how shameful that was and I resolved to try to help him get over the hangdog look and embarrassment.

"Is that a boil on your face or a nose?" I asked. "Whatever it is, wipe that sore. It's leaking."

Phan looked up and smiled, giving me a "finally you're home and you haven't changed a bit" look of joy. I walked past quickly before he could hug me.

On the computer, it took only minutes to see there was no picture or real description of Luong in the files, nor of Morgan or Hatati. Of course Nguyen needed my help. No one would recognize Luong. Those who knew him wouldn't say a word to any flatland Vietnamese.

Surprisingly, there was nothing on Mr. Liu. Being one of the few Mandarins in Cholon should have generated a huge amount of information. Either the authorities didn't care about Chinese gangsters or Liu had insiders' help to keep his file sanitized.

Tran Dai Quang. There was much about the minister of public security. My task was to figure out if there was anything that would lead us to where Quang must be hiding. He would have known immediately about the murders and the photo, coming easily to the conclusion he was the next target. I read on, paying particular attention to his recent personal life and gaining a few nuggets that could have value.

It was evident Nguyen was lost in his search. I was one of his last chances and he was willing to risk my escape to catch the killers. On the other hand, he could kiss my skinny yellow *dit* before I ever gave him anything of significance. I would betray him and everyone in this department before I aided in the capture and execution of Luong. Too many years and sneers for me to forget or forgive. I switched off the computer and stood, anxious to talk to Luong and Morgan as soon as possible. And gaze upon Hatati again.

Outside, Phan led me to a different car, mumbling something about "bullet holes" in the other one. No one was about to spoil me. This was a Renault that looked like it had been left over from when the French were our masters. The Department had a number of these junkers to be used by the lower levels, while the new SUVs were reserved for the real officers. It was hard to tell the color of this one, but I remembered watching a mamasan on a bus change a baby's diaper once. The squealing infant had diarrhea and it was the same earth tone as the wreck Phan pointed out. It did have flecks of coppery red where it was rusting through and the dents gave some character to the overall putrid green. When Phan opened the back door, the hinges screamed in protest. I slid onto the burlap bag that covered the board over the springs and sat. At least there were no windows to keep out the breeze. Phan got in the driver's seat and turned the key. The engine made a few clicks and whirs and started with a pop that exploded out of the tailpipe, cloaking the Renault in blue. I began to cough, and Phan pulled away into the traffic that had parted to keep its distance from this monster.

"Where to, Captain?" Phan asked.

"Back to Bhinh Thanh," I said.

There was something not right with the front end of the car. Phan wrestled with the steering wheel, trying to keep the Renault in a straight line. It drove like it had a flat tire.

"Keep it on the road, *cuc cho*," dog shit, I barked at Phan, slapping him on the back of his head. While I knew it wasn't his fault, there was no point in giving Phan and his minders any slack. Too bad for him and SpongeBob. For now, he had to carry the basket of dung I was about to unload.

They would be following and I didn't even try to pick out which of the Japanese-made cars was our tail. Once we got to the realm of the Montagnards, it didn't matter. No flatlander could track me inside the warren of hootches in that neighborhood. Nguyen surely didn't believe my fibs and probably predicted I would head to Bhinh Thanh anyway. I wasn't going to disappoint. It was already arranged that, if I survived, I'd meet Luong there. The fallback was Cholon, both areas that weren't welcoming for the police.

It was night. The backfires from the Renault echoed down the tight streets and lit the walls of the buildings with flames from the exhaust. I couldn't help but chuckle, putting us inside some kind of Bollywood comedy featuring bumbling police and handsome leading men. I wasn't the latter, but Morgan was. And Hatati was the beautiful female protagonist who was so stunning she seemed to be about to break out in a Miss World dance to the accompaniment of harps and violins at any moment.

On the sidewalks, it was that twilight time when citizens were deciding if they only wanted soup for dinner or would get drunk on some of the lousy sugary vodka made with distilled rice by the Binh Tay Alcohol Company, not worrying about tomorrow's hangover from the cheap booze. Some couples even dared hold hands, a custom not yet truly accepted in Vietnam. A few of the girly boys strolled by, their skintight *ao dis* slit up to their *buoi*. Penis. Swinging hips always drew whistles and "*mong an*," butt muncher, slurs. When I wasn't inhaling the Renault's fumes, I could smell the evening's Sai Gon aromas of cooking meat of unknown origin, spices from the pho that was boiling behind most doorways, ripening fruit of a hundred varieties, and raw sewage. Phan eventually guided the heap to the side of the road in Binh Thanh, close to where he had dropped me to see Hacmon not that long ago.

"Stay here and try not to wear out your *cu*," penis, I said, reminded for a nanosecond of the fact that "penis" had so many different ways to say the word in Vietnamese. There weren't nearly that number for *lon*, pussy. As in most countries, we were truly male-dominated and fixated on our dicks. One of the words was "*yinjing*" in Chinese, and the relative numbers were the same, "*xing xing tam*" being one of the few words for pussy in that dialect. A myth that was chuckled at knowingly throughout Vietnam was that Chinese men didn't have a *cu*, the legend being it was too small for anyone to have ever seen one. But there was a risk in having a *cu*. A few weeks ago, Peni Hoang had gone to the NoDam Spa in District One for a new treatment that included swimming in a small pool with young eels. The fish were supposed to dine on the dead skin we all carry on our bodies, supposedly a good thing, cleansing the body of useless crumbs. Unfortunately for Hoang, one of the eels decided to swim up his *cu*. While he tried desperately to pull it out, it was too slippery and he had to undergo a three-hour operation to remove the little fella. The images flashed across my eyelids and I nearly choked, hacking a wad of bitter phlegm on the side of the road. I really was becoming too Confucian, avoiding making a difficult decision to step into the labyrinth of Binh Thanh like any real squint would delay with empty brain chatter and internal spiritual argument.

Within a few paces, I was hidden from the view of the black Honda CR-V SUV that had parked across the street. As yet, no one had gotten out of the car and I began to walk briskly down the now muddy path, greasy from a morning squall. It took only seconds and a man in flip-flops, raggedy gray shorts, and Che Guevara T-shirt stepped out of a tin-walled hootch, beckoning me to follow. We hurried down the passageway. All the doors, or what passed for them, were closed in the huts, no one wanting to see anything and alerted by the psychic alarm that seemed to supernaturally transmit from one lean-to to the next. At least the afternoon's rain torrent had been short, and we weren't up to our ankles in slop.

For minutes, we paralleled the river, zigzagging between huts, eventually coming to a group of hootches that threatened to fall into the water with the slightest nudge. It looked as if it was the few straggly palm trees that kept them upright. No one was around. My guide disappeared around the corner of one of the sheds and someone grabbed my arm, pulling me through a curtain that passed for a door. It was Luong.

"We can't stay here," he said. "I need to know if you found out where Quang is hiding. For now, Nguyen isn't as important. We want Quang."

The tiny room was dark and sweltering. An entire life in Vietnam meant I usually didn't perspire unless it was anxiety or the heat and humidity had reached the level where a breath threatened to boil the lungs. That only happened a few dozen times a year, in a city where the average temperature is 82° F and the humidity 75 percent. Inside this small space, it was closer to 110° F and 100 percent humidity. The sweat began to form under my armpits and seemed likely to cause a sour flood in my shirt. At least the gloom assured I couldn't identify where the fetid smell that was making my eyes water came from. I moved closer to the curtain, hoping to get a mouthful of fresh air.

"I have an address for Quang's house," I said. "He's probably not there, but his file also lists a few other possibilities. Probably the homes of his mistresses. What have you found out?"

From the depths of the blackness, Morgan stepped in front of me, the laugh lines no longer curling his face. I assumed that was because Hatati was somewhere else.

"We have an idea," Morgan said.

"From your sources?" I asked. "Or Mr. Nutley?"

"Not relevant," Morgan said. "We think he's in An Pho. District Two. Somewhere just off Thao Dien Street, where the expats who can afford the air conditioning and high-class whores live. I'm sure Quang's salary allows him to live in this level of luxury. Or even higher. There's evidence the villa is home to mamasan number three. He's a loyal communist, dedicated to the triumph of the working class and spreading the wealth as well as venereal diseases."

"He must be protected," I said. "There will be guards and the latest security technology. It won't be easy."

"That's exactly why you're coming along," Morgan said. "There's lots you can help with. If we're wrong, you'll help us get it right. Besides, if I can see you, I know you're not betraying us."

"Even you," I said, shaking my head. "No yellow-belly slant can be trusted. Right? You've seen too many movies, Morgan. I'm willing to give my life for Luong. Even more, this is a chance to finally stick a sharpened dagger up their asses."

Morgan glanced at Luong, checking for his agreement. He nodded.

"What about your driver?" Morgan asked.

"Phan?" I asked. "He's too dense for them to bother with. What I'd worry about now is that they've doubtless sealed off the area." I looked up. "And that helicopter isn't for sightseeing. It's for you." The *throp-throp* sound got louder as the chopper neared.

Both Luong and Morgan glanced upward, surprisingly calm.

"Stay close," Luong said, grabbing my elbow. He moved like a Nha Nhac Classical dancer, even with the small backpack strapped between his shoulders and his sixty-plus years in this enchanted land.

Morgan went first, pushing aside another tapestry curtain and moving away from the front door. A couple steps later and he moved an old spool table aside, pulling up a metal door from under a rug. Tunnel.

Silly to be shocked. The Montagnards would have more than the river escape route, and they were expert tunnelers, having been kidnapped in the thousands during several conflicts to "help" the flatlanders dig. Starting during the French-Indochina War, the complexes reached their greatest volume during the American invasion. Only thirty kilometers from Sai Gon, the largest and most infamous tunnel warren was located at Cu Chi, now a highly visited tourist magnet in Vietnam, even greater than cheap medical care, gay bars, vets looking for redemption, and golf. Underground cities were excavated that included hospitals, dormitories, libraries, kitchens, classrooms, and bicycle generators for power. The majority of the people living below the surface had malaria and all suffered intestinal parasites. I knew much more about the tunnels than this, but, for now, I wanted to focus on anything other than my claustrophobia and the inordinate fear of reptiles. Morgan flicked on a flashlight and started to push me down a ladder that disappeared into the dirt.

"No," I said. "I won't go down there."

"Yes, you will," Morgan said.

"Hurry," Luong said. "I think I hear someone coming."

"No," I said. "I'll stay here and die with my face to the clouds. Not from a snake bite." I went rigid, my arms firmly crossed on my chest.

"You're going with us," Morgan said. "I hate this shit, too, but we can't leave you." From behind his back, he pulled out a pistol. "If you refuse, we can't let you live. They'll stop being nice and cut you till you give them whatever they want. And more." He poked me the barrel of the .22. "Go."

Two deep breaths and I looked down the ladder into the abyss. I turned and put my foot on the top rung, closing my eyes and beginning a prayer to Buddha. And Confucius. It didn't matter which one came to my aid. Only that some god keep the cobras and green snakes far away. And the scorpions, fire ants, ticks, and leeches. I began the climb downward, Morgan just above.

"When you get to the bottom," Morgan whispered, "wait for me."

My feet touched hard earth, and I had the reassuring thought that we probably wouldn't die from a cave-in. The laterite clay soil of Vietnam, a ferric soil mixed with clay and iron oxide, was perfect for making tunnels that turned as hard as concrete all by themselves once they were shaped into a passageway or room. This one smelled of mold and dirt, not the stench of unwashed thousands and kerosene. It most likely wasn't used much, maintained only for adventures like the one I was now part of. I waited, trying to get a glimpse down the passageway through the shadows.

A brief glimpse allowed by the flickering light showed me we wouldn't be hiking upright. At best, we'd be doing a duck walk squat, since the ceiling was about one-and-a-half meters from the floor and only wide enough for one of us at a time to squeeze through. The little chamber I was in was a bit wider and pushed against the earthen walls, increasing my prayers that no beast was there. Within seconds, both Morgan and Luong were pressed alongside me. Above, someone closed the hatch.

"I'll take point," Luong said. "I've been here before." He flipped on a flashlight.

"Please do," Morgan said. "I'll take drag."

"I'll just stay here and make sure no one is following," I said, reaching for the ladder.

"No, you won't," Morgan said. "You're coming with us."

Luong had already crouched and was moving away from us into the void. I stooped, waiting only a second for him to clear out. I turned back to Morgan.

"*Cao ni zu zong shi ba dai.*" Fuck the eighteen generations of your ancestors. This was absolutely the worst insult any Chinese could give and was saved only for the most important and worthy events. Since I was sure I wouldn't survive the next few minutes, it was such a time. Even if Morgan didn't know the import, he got the vibration.

"And fuck you too," he said. He pulled my hand off the ladder and shoved me down, pressing the pistol into my back.

"Move it, Charlie," he said.

"Now," I said. "you're showing your true American racist colors, peckerhead." I didn't really know what that one meant, having heard it in a favorite movie, *Deliverance,* and sensing it was truly harsh. Morgan just laughed, ramming the .22 harder into me, knowing full well I'd stall until the next dynasty began its reign. I could have called him "*mee-gook nom,*" American bastard, in Chinese. I was sure he wouldn't have got that one without translation, so I stuck with "peckerhead." As usual, my only defense was my mouth, and, predictably, that was failing again.

"Go," he barked.

It was easy to follow Luong since there was only one direction to move. I bent lower, trying my best not to rub any surface that might hold something I didn't want to know and would certainly bite me into oblivion.

The strip of land we were under was narrow and we could only be headed east toward Luong Phuoc Street. In all other directions, the Sai Gon River would block the tunnel. Phan and the watchers had to be on that road or trying to follow us in the hostile labyrinth of Binh Thanh. While I tried to keep from letting the terror shut my body down by repeating my mantra, I estimated we would doubtless emerge from the depths somewhere in the row of shops and houses across Luong Phuoc. That neighborhood wasn't part of the Montagnard slum. Still, it wasn't one of Sai Gon's most prosperous wards and was lately notorious for the illegal weekend motorbike races through its streets, where several drivers and spectators had been crushed. Mostly, I tried to stay as close to Luong as I could, hoping any vipers would nibble on him, not me.

After about ten minutes, Luong slowed, and I nearly head butted him. We were at another ladder in an open space. I stood, my knees aching for release. Morgan was right behind, and the three of us crammed into the tight opening. The light made shadow puppets on the dirt walls, and I tried to keep my focus as narrow as possible, not wanting any surprises.

"There shouldn't be any problem," Luong said. "We'll be coming out in the back room of a cashew nut stall. Just wait down here until I check upstairs."

"Do I look like a worm?" I asked, grabbing Luong's shirt. "I can't take much more of this."

"In my village," Luong said, "worms are greatly revered. They are viewed with the same respect as all creatures and are a good source of protein, unlike you. Not enough meat. And bones are hard to chew." He started to climb, and I wondered if he was being humorous. No. Solemn honesty was his character. Besides, if it was meant as a joke, it would be an original.

Morgan chuckled from behind and held me back as I tried to follow Luong.

"Stay here, worm," he said.

The few seconds felt like years until Luong whistled and I raced up the ladder as if I were being eaten by the fire ants that made this tunnel home. Morgan didn't hesitate, either.

At the top, we were in a tiny room that held woven sacks of nuts, shelves with glass jars filled with nuts, and plastic bags stuffed with nuts. The floor was littered with rat traps and dishes of warfarin that, when eaten, would explode any rat's heart after blocking their livers. The area smelled like decay, cashews, and the lavender air fresheners that hung from the ceiling.

Morgan closed the door over the tunnel, giving us a little more freedom of movement. When he stood, he took out a cell phone and pushed one key, while I attempted to slow my breathing. The mantra hadn't worked. Our escape had caused relief to wash over me like a warm monsoon.

"Two minutes," was all Morgan said, immediately stepping around me and pushing aside a curtain that hung from a rail attached to the wall.

"Let's go," he said.

No questions this time. Any distance between me and the tunnel was a lifeline. I was right behind him, Luong not far back.

We squeezed through a little booth, jammed with more cashews in various displays, mostly fifty-pound bags, and out onto a street I recognized as No Trang Long. In front of us was the normal evening anarchy of *meeping* cyclos, blue fumes, flashing neon, and the ever-present pungent scent of decay. A few seconds later and a white Toyota sedan pulled up, the driver's window down. It was Hatati. Morgan didn't hesitate to open the back door and push Luong and me inside. He ran around to the passenger side and jumped in next to Hatati. It all took less time than to pull out and examine a fingernail and we were on our way somewhere. If my hand weren't still throbbing, I'd almost have grinned as a fast left turn pressed me against Luong.

No one spoke. Hatati was an excellent driver and wove her way through the bedlam with only a single motorcyclist tumbling to the pavement and getting a few "*dit con me may tec hang,*" fuck your mother till her vagina is broken, comments. In a roundabout way, and constantly checking her rear view mirror, she eventually came to Vo Van Kiet Road and headed toward Cholon. I guessed we were going to see Mr. Liu. I was wrong. She drove through Cholon and District Five, north into District Three, stopping at a typical five-story building next to a Kentucky Fried Chicken franchise. The street level held a battery store, a boutique that advertised "We Best Short and Curly," and a place that looked to be selling old carburetors. Beside the salon, a metal door began to rise. When it was completely open, Hatati drove down a narrow passage to a small parking lot. It was pitch dark and she switched on her brights, the beams illuminating an empty space about the size of a basketball court. At the far end, a dim lamp shown over a door. Hatati shut off the Toyota and we all got out, following Morgan to the exit. His .22 was in his hand and he stopped before we went farther, signaling us to wait. My eyes began to itch with the mold smell and a sneezing attack was imminent. I stifled it and followed Morgan through the door after he motioned us forward.

Three flights of gloom, cement stairs, and spiderwebs and Morgan led us into a quiet hallway, open windows at both ends. The breeze gave us fresh evening air, and I inhaled with the pleasure I usually only found at Ma Jing's. Two doors down on the left and he went through one marked "6" without knocking, pistol leading the way. We pushed in right behind him, Luong closing the door after a quick glance down the hallway.

Morgan strode to the far wall that was mostly one big window overlooking the street and looked out, trying to see if we'd been followed. Hatati disappeared into another room that was either the kitchen or the bathroom, while Luong joined Morgan at the window. I sat down on a large couch that someone must have bought at Mo's Furniture in District One, the major Sai Gon discounter in a country where retail didn't exist. IKEA wasn't scheduled to open here until 2015. In the meantime, cheap sofas like this one that felt like an old man's bones and creaked just as loud when I sat, were better than the used fixture outlets by the Dong Thanh garbage dump. At least the cotton tapestry that covered whatever upholstery that was left was done in my favorite purple and blue colors. Nothing else but a few chairs and table were in the room and there was no sense that anyone lived here. It was a safe house and I knew all my idle speculations wouldn't prolong whatever Morgan and Luong had planned for me.

From the other room, a tea kettle began to hiss and I could hear Hatati moving around. Luong turned back toward me, taking out the satellite phone I'd seen at Liu's from the small backpack, handing it to Morgan who pushed a few buttons and put the bulky receiver to his ear.

"Winky?" he said after only a couple seconds. "News, old chap?" I'd learned from our discussions that Nutley was endearingly nicknamed "Winky."

He nodded a few times, but didn't look happy, hissing a few "bugger all" comments.

"Bollocks, Nutley," he finally said. "Is that the sum Her Majesty's finest can do?"

Morgan shook his head and frowned.

"This could be a jolly arse up," he said. "Cheers."

Before he could say a word, Hatati touched him on the arm, smiling.

"You're so cute when you try to talk like a Brit, Morgan," she said. "Nutley brings the royal out in you. What did he say?"

"He seemed a bit dodgy," Morgan said. "I'm cheesed off Winky won't give us more gen."

"Speak American," Luong said.

"We're pretty much on our own," Morgan said. "We might not be trusted in the highest ranks of spookdom. What that usually means is some politician somewhere stuck his piggy nose in and wants to make nice-nice with the Vietnamese. Probably hopes to build a links golf course on the coast around Vung Tau. Remind himself of St. Andrews." He sighed, confirming the easy Yankee acceptance of corruption in their greed-based system. "We'll be 'deniable' from here on in. At least he left us the weapons and a few other tricks. And a last ditch escape hatch." He looked at Hatati and grinned. "He did wish us a 'jolly good show.'"

All eyes to me. I was on trial and the next few answers would determine if I ever tasted another flaming shrimp or sparked another bowl of Ma Jing's sublime. I tried my best to look serene in the Chinese way they all might believe was fact rather than myth.

"OK, Charlie," Morgan said. "What did you find out?"

"Charlie?" I asked. "That's not my name and I resent your bigotry."

"Get over it, Mao," he said. "Give us a reason not to grind you up and make you into that fresh sausage that's so popular down at the Ben Thanh pork markets. You're carcass will feel right at home with the kitty meat they sell as 'delightful dog.'"

The vile aspersions were nothing new, and Morgan didn't realize I'd spent nearly sixty years absorbing much worse. Usually, it gave me time to strategize, seconds to outwit the cretins who depended on their position and prejudices to overwhelm those in a lower caste. It was normally quite simple, but Morgan was no simpleton. I placed hands in my lap and gave them my most gratuitous smile, knowing full well I had to be convincing.

"I was expelled from the Buddhist monastery for cheating," I said. "I looked into the soul of the monk kneeling beside me."

Scowls from everyone. Then, snickers. Some time ago, I'd seen a movie where the spies had more fun than the monkeys at Can Gio who ripped you off for your keys, wallet, and snow cones, scampering into the banyans and shrieking in delight. These three acted the same. And I knew they would kill me in less time than it took to swat a mosquito. At least they liked their jobs.

Age. Even in the most threatening moments, lately I'd begun to think it was all comedy. In some unbelievable stroke of luck, I'd lived nearly into my sixties. The only one in this room less than that age was Hatati. We all seemed relatively healthy, me being the most crooked. The other two could have been thirty years younger, the way they ran and moved easily, sitting, standing, and walking not being any challenge to them. At least my daily routine of one hundred katas had kept me somewhat flexible and active. Still, I wouldn't want to challenge either Luong or Morgan to a wrestling match. Or Hatati for that matter.

Hatati. She was in the tradition of the celebrated Four Beautiful Women of China, who all could have brought dynasties to their knees. Like Xi Shi. She caused fish to forget how to swim, and they dropped to the bottom in ecstasy at having viewed such perfection. Or Diochan, who made the moon shrink away in shame at her beauty. Hatati was such a goddess and I was humbled to be in the same airspace. And if she didn't believe my story, she would shoot me down like a street rat poaching her fruit cart. I waited for them to finish digesting my ludicrous soul-stealing avoidance, planning in what order I needed to divulge the few morsels of value I had gathered back at the office in order to save my cracked yellow skin.

"Bloody rubbish," Morgan said. "Don't try to deflect. We need to know what you found out. If anything." He sneered, trying to make sure he got it across clearly that I was as worthless as the husk of a durian and transparent as a jellyfish.

"Oh, I think he's got *bongs*," Hatati said. Balls. She pulled out a stiletto from her pocket and held it against my thigh. "Let's see if he keeps them."

For some reason, this beauty queen had morphed into an ugly shrew right in front of my eyes. It must be that lingering hatred every Southeast Asian, including Malaysians, had for the despicable imperialist Chinese, even if I was only a half-breed. This kind of contempt I could handle and was so common it was almost boring. The years had forced me to develop then hone my verbal and mental skills. If I couldn't beat them with my martial arts moves, I could humble them with my sharp tongue and fast thoughts. These three were professional intelligent adversaries, the hardest to defeat. Insults and fables weren't working. The stupid ones got angry, while the smart enemies bided their time. Like Nguyen. As Sun Tzu said, "The intelligent general will use those of the highest intelligence to spy." The three in this room were all spies.

"No more panface tricks," Morgan said. "We have more information than you might think. If I feel you're lying, Hatati will make you eligible to play the eunuch in some rich Chinaman's harem."

"When were you last at the beach?" I asked. "You look like you could use some relaxation. I'm sure Ms. Hatati would enjoy a day of sand and sun. Luong would be a great chauffeur for the journey now that he's given up driving oxcarts." I smirked almost as loudly as Morgan's sneer.

"Go ahead, Hatati. Nick the right one first," Morgan said, nodding toward my groin.

"Phu Quy Island," I said quickly before my right gonad was rolling across the floor. "It's also called Mackerel Island because it looks like a cod climbing from the sea, if that makes any sense. Quang has a villa there. I think that's where he is."

They looked back and forth between each other, apparently deciding if I was going to become the newest soprano in the Sai Gon Men's Choir.

"Where is this 'Phu Quy?'" Hatati asked, putting a bit more pressure on the tip of her knife.

"East of here about 160 kilometers to Phan Thiet City on the coast," I said. "Then another 100 kilometers southeast in the South China Sea. It has been a place for the fishing fleets to dock and load supplies for centuries. Now, it is welcoming tourists for its white sand beaches and charming pagodas." I smiled, enjoying this chance to be a tour guide rather than a mongrel.

"Go on," Morgan said.

"There's no airport on Phu Quy," I said. "If you want to get to Quang there, you'll need a boat. Or a helicopter. Maybe your comrade Nutley can get the queen to send a Royal Navy submarine. It's mostly coral and rock with some jungle and a few hills. Night would be the only time for an assault."

"Why do you think Quang is there?" Hatati asked.

"In our classless worker's society, every one of the proletariat has a vacation villa," I said. "We are truly equal here. Our mansions are a place we all go to when we are pressured."

Luong snorted, obviously feeling cheated he hadn't found his own deserved private escape home. Maybe he had chosen a chalet in the mountains rather than a manor on the beach. I sighed, showing I was sympathetic to this omission. As usual, he didn't display any emotion on his face.

"Answer the question," he said. "I spent too many hours ear-to-ear with you in the mud while you explained in detail the scientific reason worms were blind to be sidetracked by your trivia." He moved a few inches closer, and I was now pinned in like a Sai Gon traffic jam. "I know when you're just wasting time. Now, for the last time, do you have solid information to support your belief Quang is on Phu Quy?"

The air in the room was getting thin and stale. Too many bodies pressed together, with me in the middle of the clench, all recycling the same humid night air.

There was no compelling reason to stall any longer. If I was on the team, a decision already made, I should absolutely cooperate. For some reason, submission was nearly impossible for me. That was a tactic that needed to be detonated. Even if the Communist Manifesto said there was "no capitulation to the foreign pressure," I was well beyond the slogans that had been hammered into my brain through hours of indoctrination in the sweat shop of the camps.

"Confucius say," I said, "man who gets cut in the balls is left holding the bag."

This time, Luong kicked me in the shin hard enough that I wasn't paralyzed, but certainly paying attention.

"Sorry," I said, bowing. "The time you so politely gave me to return to my office was quite productive. Along with what I'd already heard about the hardships experienced by our leaders in finding good servants and clean running water at their holiday homes, I knew about Quang's beach hideaway. Besides, there has been a noticeable movement in the last few days of thug bodyguards from headquarters who pass as domestic help. All toward Phu Quy." I shrugged. "I can't be sure, but I believe there would be no better place in the country for him to hide. An island that has probably been turned into a fortress."

"That seems weak," Morgan said. "Why else do you think Quang is on Phu Quy? Do you have any real proof?"

"You mean like reading the tea leaves?" I asked. "I do know how to use a computer. The one they gave to me may have been five or six chip generations old. That was then. Now, the inside is what matters, and there are very few machines in this country as up to date as the one in my office. Information wants to be free, as they say, and I've learned how to let it tell me countless secrets." I was starting to get a little queasy. While I tried to keep as many nights as possible far away from Ma Jing's dreamworld, this time of the evening meant there was a physical pull toward the long pipe. I steadied myself against the wooden chair beside me. "May I sit down?" I asked.

"Of course," Luong said, likely the only one besides me who cared whether I left this room.

Taking a seat, I scratched the fingers on my good hand together like I was scoring a ball of opium, trying to decide what to tell these assassins. Everything, I thought. In for a dollar, in for a dong.

"I've found the passwords to every government official of any importance," I said. "It is one of the reasons I have not been executed and am allowed to continue to poke the beast in the eye with my mouth. I know too much. They don't understand how or why, but they do know I'm aware of the numbers and amounts in all their foreign and domestic bank accounts. I also have access to all the intelligence files and a way to hide my tracks." I was getting thirsty, another result of nerves and opium starvation.

"Is there any water around here?" I asked.

"You haven't had your tea," Hatati said, handing me a cup. I drank, looking up after my throat was moist again.

"Do you think someone of my mixed background would rise to Captain of Detectives only because I am a brilliant investigator who has an exponentially higher closure rate than anyone else in the country? Is there a slim chance my barbed comments would be tolerated even if I was a purebred Vietnamese with Uncle Ho as my grandfather? No. They're afraid of me. But that won't allow them to condone my involvement in the assassinations."

"OK," Morgan said. "You've convinced me. I won't put a bullet in your head. For now." He shoved the .22 in the waistband behind his back. "So, tell us what we want to know."

There'd been enough excitement and epinephrine to make me ignore the searing sensation in my nail-less fingers. The pain was a dull constant and now it flared up like a pimple on an acned child. I tried to focus on exactly what I'd read in Quang's file.

"There are many reasons Quang should die," I said. "Not the least is that he is responsible for genocide in the Central Highlands and of Luong's people. I don't suppose you're looking for justification, but I would like to tell you of one such episode that you may not know." I looked to them for agreement. All three of them remained standing and Luong was the first to nod.

"Go ahead," he said.

"In the Highlands close to the Chinese border," I said, "there is a town called Lao Cai. It is primarily a city where Degar villagers come to do their trading and a summertime mountain escape for lowland Vietnamese. Western missionaries and health workers have made an impact there, building a hospital to house sick and dying local Montagnards who have relied on roots and bark for their medicine for centuries." I took another sip of the now-cold tea. "As you know, the lowland Vietnamese have never stopped persecuting the Degars and other mountain tribal people, including the Hmongs. During one of the recent crackdowns, many villagers were wounded, both by gunfire and torture and managed to get to Lao Cai for treatment. The officers in the Vietnam People's Army knew the survivors would most likely end up there out of desperation. The head of this latest operation was Tran Dai Quang. When his agents were sure the maximum number of Montagnards were in the hospital, he had them block the doors and throw in Molotov cocktails, burning everyone inside to briquettes. The media was told it was an 'unfortunate event caused by faulty gas canisters supplied by greedy Western medical corporations.' No one questioned the official response except for those who had witnessed the carnage. No one cares about them. The international community is happy that Vietnam is entering the world economic community, and nothing should slow down this development."

"I know this," Luong said. "You have proof?"

"I can get copies of the files if I make it through whatever it is you have planned. And they believe I'm not part of the plot."

"Show us," Hatati said, walking over to a closet and opening the door. She reached inside and came out with a laptop that had a bulge like a huge boil on the side. I had never seen a PC like this one. She opened the lid, pressed the "power" button and set the computer on my knees.

"It's hooked directly to a satellite like the phone," she said. "Every keystroke you make is encrypted. You're on the web already."

I looked down and was amazed to see that Google was already up as the home page, the cursor blinking. This one was certainly state of the art.

"Show us what you're talking about," Hatati said. "If you're such a computer phreaker, we want you to take us into Quang's secured sights."

A few keystrokes and we were looking at Quang's private files. In Vietnamese. I would have to interpret, knowing Luong would detect if I was being deceitful. I was aware that every move I made was surely transmitting back to London and MI6 headquarters. That no longer mattered. I'd joined the visiting team and had to live or die with the consequences. I scrolled through much of the information, finally stopping at Quang's most recent entries. Sitting back, I pointed to the screen.

"See," I said, "he's making plans to go to Phu Quy."

Morgan and Hatati glanced at the screen and then turned to Luong for confirmation.

Luong read for only a few seconds and nodded.

"It looks like you're telling the truth," Luong said. "Quang is probably hiding out on Phu Quy." He looked first at Morgan and then Hatati. "Now, what are we going to do? And what about the murderer Nguyen?"

"I can always find Nguyen if I'm kept alive," I said. "His job is to tail me. He might be in the dungeon now, getting a manicure because he and his men failed. I don't think so. They'll bluster and let him go to find me, threatening to exterminate his entire family if he doesn't succeed. Any contact means he's redeemed. For now, Quang should be our focus."

"Get as much information as you can on Phu Quy," Morgan said. "I'll make a few calls and find out if there will be any help or if we're totally off the board."

"Do you have a printer?" I asked.

Hatati went back to the closet, returning with a small printer and setting it down on the floor beside me.

"It's wireless," she said. "Just hit the print key whenever you want a copy." She smiled and moved around behind me to watch.

Luong was at the window and I could hear Morgan speaking softly to someone on the satellite phone in the next room.

First, I went to Google Maps and printed an image of the island. Then, Wikipedia. That site was relatively useless, so I began a search engine query of Phu Quy, focusing on the terrain and possible access. Within minutes, I'd printed a number of pages and had a rudimentary knowledge of the place.

Lastly, I went into the Security Forces files, tracking the numbers of and location of police and military. Storming this island wasn't going to be easy. I stood up and walked over to Luong.

"I hope you can swim," I said.

"You too," he said. "You're coming along."

"Where did you learn? I've never heard Degars were water people. Primitive hunter gatherers and heathen animal worshippers not worthy of being called Vietnamese is the party line."

"I've been out of the mountains to do more than hawk colorful hats to the tourists and trade boar skins and tusks."

"Well, don't count on me to rescue you if you're drowning. Dog paddle is about all I can do." I tried to look convincing, staring into Luong's eyes. "I believe I'd be of more help if I stayed here and monitored Nguyen's movements."

Really, being on a boat in the middle of the night was terrifying to me. I could face a firing squad knowing death was coming in seconds, and it wasn't as scary as the vision of an unseen shark nibbling on my toes.

"Stop whinging," Luong said. "You're coming with us. Can you shoot an AK?"

"Of course," I said. "I had to go through police training. Even if they don't let me carry a weapon, I do know how to use one."

Across the small room, Hatati continued to study the printouts. It was getting late now, and, Ma Jing's being an impossibility, all I wanted was to go to sleep, cradling my still-pulsing fingers to my chest. I could barely process all that had gone on today and longed for a few seconds of closed eyes.

Morgan came back, holding the phone at his side. He glanced at me and stopped.

"Captain Fang," he said, "you look like a dried lizard skin. You need some rest. Lie down on the couch while I speak with Luong and Hatati."

For once, I didn't argue or make a cynical comment. I did what he said, not even bothering to give Morgan a comic salute.

Morning traffic noise of bleeping motorbikes and honking horns woke me. I opened my eyes to wide-open windows that let daylight flood the room. I could hear murmurs from the kitchen and smell coffee brewing. It took a few seconds to figure out where I was, but the rich smell drew me to the other room.

"*Chao buoi sang*," I said. Good morning. Three heads nodded, and I joined them at the folding table. They didn't seem in the least tired, and I wondered if the amphetamines the Americans were famous for using had kept them awake.

"We're just planning breakfast," Hatati said. "We've got a big day ahead. What would you like?"

Typically, I wasn't much for breakfast, but when I did eat, I stayed with the traditional Vietnamese morning dishes.

"Noodles with beef marrow, oxtail, flank steak, cloves, ginger, and onions would be fine," I said, bowing.

Hatati stood and walked over to the cupboard, opening the door.

"How about a bowl of Special K?" she asked. "Milk?" She went to a small refrigerator.

When it was all in front of me, I ate and drank my cup of coffee while Luong, Hatati, and Morgan talked among themselves, acting as if I were a gecko on the wall. I was probably destined to be the getaway driver, not a soldier on this operation. From that point on, I didn't pay too close attention, instead wondering how I'd stay alive without defecting to the West.

After my last spoonful, Morgan spun toward me.

"You'll be carrying a pack with rope, C-4, plus an AK-47, a pistol, knife, radio, and grenades about two miles, mostly uphill," he said. "The weight will be around forty pounds. Can we count on you not to have a stroke?"

"Can't I hire a porter?" I asked.

"No. In fact you'll be going in first. If it's a trap, you're the one we can spare."

"Oh, here we go again. Sacrifice a squint."

"There are a few billion of you anyway."

"You know what my people call you whiteys?"

"No."

"'Mayonnaise' is a nice one. I prefer 'turd mold.'"

"Careful or I'll drop a rock or two into your pack and take out all the bullets in your rifle."

"I suppose you'll want me to be the executioner too."

"No," Luong said. "I get that pleasure. You're just a donkey."

"When does the adventure begin?"

"Tonight," Morgan said. "We'll leave this afternoon. Luong and I have to go out and get supplies. Hatati will stay here with you and explain the details." He got up from the table. "While you're lounging around, check on the laptop if there's any change you can find in Quang's position."

Hatati and Luong followed Morgan into the front room and I gazed at the small pool of milk in the bottom of my cereal bowl.

A poem. It resonated in my head, written by Nguyen Hue many years ago.

> With the army on hasty march at night
> The calm Prince quietly pulled out the dagger
> He had long before hidden on himself
> And aimed it at his neck ready to die.

I was no "Prince." I wasn't even close to a royal. More like the lice in the Prince's hair. But I wasn't prepared to be a suicide, even if a spin on my reincarnation wheel didn't frighten me. As recently as yesterday, I might not have felt this optimism for life. Now, I was finally snared in the web of something that mattered other than the next bubbling bowl at Ma Jing's. For the first time in memory, I was interested, not sitting on my *dit* thinking of how words were my sword and whether I'd win the eternal duel with my lashing wit. I wanted to be alive and would follow these three criminals straight to the hangman. I was convinced I wasn't like the Prince of Hue's poem. There was no dagger aimed at my neck, only choices. There was not a single doubt about the "team" I was on, whether or not it was my final game. I stood and went into the main room, not bothering to clear the dish or put away the Special K. I chuckled at the thought that any of that mattered in the universal comedy I had jumped into with an open mind.

Morgan and Luong were at the door on the way out. Morgan stopped and gave Hatati a hug, wrapping his arms around her as if she were porcelain, whispering something tenderly in her ear.

The door closed and we were alone.

"I wondered how long it would take for you to get rid of them," I said. "Now you finally have me all to yourself."

"I won't even bother with the warnings. You know as well as I do that I've been trained to kill in ten ways unarmed in less than five seconds."

"And to think I believed you were such a gentle spirit. Like Tara, the goddess of love, who is reincarnated in every beautiful woman."

"In your eyes, I should be considered Asara, the god of war."

"You know your teachings. I thought Malaysians were mostly Muslim."

"I've studied many religions. Now, I'm devoted to killing Quang."

"Please tell me how you are going to do this and my role."

Over the next few hours, Hatati explained the operational plan, along with the fallback positions and contingencies as best as they could predict. I was impressed with the amount of technical supplies, equipment, and armed support Morgan had organized. This shouldn't have been a surprise after hearing his conversations with Nutley. MI6 was bound to have agents in place, and their access to arms would be nearly unlimited, especially since they were in bed with the CIA and could call on the cousins for help if needed.

The most amazing part of the details Hatati displayed were the pictures of a secluded villa on a hillside off the dirt road leading to the top of Cam Mountain, where a solar-powered lighthouse stood to guide the fishermen who were the prime residents of the island. There were photos of the entire land mass. The series of snapshots zoomed into the house that stood out for its size, splendor, and location, overlooking the diamond-clear water lapping on the white beach. In the highest resolution, several military Jeeps and civilian SUVs were parked on the driveway, and there was even a still of an armed guard smoking a cigarette on the deck beside the swimming pool. No other houses were nearby and the terrain was mostly rock sprinkled with small scrub brush. There would be little chance to sneak into the home in daylight.

Hatati showed no anxiety as she described the features. Nor excitement. It seemed like planning and carrying out an assault on a heavily guarded site was something she did most every day. She pointed at a medium-range picture of the house.

"That's where he sleeps," she said. "We believe there are always at least four guards patrolling and four sleeping or resting in the basement servant's quarters. It won't be easy, but we've had more difficult targets." She swiveled toward me. "Do you think you're capable of running a garrote around a man's neck, cutting through his throat to his larynx while he struggles in a final death dance, his spurting blood making your fingers slick?"

"No problem," I said. "And maybe I can drown a sack of kittens in the bay afterward."

"This is no time for your cynicism," Hatati said. "You will most likely be called on to kill someone. I want to know if you're up to it."

"If they are Vietnamese," I said, "they have inflicted thousands of little cuts on my body and soul, and I am nearly bloodless. I will show them no mercy." I held up my nail-less finger. "This is only the most recent wound."

"Good," she said. "And if you hesitate, I will shoot you myself. And if you can't keep up, I will shoot you again."

"Won't I already be dead?"

"I don't miss."

I scratched the stubble on my chin, making sure I looked confused.

"Now that you've told me how cruel and ruthless you are," I said, "how did you get all this intel in so short a time?" I waved my hand over the pictures and printed documents.

"The man you've heard called 'Nutley' can do magic," Hatati said. "I believe he has friends all over the globe, many in a place called Langley, Virginia. Do you know what I'm talking about?"

"Pardon me," I said, bowing like a peasant. "I am a lowly half-breed Chinese. I only learned yesterday, with your kind guidance, that I should use that soft white paper on a roll in the loo to wipe my bum after a runny shit. I always thought it was for leaving messages." I bowed even lower. "Please be so kind as to tell me about this 'Lonely, Vagina' place. It sounds extremely inviting to me."

If she would have been drinking the tea that had now gone cold, I'm sure she might have spewed green liquid all over me and the dossier below. Of course she didn't. She was a professional. Signs of emotion were off limits. She just glared.

In order to keep her from using me as a practice dummy, I smiled, letting her know I was playing the harmless buffoon, a character I was used to portraying.

"Did you use carrier pigeons?" I asked. "Or does this 'Vagina' place demand something much bigger?"

"Enough," she said, slamming her palm on the table. "When all of this is finished, I'll be able to clear up your newfound 'Vagina' fetish. It will include handcuffs."

"I'll be waiting with my hands in my pockets," I said.

"The information we have is fresh. The photos are from the KH-13 spy satellite's latest orbit and only a few hours old. If needed, we could have read the time on the guard's watch. We don't need that kind of resolution."

"In order to make a nighttime strike on Phu Quy, we'll need things like, uh, boats."

"As I told you, there are people who have long memories. Men who want nothing more than to eliminate Quang before they die. He didn't just murder Montagnard women and children in the Central Highlands. He and his comrades butchered and tortured many Americans too. As long as these survivors can have 'deniability,' they will do whatever they can to help us. And some are in very lofty positions."

"I guessed as much. When do we leave?"

"We'll know the exact time when Morgan and Luong get back. I wouldn't count on having a green omelet and spring rolls for lunch, though."

"I was thinking more of sweet and sour spam."

"None of that nuoc cham sauce. It will make you too thirsty, and you have to concentrate on killing."

"Easy. I will massacre more Vietnamese than I eat hot fish paste."

We danced a few minutes longer, Hatati outlining the skeleton of the plan as she knew it. I felt exhilarated, finally able to be the man I'd seen in my visions. Then, the door opened. Morgan and Luong walked in, both carrying heavy bags stenciled with "Team Vietnam" in gold on the sides.

In the kitchen, Morgan and Luong unloaded the arsenal, both of them taking turns snapping out the slide release on Sig Sauer P226s and other types of pistols and examining the latest model of the M67 fragmentation and smoke grenades. They both "ooh'ed" and "ahh'ed" over the treasure trove, paying particular attention to the slabs of C4 explosive and the detonation caps. Morgan threaded the silencer onto a .22 and hoisted it like it was his baby. Hatati joined in as if she were the last one to the party. I watched, hoping to learn how these unfamiliar foreign weapons worked. Most Vietnamese police still used the decades-old Chinese knockoff of the Browning M1911 .45 caliber pistol, and these grenade launchers could have come from Star Wars as far as I knew. I crossed my arms and didn't join in the frenzy.

"Where's the big guns?" I asked. "You can't stop Asian elephants with pea shooters."

"In the car," Morgan said. "The rifles and dark clothes are stored in the garage, waiting for us. We'll be leaving in an hour or so." He snapped the firing pin on a pistol and began to load the cartridge chamber with a pile of bullets Luong had dropped on the table. "Pick your weapon."

They all seemed the same. I chose one of the Swiss revolvers no one else had touched. On contact, it felt like it was part of my hand. The pistol seemed more comfortable in my fingers than the wooden-handled garrote and fighting knives that were also in the heap. This was not part of my daily routine, unraveling clues in my head being the norm. Physical action was left to the cretins who spit on me when no one was looking. I even puffed up my skinny chest. A man of action was the new me and I didn't know how the jacket fit.

"Go ahead, Quang," I said, pointing the pistol toward the window, "make my day." I dry shot the revolver and blew on the tip of the barrel.

This time, even Luong snorted.

Over the next hour, we checked and prepared all the weapons, took turns refreshing in the bathroom, and ate *banh mi* sandwiches, the Vietnamese version of a baguette. These were filled with *gio thu*, headcheese, a combination of pork ears, tendons, skin, fat, and other pig brain parts, all on a freshly toasted bun from an ABC bakery downstairs.

By early afternoon, we were on Highway 1A, heading east about 150 kilometers to Phan Thiet, where we'd find the Zodiac that would take us to Phu Quy. On the way, Morgan, Luong, and Hatati discussed operational plans, leaving me out. That was fine. I wasn't a military strategist. My forte was liars. Everyone lied when under investigation. The challenge was to pinpoint the when and then find out the why. None of these three were being deceitful, their noses all pointed toward one grub. Quang.

The satellite phone that lay on the console between Luong, the driver, and Morgan in the passenger seat rang several times. Morgan didn't talk much, only nodded as he got more intel and updates on the rest of the equipment he wanted. He seemed pleased and sincerely thanked the person on the other end of the line. After the last call, he turned toward Hatati, who was in the backseat next to me.

"Everything looks like a 'go,'" he said. "Nutley has arranged the lot the way I asked. Now, it's up to us. He thinks it's the 'mutt's nuts' we're going after the wanker but doesn't want any pissing about or he'll have us all 'sacked.' Permanently."

"And you let him play into your Anglophilia as always," Hatati said. "You know he doesn't give a rat's arse about us. He's always a dozen moves ahead, and we're just pawns to be sacrificed if it fits the queen's interests."

"Sod off," Morgan said, grinning. "I was just practicing being limey. The important thing is the Zodiac is ready and it's all up to us tossers now."

"Sweet Fanny Adams," Hatati said with a growl. "Isn't that smashing." She punched Morgan on the arm. "Please, no more. Speak American English."

The trip was only a few hours, and it seemed Morgan and Hatati wanted to spend the afternoon joisting since we had already rehearsed the assault on Phu Quy several times. I wished they'd get a room, maybe at one of the Eden Hotel chain sites, known for their hourly rates and "magic finger" beds.

As we got closer to Phan Thiet, the sparse jungle turned rockier and the sky became blue rather than the murky gray of the tropics. Ocean breezes allowed Luong to shut off the air conditioning. Traffic on the paved highway had been mostly cyclos and tourist buses, sprinkled with a few police Toyotas and fruit carts that looked as if they were about to tip over from the uneven weight of their cargo.

Finally, we reached the harbor. The crystal-blue water in the bay held hundreds of sampans and larger trollers at anchor, evidence of a thriving fishing business and perfect cover for our outing. It would be easy to weave through the boats, making it difficult to follow our movements.

A few hundred meters north of the market that stretched from the main road to the beach, Luong parked the SUV inside a thatched hut. He got out and pulled a curtain over the door. It was as if he'd been here before and knew exactly what to do. For me, it was reminiscent of the whoretels that had popped up around Sai Gon, modeling the Bangkok system of motor inns where the curtain was not only pulled over the entrance but also on each and every parking spot in the garage. Discretion was the purpose, and angry wives often had sharp fingernails. My personal favorite was the Rub and Tug on Le Loi, where Phan would hang out in the basement and tickle SpongeBob while he waited for my business meeting to climax.

The mood had shifted. No one was smiling or joking. Not even me, even though I was dying to tell them the old line while we were in the darkness. How many Buddhists does it take to change a lightbulb? None, change must come from within.

The garage was constructed of thick bamboo poles and palm fronds for the roof. Plywood had been tacked to make the walls. The whole thing would have vaporized in a strong breeze. It smelled like sand and we had escaped the worst of the Sai Gon scent, only a trace of the sewage smell mixing with the aroma of motor oil. The feng shui of the shed was missing all of the five elements other than wood and was classic early twenty-first century beach rubble. Morgan and Hatati went to the back of the vehicle and began to unload the gear while I took out the few things we'd need that were still on the other seats. Luong went to the door, playing the role of sentry.

From a crack in the curtain, I could see the sun was already beginning to set. Morgan motioned for us to change into the black costumes. When we finished, taking turns watching outside, he took out black balaclava masks that hid everything but our eyes. After we checked the weapons, the last thing was the headsets, transmitters, and receivers for each of us. Morgan had already demonstrated their use back in Sai Gon. Now, we made the final checks. There was very little chitchat, everyone focusing on preparations. By the time we'd finished, it was completely dark.

Someone had chosen the perfect spot for our launch. There was enough light from the market to put us in deep shadow as we crept through the palm trees toward the water. There were no people about, most of the action on the other side of the shops where the restaurants and bars were much closer together.

At a small dock, Morgan led us to a Zodiac Seahawk 800 inflatable with a Yamaha 350 horsepower V8 engine, all as foreign to me as meat that had to pass sanitary inspection. Morgan had given us a few details about the black boat. He had assured everyone it would be waiting, and he could steer the brute, even going over one hundred kilometers per hour. I hoped the speeding boat didn't disturb the Con Rit, huge snakelike creatures that lived in the sea up and down the coast of Vietnam. Legend had it there were massive treasures just off the shoreline in sunken sampans drowned by the Con Rit and protected from scavengers by the razor-sharp teeth of the green and gold monsters. We dropped our duffel bags in the swaying boat and climbed aboard, Luong sitting on the bow, Hatati and me in the middle, and Morgan taking the captain's spot. Luong unhooked the moorings and we pushed off, utilizing the paddles Morgan had drilled us in. Back in Sai Gon, he had demonstrated with brooms since at least two of us had never done anything like this before.

The trip was going to take awhile, since it was fifty-six nautical miles to Phu Quy. Once we'd rowed out of the harbor, zigzagging between anchored sampans and trollers, Morgan pushed a switch, and the V8 roared to life, nearly shaking the boat into tiny rubber dinghies before we howled into the night. Seconds later, we were bouncing over the gentle waves headed southeast and I was already puking out the headcheese over the side, my hands wrapped through the rope that surrounded the boat, the only thing that kept me from being tossed into the jaws of Con Rit. The Confucius saying that "when you have faults, do not fear to abandon them" resonated as I dumped my stomach into the South China Sea.

It was pitch black and I had no idea how Morgan kept us going in the right direction. It must have had something to do with his spy skills and a compass. I wasn't capable of any strong opinion, since my head was over the side, staring at the depths as my body spasmed. Eventually, the retching only brought up air and a tiny bit of bile with no chunks. I looked up, seeing the beams from a lighthouse scanning the horizon straight ahead. It had to be Phu Quy or else Morgan would have turned in another direction.

Within minutes, he shut down the engine and gestured to us to begin paddling. The course was directly at the lighthouse. When the lamp turned south and east, we could see the flickering lights of the small city a few kilometers away. More importantly, the outline of the house we'd studied in the satellite photos was coming into view, sitting by itself and the closest building to the path of the beacon. Morgan motioned for us to row fifteen degrees north, now pointing at a large rock just a few meters off the shore. It was where we planned to stow the Zodiac. Morgan got us close enough for Luong to jump out and secure the boat to a smaller boulder.

There was a tiny area of sand about the size of a dumpling cart, and we used the space to unload and fasten our weapons. I'd been ordered to take the tail, no one trusting my climbing or vision skills. Phan Xi Pang was the highest mountain in Vietnam at 3,143 meters tall. I don't think I would have made that one even on the back of a water buffalo. Here, the height to

Quang's place was closer to that of a five-story building, protected by rocks and Pitaya cactus. As we passed slowly, I could smell the plant's delicious pink fruit, a delight I loved on vanilla ice cream. While the trek was in the night, reflections off the rocks from the beacon gave us enough light to see. Morgan was obviously well-trained in guiding us behind boulders and cactus, hiding our movements.

Below the wooden deck that stuck out on the ocean side of the villa, Morgan gave us the hand sign to stop. He pointed to Luong, and the two of them headed around the right side of the home, Hatati going to the left. I was to stay here and only come out if automatic fire started. Certainly, there would be a man on the deck above me. I tried my best to be calm and listen for any commotion.

It came within seconds. First, the rattle of a rock below where Hatati had disappeared, followed by someone running across the deck floor over my head. Then, a slight *phuupp* sound and a man's grunt. We all carried AK-47s and the silenced .22s. It must be Hatati had killed or wounded a guard with her Hush Puppy, the suppressed weapon that had made Morgan a legend. She probably wasn't strong enough to use the garrote. I didn't hear a rifle or body clatter to the wood, so she had to have eased him down. This was my signal to follow.

Around the side of the villa and through an open gate, Hatati was crouched over a motionless man. When she saw me, she stood, immediately going to the sliding doors on the sea side of the villa. We both had our pistols drawn, AKs slung around our necks. Our task was to make sure there was no one else on this side of the house. Hatati would go inside and I would stay as sentry outside. She slipped the door open and vanished.

The rest of the operation was mapped out so that Luong would make his way to Quang's bedroom, disabling anyone who got in his way. He would kill Quang, while Morgan found the other guard on patrol and took care of him. Then, they would go to the basement and incapacitate the other two sleeping sentries. That was the stated mission.

Incapacitate. Disable. Immobilize. All words that had no meaning in this place, on this night. Maybe it was an attempt to not offend the gods and call murder by its real name. Quang and these men would all be dead before we were on the Zodiac. Everyone knew it. The dance was the same. There would be no collateral damage. There were no innocents. If they suffered first, no one would have nightmares. Not even me. And there would be no jokes. We weren't psychopaths.

A few muffled sounds came from the house. No shooting. I watched the road, making sure no one was coming our way. If a vehicle appeared, it could only be headed here or the lighthouse. No one did and we were soon assembled on the deck. I could tell Morgan and Luong had lost much of their cargo, but it was no time to ask why.

Again, Morgan led the way off the deck and onto the rocks below. We weren't so focused on remaining silent, speed being the objective. It took just minutes to reach the Zodiac, and we threw the gear in, Luong untying us and pushing off. There was no way to debrief with the 350 horses making us fly. I held on, hoping the yacking wouldn't have enough stamina to keep my head over the side for the entire voyage.

At Phan Thiet, we reversed our path, packing everything we had taken on our backs. Morgan took out an Ultima fighting knife with a terrifying serrated edge. He plunged the blade into the boat, watching as the air came out and the boat sank, engine and all.

Back in the garage where the SUV was hidden, we unloaded, Hatati and me taking our places in the backseat. Very few words had been said. Now, Luong and Morgan stood at the front of the vehicle, a cell phone in the Night Snake's hand. He punched in a number, looked at Luong who nodded, and hit the "Send" key. A few seconds of silence and the rumble of a distant explosion rippled across the water. Hatati smiled, and I knew part of the plan had been kept from me. Morgan must have left the bundles of C4 with a detonator synched to a mobile phone. The villa would be nothing but woodchips and glass shards now. Leaving the bomb behind was why he looked so skinny on the return.

"I guess he didn't care about the picture or the cobra," I said softly to Hatati.

"No," she said. "He was the last. Except Nguyen. When he's terminated, we'll be leaving your beautiful country."

Luong opened the curtain, and, when it was pulled aside, he and Morgan slid into the front seat. We backed out and sped down the 1A toward Sai Gon. We wanted to get there well ahead of daylight and before the search for the saboteurs could be organized. So far, we were on schedule. Morgan turned around, his arm over the seatback, looking at Hatati. There was blood on his hand and shirt.

"Are you OK?" he asked.

"Yes. Even a weak woman can take care of herself," she said, patting him on the shoulder like he was a lost little boy. "I notice you didn't ask the captain."

"Oh, glad you asked," I said. "Other than the boat ride and depositing my banh mi in the sea, it was like most nights at Ma Jing's. This is all a dream, right?"

"'Fraid not, mook," Morgan said. He held up his bloodied arm close to my face. "That red stuff came from Quang's carotid artery. He got a little fidgety when Luong pulled the garrote tight around his neck. I had to help hold Quang still while he kicked out. The old bastard shit his pants, but I didn't get any on me if you were about to ask about the smell. That's the essence of Vietnam, not me."

"How many guards?" Hatati asked.

"One by the front door," Morgan said. "Luong took him out with a knife strike. I was right behind and helped the man to the ground. Luong and I decided they all needed to die or we probably wouldn't make it out even if the CIA helped. Only one guard was awake inside, and he was reading a copy of *Hot Asian Sluts* in the basement bathroom. I wasted him and the one sleeping with the Hush Puppy. Upstairs, Luong took point. He can smell flatlanders and he led us straight to Quang. As agreed, Luong took it from there. Then we set the charges and met up with you for the scenic cruise back to Phan Biet. Pretty basic. It almost felt like no one cared enough to protect the old killer very well. Signs of the 'New Vietnam.'"

"No snags?" Hatati asked.

"No," Morgan said. "Went as planned." He bent down and came back with something in his hand. "This is for you, Captain. Found it on the table beside Quang's bed. I hear you guys believe in this stuff."

It was a horn. Curved like a scimitar and about a half-meter long, rough and pitted on the outside. Even in the darkness of the SUV, I was pretty sure it was from a rhino. Among all the other myths that seemed to sustain Vietnamese culture, this one had become extremely popular. For the rich of our classless society anyway. The folklore alleged that ground up rhino horn or edible chunks of skin and other bone could cure many ailments including fever, anxiety, boils, impotency, barrenness, and devil possession. Vietnam had become the world's biggest client for these poached animals that were now nearing extinction. It was said a mature horn could bring as much as 250,000 USD or approximately 5,209,417,047 dong, based on the currency conversion rate that fluctuated by the minute.

The rhino smugglers made a less lucrative living sneaking in heroin that, pound for pound, was areca nuts compared to rhinoceros parts. The going price in South Africa was about $10,000 for a snout. Even the diplomatic core had gotten involved. In 2008, Vu Moc Anh, an official at the Vietnamese Embassy in Pretoria, was caught by undercover cameras accepting rhino horn from a known trader. It was shown he had been involved in the illegal traffic for years and paid for his mansion outside Hue with the proceeds. Several times, the Saigon drug squad had arrested dealers who had quantities of heroin from the Golden Triangle and rhino parts for sale at the same time, the heroin going for the paltry sum of about $3,000 per kilo. I put the horn on my lap, knowing I would donate it to Nguyen Trung Kien, the leader of the Vietnamese Anti-Poaching League for use in his campaign to educate citizens on the absurdity of their fantasies.

Along with the sale of rhino parts, Vietnam had lately been named the world's biggest exporter of rare animals, birds, fish, and reptiles. The black market thrived on nearly extinct species, and there appeared to be no limit to the shameless slaughter as long as there was enough dong to pay for a country club membership, a yacht, and several mistresses. It had recently come to the public's attention that the wealthy kept rare species in their home for fun. Like owning a stolen Picasso, it was a sign of their superiority in a land of equality.

The thoughts of slaughtered rhinos had sobered me. Hatati, Luong, and Morgan continued to decompress while I wondered why dead animals meant more than dead Vietnamese. Easy. No rhinoceros had ever insulted, tortured, or discriminated against me. The beasts were helpless to the whims of those who carried the guns. I shook my head, knowing this line of thought wasn't going to bring any further enlightenment.

Outside, it remained dark on 1A with the occasional streetlamp highlighting a small store, mostly selling Coca-Cola and local handicrafts like bamboo carvings and painted ceramic bowls. As we approached Sai Gon, cars and cyclos appeared, most likely workers going home or leaving for morning shift work in the meat, fish, and flower markets. The closer we drove to the city, the more activity was apparent, allowing us to blend in with the early traffic.

By the time we pulled into the underground garage at the safe house, the debriefing was over. We unloaded the SUV, taking all the gear upstairs to the apartment. Inside, we took turns cleaning up in the bathroom and changing clothes. The fridge was filled with cold Tiger *bia,* and we sat around the front room, toasting.

Luong was the only one who didn't act complete as far as the dead commissars went. It had to be about the woman H'Khar and the final act of vengeance in this chapter. Luong was crafting a book, a litany of dead Vietnamese devils he sent to eternity, and Nguyen would play a role. His mission wouldn't be complete until H'Khar's and the other's murders were marked totally paid. There would be no celebration until then and probably never, since the Socialist Republic of Vietnam would still exist no matter Luong's body count. He sipped the beer, unsmiling, and offered little to the conversation.

From my vantage point, I could watch Morgan and Luong without ever letting the masterpiece of Hatati out of my sight. I watched her grin, laugh, cross those stunning legs, and touch Morgan warmly, jealous of this white man's incredible luck. I'd once heard an ex-GI refer to his buddy as an "Opie-looking motherfucker," finding out later it had to do with a popular American TV show in reruns on Video 4. Morgan looked nothing similar to that Opie, more like an older Willem Dafoe in *Platoon,* one of my favorite movies because there were lots of deaths on both sides. I listened to their banter, making an occasional comment, waiting for a chance to find out what I really wanted to know. Eventually, the conversation began to wind down and my opportunity came. I sat forward, looking straight at Morgan.

"I'm mystified," I said. "How did you ever happen upon a treasure like Hatati. Here, you would have to be worth a few trillion dong to be with such a gem. Are you rich?"

They both nearly choked on their beer. Hatati nodded at Morgan, giving him permission to proceed.

"She seduced me at a casino in London," he said. "I believed she was a damsel in distress. I'm a sucker for that act." He took another mouthful of Tiger. "In reality, she was working for MI6 and Nutley was her minder. I was totally fooled. She led me by the nose around the globe. Or maybe it was another body part." He laughed, not in the least embarrassed. "Yes, I do think it was. Well, whatever, her and Nutley made sure I terminated a number of targets, both of their and my choosing. Luong played a part in the Vietnam incidents. Since then, we've been relaxing at my place on a tiny Greek island. That was until we got Luong's call. As you know, I owe him many lives."

"Please excuse me," I said, looking at Hatati, "but what is your version? You are obviously too good for this old man."

Even Luong chuckled.

"The way he told it is true," Hatati said. "I was paid to introduce myself. Otherwise, it would never have happened. He easily fell into my web. He is a very lonely man, and women have not been significant in his life." She shook her head back and forth, long black hair swinging from side to side. I was about to faint. "I think he might have assassinated the queen if I asked."

The green eyes. Maybe the feature that put her in another universe. Of course she was the most stunningly beautiful woman I'd ever seen. I'd viewed thousands of gorgeous females in this age of the movies, magazines, porn, TV, and Internet, plus many in person. None had those eyes. It was as if the two most priceless dazzling emeralds in the world had been implanted in her face. Not even Miss Ireland's could compare. Certainly, no one in Southeast Asia. I couldn't take my eyes off hers.

"Do you want the queen dead?" I asked. "I'll do it."

More guffaws.

"No," Hatati said, "I've got my man." She patted Morgan's arm like he was a puppy.

The satellite phone buzzed. Morgan had laid it on the end table beside him while we chatted like any four killers would after a successful massacre. Morgan picked the receiver up, pushing one button, and held the handset to his ear, not saying a word. He listened for a few seconds, his head bobbing up and down.

"Roger that, twonk," Morgan said. "And stop sucking on that Cohiba. You're words get arsed up." He glanced at Hatati, only a tiny smile bending his lips. "And thanks for all your help. Couldn't have done it without you, mate." He listened for a while, sitting back on the couch. "One more little piece of work and we'll be back on Mykonos. We'll keep that classified for now." He pressed another key and set the phone back.

"The gaffer's chuffed that we're staying on," Morgan said, referring to Nutley and looking back and forth between Luong and Hatati. "I didn't want to listen to him squeal. He thinks we're in real danger of being caught and he doesn't want us to grass on MI6."

"Those Brits," Hatati said. "It's always all about them. What that country needs is a few good dentists and a conscience."

"I've got holiday time due," I said. "We could visit Big Ben. I've never been outside Vietnam and I love tea and fish and chips."

"Enough," Luong said. The rest of us stiffened, surprised at his abruptness.

"We have to plan how we are going to find Nguyen," Luong said. "And kill him. Only then will I be able to enjoy your juvenile jokes."

"You're partly right," Morgan said. "We do need to start thinking about locating Nguyen. But I don't believe you'll ever be able to appreciate our kind of humor."

"Children's?" Luong asked, shaking his head back and forth. "I am too old and have seen too much for the trivial. Bleeding out Vietnamese is about the only thing that makes me laugh."

"Remember when we rescued Tran from the firefight?" Morgan asked. "We watched the Southern Cross from a rice paddy, surrounded by NVA. To keep the baby quiet, you let him suck on your finger while I stood guard. I caught you smiling. Do you recall what it feels like to enjoy anything but killing?"

"Yes. Not all of them have to die. Only crawl on the earth blind, deaf, dumb, and wailing for mercy. They'll not get any from me."

"You sure know how to ruin the party."

"I've never been to a 'party.'"

The mood had changed. There would be no more banter, and my destiny would soon be known. It was time to focus on my continued existence, not silly and boorish teenage behavior.

"Speaking of parties," I said. "What is a one-word party joke?" Everyone looked blank. "Communism." It fell as flat as it sounded. It was time to focus on seeing the next Chinese New Year, coming up in a few days, and one I might not witness unless our tactics were sound and I was the model of cooperation. Coincidentally, it was soon to be a Year of the Snake.

"You know that in America, you can always find a party," I said. "In Vietnam, the Party finds you." I waited for a response. Silence. "So, I can do karaoke too." Stares. "Or should we decide how you'll let me free so I can get to Nguyen and Luong can strangle him?"

"Yes," Luong said, showing the face of a doctor giving the diagnosis of lung cancer caused by inhalation of Dow Chemical. "What do you propose?"

The choice was to continue playing the buffoon or demonstrate I could be of value as a player on this Murder, Inc. team. I crossed my hands on my lap and tried to look as grave as Luong.

"Of course," I said, "I can't just shuffle into headquarters as if nothing has happened. I don't know where he lives or much about him and don't think I can find where he is. If the goal is ultimately to get to Nguyen, I have an idea. "

"Go ahead," Luong said, finally showing some interest in anything that came out of my mouth.

"I have his cell number," I said. "He told me to stay in contact. I haven't. One fundamental reason is, I don't have a mobile phone. Nguyen forgot that he and his masters never trusted me with one. Or a weapon. Phan made all my calls."

There was an infestation of geckos in Vietnam. For some bizarre reason, they seemed to appear in every room where I sat, even the ones where I was losing a fingernail. It could be I rarely paid attention since they were as common as bamboo. This one had more yellow spots and a thin red line on his green crinkled side. Maybe he was one of the new local variety recently identified by a German scientist and named "Cryptus" for the lizard's bent toes and scales. This one was as still as Luong. I brought my eyes back to the Montagnard, knowing he was the one I had to convince.

"Let me use a phone," I said. "You can monitor the call. I'll set up a meeting; Nguyen will object, but he'll be even more frantic after Quang's killing. I think he'll go along with it, believing he'll be able to trap me. We'll make sure he has a surprise."

Luong sat forward like he was waiting for the punch line.

"Where do you feel most comfortable in Sai Gon?" I asked.

"Binh Thanh," Luong said.

"He'll be under so much stress," I said, "Nguyen won't be able to refuse. You know the area. You tell me what you want. I'll make the call."

Luong, Morgan, and Hatati traded glances. It appeared they at least temporarily agreed to discuss my strategy.

Over the next half hour, plans were formed. I didn't contribute unless asked. The three of them had participated in operations like the entrapment of Nguyen now being thrashed out. I was a homicide detective, not an assassin. Or spy.

It was getting to be midmorning, and I was worn out. Not even the occasional question kept my eyelids from flickering like a firefly. I was resigned to whatever was coming in the next level of my earthly incarnation, even if I had hopes and dreams that it meant a few more dead Vietnamese who had tormented me and their countrymen for too many years. My head slumped onto my shoulder and I was already into REM.

"Wake up, Kung Fu master," Morgan barked.

Eyes open, the room was way too bright, and this *gwailo* ghost was standing above me, shaking my shoulder as if he were testing to see if I was a spirit or just another passed-out overdosed dog eater on the couch. I grunted, letting him know I was still in the kingdom of the living.

"Please step away," I mumbled. "There's too much light bouncing off all that white skin. It hurts my eyes."

"Now, now, Captain Fang," Morgan said, "don't be such a bigot. Even I know the Chinese are the most racist people on the planet. I'll let your slander of whites pass for now. Only because you can be of help. The minute I change my mind, you'll be providing the protein in a bowl of spicy pho. Your people wouldn't know the difference between your meat and a Labrador's."

We must have a little time or this tap dance would have ended much quicker, and Luong would have commanded us to stop the infantile sparring. I made up my mind to move things along and not cheapen the scheme with my thin skin.

"I have just one question," I said, looking at Morgan and slowly sitting up. He nodded for me to go ahead. "What do you call a white man with a sheep under each arm?" He shook his head. "A pimp."

This time, Luong didn't bother scolding. He stared back and forth between Morgan and me, with one glance at a chuckling Hatati.

"If Morgan is correct," Luong said, "even the dinosaurs of the Vietnam People's Security Forces may have the ability to track cell phone locations. Do you have Nguyen's private number?"

"Yes," I said. "I believe so."

"You will not call from Binh Thanh," Luong said. "Since we will not be here much longer, this area of the city would be better. Please go downstairs and call him. Say you'll meet him in Binh Thanh in an hour. In the same place he knows you were dropped off before. Since we no long care if they track the phone, don't worry about how long it takes. Be convincing."

"He will ask questions," I said.

"Tell him all will be told when you meet."

"He will most likely bully me. At least I have no living relatives he can threaten me with."

"Don't worry. He'll try to organize a trap as fast as he can. Tell him he must come alone and will be watched. This is all so obvious. He knows he will have armed police or military with him, but all we care about is getting a clean shot. After he's dead, there's no chance for them to catch us in Binh Thanh, no matter how many men and helicopters they have." Again, a rare smile. "There are many tunnels, and, just like the Americans, they won't find them all. Or even a fraction."

"But won't all the people who live there be severely punished?"

"They will know nothing. And, all my Degar brothers and sisters would gladly die to avenge years of persecution in our homeland. Besides"—he turned to Morgan—"he has contacts in the Western press. There will be newsmen around. Morgan's alerted them, tantalizing the reporters with details of the ones who've already been killed."

"So this needs to happen soon?"

"Yes. Make the call. I'll come along. Morgan and Hatati are going to the car. We'll meet them on the street."

The hesitation was only the time it took me to get over my amazement about the length of the speech Luong had just made. Even in the middle of a dark monsoon night, his stories were told in quick, quiet staccato with little background. He conveyed the horrors without embellishment and rarely spoke during daylight hours when the guards would have rather clubbed us into the mud than allow even a short conversation. I couldn't remember when Luong had used so many words. Never in English. I would by no means lose my trust in this man. That didn't mean it could stop from shocking me that an illiterate hill tribesman had become comfortable in the language and customs of the capitalist West. He could drive a car and use a satellite phone, skills I barely had myself. Luong was now like the popular Vietnamese legend Tru'o'ng Chi, a poor, lowly, and forsaken fisherman who was transformed into a nobleman in order to find the love of the princess My Nu'o'ng. This Montagnard had mutated out of hate, not love. Still, he was a different, but still dangerous, spirit. I stood up, wanting to quickly get to the next skirmish of this battle.

"Lead the way," I said. "If I'm going to die, I can't think of any other Degar I'd rather be with."

"You don't know any others," Luong said.

"Sooo, am I lying?"

"Just follow me. And shut up. For once."

We went out the door and down to the street. Around the corner, in front of the Hurmes authentic leather bag shop, where everything was made of plastic and sold for less than ten dollars, I wondered what variety of pig the purses came from and if it took more than a gallon of petroleum to manufacture. Luong brought out his mobile and I gave him Nguyen's number, the one I'd memorized.

"*Xin chao*," Nguyen said. Hello.

He wouldn't have recognized the number. If he'd known it was me, he would have growled out some kind of scorn, like, "speak to me, *cho cai*." Bitch.

"Now I'm your bitch too?" I asked. "And here I thought we meant so much more to each other."

"Where are you?" Nguyen asked.

"Not as important as where I'll be in an hour."

"Where?"

"Binh Thanh. Where I've been since I was released."

"You were not in Binh Thanh."

"Oh. And I thought I was. Must have been someone else."

"No wisecracks, fool. Where have you been?"

"I told you. Did you miss me? Have you been looking? And I didn't know you cared after pulling out my fingernail and giving me a cold shower."

"You will pay for this."

"I don't make much salary, about a quarter of what other detectives are paid, but I do have a little money hidden away."

"It will be more likely a few body parts and blood."

"And so I would want to meet you why?"

"Because, if you don't, eventually we will find you. Then, it will be worse. In the meantime, we will interrogate every family member and friend. We will not be delicate."

"Good. I don't much care for my remaining relatives. If I had any. Feel free to start with their toes and move upward. As for friends, I can't think of any except for a few on the police force. You can have a go at them too."

"We will destroy you. You will never be able to walk, let alone work."

"My, my. I can hardly wait to see you."

"Where?"

"I have conditions. First, you come alone. Second, you will give me your oath I will not be harmed. Third, I can continue in my detective position. There may be more. Those will do for now."

"You've heard there's been another killing? This one was mass murder, not just a commissar."

"No. I've been out of touch lately."

"Is Luong involved?"

"Who?"

He waited, and I could hear him spit. There were cars in the background and that incessant *meep meep* of the cyclos. Nguyen must have been on a street, waiting to get into a chauffeured car and make arrangements to have me killed while he drove to the rendezvous.

"I will expect you to tell me everything. Anything less, and it will go hard for you."

"Well, it's been a while since I've been hard. I'll be looking forward to it."

"Time is getting short. I want to know the meeting place. Now."

"Binh Thanh. Where Phan dropped me. You know the spot. I'll be there in one hour and will only show myself if you're alone. The rooftops will be watched and the sky, too, if you plan on sending a helicopter."

"Will you come with me?"

"If I trust you and what you have to say. I think that could be like praying the cobra doesn't strike."

"I'll be there. Make sure you are."

"Can hardly contain my glee."

Nguyen disconnected, and I threw the cell into a rubbish can next to the sidewalk. Luong had stood beside me the entire time, keeping guard in case of a passing patrol or anyone suspicious. There had only been two girly-boys in thigh-high, leopard *ao dis*, blonde wigs, and fake, pointy tits. Luong hadn't bothered to respond to their, "Hey, big boy, wanna have a swell time? Two for one day" chirps.

We moved quickly around the corner, away from the TOT NHAT BUOM at Hurmes. BEST SAIL. Morgan and Hatati had already pulled the SUV from the garage and were parked on the street, waiting. When they saw us approaching, Hatati jumped out of the driver's side, and Luong replaced her. I got in the back and Hatati followed, leaving Morgan in the front passenger seat. Luong immediately steered us into the maddening afternoon traffic, headed southeast toward Binh Thanh, and I wondered if it would be Buddha or Confucius who got me through the next few hours with at least a few bits of my body still functional. For some reason, I felt the need to pray. One way or another, my "miserable" life was about to change dramatically.

While the call of Buddha was closer to my heart, as the years drifted by in an opium blur, I seemed to be floating more toward the teachings and philosophy of Confucius, that Chinese master Kong who died nearly five hundred years before Christ but a few hundred years after Buddha. It could be only an attempt to connect with my northern Mandarin ancestors. Again, as a half-breed, I was torn between two religions and cultures. It wasn't as if I spent hours of every day trying to get in touch with my true self. Still, there were fundamental questions that bothered me. While Confucianism is a philosophy, Buddhism is a religion. Anything that smacked of the doctrinaire or political was creeping further away as the time passed, replaced by suggestion or discourse. Too much time being told exactly how a true pure socialist Vietnamese should think and behave.

While it was my experience, I couldn't quite get my head around the idea that "life is filled with pain and sorrow." If I followed that tenet, there was no reason to leave Ma Jing's. Sure, I did believe "the cause of all suffering is people's selfish desire for pleasure." Besides, Confucianism didn't promise or teach anything about the afterlife. No earthly sacrifice or worship was described like "ending all suffering by ending all desires," a major principal of Buddhism. I was still too alive to abandon every one of my cravings and joys. For this adventure, I'd stick with my Chinese roots and keep homage to the last of the Five Confucian relationship values, "friends." Still, I was in the dark about what would happen next in this drama. Like Confucius, I knew that "faced with what is right, to leave it undone shows a lack of courage."

At least the years spent drifting in the clouds at Ma Jing's gave me experience in the realm of imagination. Nguyen would meet me, and he may or may not be protected by a squad of heavily armed men, ready to shoot me down like a rabid monkey. We needed to be prepared for an assault and neither Luong, Hatati, nor Morgan had chosen to share their plan with a lowly Chinese junkie. I fidgeted in my seat, finally unwilling to let my future be so vague.

"Morgan," I said, "I believe it was your former commander, General Westmoreland, who said, 'In Vietnam, I was participating in my own lynching, but the problem was I didn't know how I was going to be lynched.' I feel exactly the same."

"A student of war, eh?" Morgan asked. "You quote Sun Tzu, Mao, and Westmoreland. I'll bet you have a lot more dung in that oversize brain of yours."

"You're avoiding," I said. "Please be so generous as to tell me your strategy. I will be risking my life, too, even if you have little belief in its value. I think you owe me that small courtesy." I bowed.

"Tell him," Hatati said. "It could be the last act in his *chuangi*." I knew that was a form of traditional Chinese play that rarely ended in anything but a tragedy.

"We have people watching," Luong said, "and will know if the number of police grows and exactly where they are. We should arrive before most of

Nguyen's people. If not, we'll have identified their locations." He looked at me in the rear-view mirror. "You're the bait. If I were hunting a rare *duoc* in the forest outside Dalat, you'd be the rotten banana. Like you, those monkeys are almost extinct." No smile, just the facts.

"How fun," I said. "I get to be the main course, while you lurk in the bushes, diddling yourselves."

"That about sums it up," Morgan said. "I will guarantee if or when you are shot, there will be a few dead policemen, including Nguyen, bleeding out on the road."

"Is there some objection to giving me the details?" I asked. "I feel like I'm back in the camps. Kept in the dark and fed *cut*." Shit.

"At least *cut* has a tiny amount of protein," Luong said. "There were nights where we would have given up our *lo dit*, asshole, for a bite of shit. Unfortunately, we would have had to drink it, since the dysentery never left and eating leaves only made the diarrhea worse." His focus was back on the road chaos in front of him. Surprisingly, Luong was a good driver, able to avoid the slow-moving carts and crisscrossing cyclos that appeared out of nowhere, seemingly more intent on suicide than reaching any destination.

"Spare me the memories," I said. "I was there groveling beside you." I sat back and watched a beautiful Eurasian woman, her head covered with a white umbrella, strolling on the sidewalk as if she were in summertime Paris. "What I'm asking is simple. Like, do I get to carry a pistol? Where and when do I get out of the car? What do I do when I meet Nguyen if that happens? If things go bad, is there a hiding or meeting place?"

"Stop torturing him," Hatati said, a stern look on her gorgeous face. "If you won't tell the captain, I will."

"Go ahead," Morgan said. "We won't treat him like our minders have always behaved with us."

"If you're talking about Nutley," Hatati said, "I agree no one should act the way he does. Silly, juvenile jokes and as little information as we can force him to share."

Both Morgan and Luong nodded.

"A few years ago," Hatati said, "Nutley sent me to Phnom Penh to infiltrate a supposed terrorist cell of mostly women. They had been slowly moving

from southern Thailand into Cambodia, and he said these fanatics were affili-
ated with the Sunni Islamic Resurgency radical group. That all made sense.
What Nutley neglected to tell me was the women were all veteran guards who
had spent years in the Khmer Rouge S-21 prison, specializing in the use of
white-hot metal prods in order to get some of the thirty thousand prisoners
who went through the gates to confess to being spies. I think it has been
decided only three prisoners ever survived." She stopped and looked out the
window where a cyclo was being pulled from underneath a Mitsubishi garbage
truck, the driver and his female passenger still lying in the street, her *ao di*
ripped and showing bleeding legs. "Even worse, Nutley implied the women
were amateurs and relatively harmless, so I didn't need to have weapons." She
shook her head and frowned. "I've never been around such evil. Those women
would have torn my skin off and made handbags, using my teeth for zippers.
Luckily, it didn't take long to discover what fiends they were. I'd snuck in a
knife. Nutley said it would be too dangerous to go in armed, so no pistol. Had
to kill one. I got to the safe house in Dangkao with the others close behind. I
was told they were relatively peaceful." She scowled more.

"Is that true?" Morgan asked.

"Maybe," she said. "It's 'need to know.'" She smiled, reaching over and
patting my arm.

"So, the point of that fable is I get to carry a knife?" I asked.

"I think you might need a Leopard 1 handheld missile to survive this
one," Morgan said. "And that might not be enough firepower." He grinned
like he'd just been dealt a Wong at the Pai Gow table.

Hatati reached forward and gently boxed his ears. Then, unable to control herself, she began stroking his neck and cooing softly.

"Get a room," I said. "We'll be passing the Faifoo Hotel in a few blocks.
They charge by the minute. I'm sure Luong and I can spare five."

"You're just jealous," Hatati said, not bothering to remove her hand.

Women. They sensed when a man lusted for them like a dog for a
human leg. Usually they could easily take advantage of a man's weakness
and lead him blindly around, the promise and scent of sex taking the place
of a nose ring and leash. Most times, I wasn't victim to this temptation,
more interested in smoking the Chinese molasses than burying my *cac* in a
lon. But I did appreciate a masterpiece like To Ngoc Van's *A Girl by Lilies*.

Hatati was even more spectacular and I could reach out and touch her, not just appreciate beauty on the wall of the National Museum. The truth. I was incredibly envious, even beyond my cloud-blurred comprehension. In response, I did the "tsk, tsk" thing that was so common in avoiding reality.

"We're getting close," Luong said. "I suppose we should tell Captain Fang what we have in mind."

"Brilliant," I said. "Do I get to name my heirs?"

"No need," Morgan said. "We're skilled at these kinds of ops. Haven't lost anyone yet. Not this trip anyway." Morgan swiveled toward me, trying to keep the corners of his mouth from curling into a grin. "Oops. I forgot about the agents in Belgrade. Oh, and the two on the clusterfuck outside Minsk. Those weren't Nutley's fault at all." He shook his head back and forth. "The one in Dublin was." He faced forward and I could tell by his shoulder movements he was silently laughing.

"That's fine," I said. "I'm less afraid of being shot than a return to the basement at headquarters. I think I'll just turn myself over to Nguyen and beg for forgiveness."

"Do you think you'll get it?" Morgan asked.

"We're within blocks of Binh Thanh," Luong said. "Give him his orders."

That was the Luong I had shared nightmares with, a man who was sure of himself and his destiny, willing to steer things as best he could, even with an AK-47 at his temple. I sighed, thanking him for always willing to be the director as well as an actor in his and the Montagnard's movie.

"Don't bother," I said. "I've decided to surrender, since you all don't seem to care about the fate of a half-breed."

"Stop the nonsense," Hatati said. "Give him his instructions. They're not that complicated."

"Oh, so even one as slow as me could understand?" I asked.

"Get rid of that chip on your shoulder," Morgan said. "Or I'll cut it off with my Ka-Bar." A much-loved fighting knife used by many special forces soldiers.

I bowed. "Please proceed," I said.

"It's simple," Morgan said, facing me from the front seat. The blankness on his face told me it was time to be serious. "You stand on the street and we try to make sure you're not ground into *gio*." Sausage.

"Speaking of food, can we stop and get doughnuts first?" I asked. "It could be my last meal. Doughnuts Doughnuts is just ahead. They make the best Fruity Pebbles in the city."

"Not a chance," Morgan said. "That's where the cops hang out. We'll have you on station in just a few seconds." Morgan faced me, his arm over the seat back. "After we take care of Nguyen, we'll treat you to haute cuisine at Le Bordeaux, the finest French food in the city. We could walk there from here, if there're no bullets flying past." He turned foward. "We're here. Showtime."

Luong steered the car to the side of the road. On the sidewalk, two men were trying to look casual. Their thick brows and prominent cheeks screamed "Degar." These Montagnards, dressed in Sai Gon chic of black slacks and white shirts, were as inconspicuous as "turds in a bamboo salad" according to Luong. Both could never be mistaken for lowlanders with their flattened noses and easy stares, hinting more of Australian aborigine than Kinh, the majority of Vietnamese people. The bulges under their untucked tops looked like huge tumors, but the shapes were obviously pistols. They didn't smile and scanned the street and buildings across the road in a way that made them out to be ex-military in the way they quartered the horizon and stood with their feet spread shoulder width. When I got out, they silently disappeared and I wondered if they were opium apparitions.

"Stay there," Morgan said. "You're being guarded."

"Ever heard of a 'drive-by'?" I said before he could buzz the window up. There was nowhere to hide unless I ran.

"We're not in LA," Morgan said, as Luong pulled away. "Here, they use AKs and grenades," and they were gone.

It would be a few minutes before Nguyen and his troops arrived. The question was how many there would be and if Nguyen would present a clear target. It wouldn't have to be much. I'd heard from Luong about Morgan's skill with a sniper rifle as well as his preferred Hush Puppy. Within a hundred meters, there was no missing. Nguyen would want to speak to me before I was used to fertilize the paddies, so there would be a period of confusion that Morgan and Luong were more than capable of exploiting.

On the street, there wasn't a lot of traffic. It was too late for the morning rush hour and too early for the evening anarchy. Still, it was relative. Taxis fought with mopeds, cyclos, buses, and motorcycles for the small spaces unfilled by pushcarts and bicycles. The din was less deafening, since most of the drivers didn't seem to think Buddha was calling them and there were more blessed days to come on this planet. Things were moving, and I thought the first indication that Nguyen was near would be a sharp drop in the traffic. If he had enough time and people, he would close off the street.

Wafting from the river, not more than fifty meters behind me, the aroma of Sai Gon sewage coated my nose, drowning out the sweet perfume from the flower stall across the road and the smoking sausage cart that served quasi-meat floating in clotted blood and served with stirred vegetables, some that could be identified. The block was a normal space in Binh Thanh. Knockoff CD and DVD markets were next to tire repair stores, camera and TV shops, and clothing door fronts, featuring "Ralf Loren" and "Kalvun Cline" originals. Overhead, the afternoon rain was building in the gray clouds, threatening to drown even the rats that scurried past in the gutters. I yearned for a quick hit on the pipe at Ma Jing's and wondered if I'd inhaled my last breath of heaven. I was standing alone and unarmed, totally not in control of my destiny, reciting Buddha's words "do not dwell in the past, do not dream of the future, concentrate the mind on the present moment."

The sound came first. Squealing tires and horns blaring even more loudly than the normal *meep* of hundreds of cyclos jockeying for position. Drivers swerved aside, some getting thrown to the pavement, yelling "*du ma may*" or "go fuck your mother" to the black SUVs that were clearly from the security forces. It all happened so fast, I didn't even have time to piss myself or surrender to the fight-or-flight reflex. Instead, I let my jaw drop in awe of the spectacle, knowing full well I was the dCON in the roach trap and there was little alternative than to act calm, a performance worthy of an Indochine film award.

The two Montagnard men who had been trying to be invisible surrounded me before I could run, one-stepping in front as a human shield. The SUVs slid to a halt and both men drew pistols, aiming them in the general direction of the three security force vehicles. If it had been the police, they would have arrived in Hondas or old Jeeps, but this operation was way above the pay grade and clearance of a regular Sai Gon cop. I couldn't see inside the blackened windows. Within seconds, the doors burst open, and men began to scramble out, Nguyen from the passenger seat of the middle SUV. If Morgan, Luong, and Hatati were coming to the rescue, now was the time.

Before my guards or any of the security forces could fire their pistols, the sound of both of the Dragunov sniper rifles I'd seen in Morgan's arsenal boomed from the shanties behind us. We were close enough to hear the gas discharge after every shot as the 7.62 rounds thudded into another target. Between the lookouts and the riflemen, it was less time than a deep breath before the pavement was littered with bodies, none Montagnard, Caucasian, or half-breed.

Obviously, no one had aimed at Nguyen. He was still moving quickly toward me, a Russian-made Makarov PM revolver pointed at my stomach. In the silence that shattered the barrage, he pushed the handgun into my side and shoved me toward the open door of the front SUV. Someone had shot out the tires of the other two and Nguyen instantly recognized he had only one chance.

Reaching the car, Nguyen shoved my quivering body inside and used the butt of his pistol to slam me on the skull. I slumped to the seat, unconscious. When I awoke, in what must have been only a few seconds, the Makarov was jammed into my side, and Nguyen was swerving through traffic on La Duan Street, barely avoiding killing a pedestrian or motorcycle driver every few yards. I watched in terror as he broke through the mayhem like an elephant in saw grass.

The mystery was twofold, and I didn't want to make it some kind of Chinese riddle. First, why I was alive? Next, why Morgan and his comrades hadn't prevented me from being taken? They could easily have shot Nguyen, and I wondered why he wasn't the primary goal like they'd told me. If they'd killed him when it was simple, it would be all over. Morgan and Hatati could head back to their Grecian paradise, and Luong could hike into his beloved mountains. And me? Thanks, Morgan. I was completely at the mercy of whatever was about to unfold if we made it to wherever he was headed without a fatal crash.

"*Don lon que, dee chaw,*" I said. You're having your period, bitch. "Slow down and smell the orchids, not just your tampon."

The slap came so fast I didn't have time to register the pain on my cheek before his right hand was back on the handgun. When the blow came, Nguyen hadn't taken his eyes off the cars, people, and cyclos he was barely missing as he slalomed around corners and jumped curbs.

"Your childish attempts at humor make me sick," Nguyen said as we clipped a vegetable stand. Piles of water spinach fell to the pavement next to heads of cabbage and pak choi, making a slippery green blob as the vendor shook his fist and tried to stay upright in the slime. "If there were time, I would kill you now and make the country a happier place."

Rubbing my jaw, I wondered if I cared if my passing came now or from a blowtorch in a dank basement.

"The best part of you was flushed earlier today when you took your morning shit," I said. "If you weren't so full of it, you'd just shoot me now and quit with the empty threats."

"Old man," he said, "you have no idea what I'm capable of or what's going on. If you'd shut up, you'd find out. And maybe we'd both survive." He squeezed the steering wheel firmly and jammed the gun harder into my side. "Now let me concentrate on driving before we both die at the hands of a fruit stand."

"Fruit stands don't have hands," I said, shaking my head like he'd just misspelled "duh." But, I chose to stay quiet and not jeopardize our lives threatened now by an oxcart filled with bags of rice that appeared out of an alley. The beast saw us coming and started to buck, just as we raced past, his huge horns piercing the sky.

Since I'd been struggling lately with my personal code and whether it should be guided by Buddha or Confucius or Ma Jing, I examined the wisdom of the first two and lusted for the third. As it regarded the current mess and Nguyen, Confucius had it spot on. "When we see men of a contrary character, we should turn inwards and examine ourselves." I did just that, unbalanced at the possibility Nguyen may not be who I thought and why I believed that could be true other than out of desperation.

By now, we'd reached the Ho Chi Minh City Highway and didn't have to worry so much about oxen and food carts. The traffic was flowing. Nguyen expertly zigzagged down the four-lane road, obviously knowing where he was headed. I had no idea.

In a few minutes, Nguyen turned back toward downtown on Hai Ba Trung Boulevard. This route could take us to police headquarters or to the Rex Hotel for a mimosa at the rooftop bar. He took the pistol out of my side and slid it into his still fresh, uncreased jacket. This man would retain his movie star looks and calm in front of a firing squad. He slowed the SUV and bent toward me, his black eyes simmering charcoal and a Hollywood smirk on his face.

"That story you told me about Luong and the Night Snake," Nguyen said, "you left out a few details. One is Hatati. Two is all three of them and their relationship with MI6, especially a man named 'Nutley.'"

Once, I'd gone to my office, closed the door, and wondered why I continued accepting the abuse of my comrades without committing murder. I took a deep, cleansing breath and tried to relax, dreaming of the upcoming release at Ma Jing's. Still, there was paperwork to finish, and I opened the desk drawer to get out a pen. I stuck my hand inside and touched something I couldn't comprehend. Looking down, I realized it was a giant Emperor scorpion close to a foot long. Its fat black claws tickled my hand, and I knew a sting could kill me if I didn't pull away fast. I did, my heart about to detonate in my chest and my head twirling like a dust devil. Not even that hideous arthropod surprised me more than Nguyen's short revelation. I breathed again deeply, hoping a repeat gesture would bring some peace.

"Shocked?" Nguyen asked, grinning wider, his sessions with the orthodontist and teeth whitener clearly visible.

"If you told me your mother wasn't a whore," I said, "I'd be even more stunned."

"Now, now, Captain Fang," Nguyen said soothingly. "It's time we call a truce. Save the trash talk for your real friends. If you have any. Or pay enough."

"You're not going to tell me you're involved in all this," I said, making a circular gesture with my still-throbbing hand minus two fingernails.

"Have you heard of 'need to know'?" he asked. "Suffice to say, I'm aware of what you've been up to and could have had you executed a few days ago. Or most anytime since."

"And why didn't you?"

"If you haven't grasped this by now in your monkey brain, we're on the same team."

"And the old Degar woman you murdered?"

"I told you it wasn't me."

"Who did it?"

"I have my suspicions. No proof."

"You're telling me you're friends with Luong and Morgan?"

"Not exactly 'friends.'"

"Fellow travelers?"

"Why do you think I speak such fluent English? Cambridge? Oxford? MI6? Get the clues? You are a detective, aren't you? Put it together yourself."

"Oh, you're a spy recruited by MI6 while studying in England. A true cliché. Were you on the sculling team?"

"How did you know? I was a middle rower on the Oxford Old Blues Crew."

"Now I know you're lying. That is easy to check and I don't believe you. There's never been a Vietnamese rower on any Oxford Crew."

"Check the Oxford University Boat Club website. You'll find my picture for the 2001 squad."

"So you went from Oxford to MI6 on the Thames? Trained in the art of spying? Learned how to peep through windows?"

"Yes. Yes. Yes."

"And how to assassinate the queen's enemies?"

"Need to know."

"Then you came back and joined the Security Services here?"

"They were the ones who sent me. Someone needed to learn what the capitalist pigs are doing and have planned for us in their campaign for world domination."

"Sure. They want our shrimp and fish balls."

"Golf courses and massage parlors. Just like Thailand."

"And now you're a double agent?"

"Need to know."

"Yes, I do. If you want my help, I need to know. I will not betray Luong and I really have no country, so don't try any 'loyalty' *cut* on me." Shit.

Silence. By now, Nguyen had slowed the SUV as we approached the center of the city. I had no idea if the next stop was police headquarters and a reunion with Lat, the court torturer, or a drink on the terrace at the Majestic, watching the palms sway in the afternoon breeze and sipping a frosted mango martini, while fat, old white men in safari shirts and cotton slacks entertained their young Vietnamese "dates."

But we didn't stop in District One, heading immediately to Cholon and Chinatown, the part of the city that was most like home to me. Nguyen drove straight toward the alley where I'd recently been taken to see Mr. Liu. He parked and the same man stepped out of the shadows, jumping into the driver's seat as Nguyen got out.

"Follow me," Nguyen said. "We're expected."

My feet hit what might have been the ground and I was floating as if on a cloud of Ma Jing's finest Laotian Brown, wrapped in banana leaves and 100 percent pure. This had to be a dream. I was gliding toward a door I knew led up the steps to Liu's apartment with a man who had my fingernail pulled out and shot an old Degar woman, a sworn enemy of Luong and Morgan, the atrocities I knew about. There were surely a lot of others in his scrapbook. The only thing that could have surprised me more was meeting Luong, Morgan, and Hatati.

The instant that thought resonated in my muddled head, another SUV appeared in the alley. Luong was driving. When he stopped, a second faceless man appeared from the depths and drove the car quickly away while Luong, Morgan, and Hatati hurried toward the door being held open by Nguyen. They nodded at one another while I tried to keep from fainting. There was one question that kept pounding in my head like a Tibetan monk's call to prayer: How could it be?

Nguyen pushed toward the stairwell.

"Move it," he said.

Luong was there before the words were out, smiling and giving me a reassuring nod that looked more like he was standing over the corpses of a dozen lowlanders he'd just slaughtered than encouragement. I let him nudge me, my guide to the next level of this strange life. We climbed the stairs and entered Liu's dwelling, the old man himself holding the door open.

This time, I was less nervous than mystified. The priceless silk Song dynasty tapestries, displaying magnificent images of ducks and cranes, which hung on the walls were of less interest than why I was here. And still alive. I didn't wait to be asked and took a seat on a hard-backed chair that must have been worth more than I'd make in three lifetimes. It was straight and rigid enough to remind me that money didn't guarantee comfort, even if it was crafted a few hundred years ago for an emperor.

The shades on the windows were still closed. Luong, Morgan, and Hatati took seats, and Mr. Liu began the ritual tea offering. There was little conversation other than "sugar" or "cream, please." Everyone seemed to be waiting for the elephant in the room to begin trumpeting. Me, I was approaching a coma and didn't want to slip into the universe of the unconscious, a desired world in the past. I waited, trying to keep my eyelids from being welded together from the pressure.

"So, things must have worked out to our satisfaction," Mr. Liu said, bowing after he'd finished pouring the tea that smelled of lavender and oranges. "And you didn't have to shoot Mr. Nguyen."

"No," Luong said. "No matter how much I wanted to." No smile. His back was as stiff and straight as a bamboo culm, and his face betrayed nothing but annoyance.

That made Morgan chuckle.

"My biggest challenge when I'm with Luong," he said, "is to keep him from using a tactical nuclear warhead on the lowlands. I think he would anyway if he could get his hands on one."

"And my biggest challenge with you," Hatati said, looking at Morgan, "is to keep you away from the targets. You like to be up close and personal. Watch them die and try to get your morality play questions answered before you blow their heads off."

"Since I've now been inducted to the team on the side of righteousness," Nguyen said, "I'd like to know what comes next." He glanced at me, nodding. "And tell me again why we need this crocodile lizard."

"We don't anymore," Mr. Liu said. "You can go ahead and make *bo kho* out of him in the cooking pot." Stew.

Nguyen lunged toward me. There was no time to react, and, besides, I didn't have any martial arts moves in my repertoire to respond to his attack, being soundly on another planet and completely outnumbered. Before he could reach my throat, he stopped and the room erupted in laughter. This time, I did faint.

I awoke from my blackout to someone slapping me gently on the face. It was Nguyen, and it was the first time I'd seen what appeared to be an authentic smile creasing his mouth. Of course, that ignored the moment when the fire hose pushed me around the barren room at police headquarters. I thought that might have been today. Or yesterday. It was all melting together in my brain as one huge clusterfuck, a word I'd heard Luong and Morgan use.

Nguyen stopped once he saw I was awake and moved back to his chair, a superior and satisfied look on his face.

"*Con bat hieu*," I whispered. This was the worst insult a Vietnamese could utter to a countryman. It meant "you have no filial piety," and was as close to saying "motherfucker" and truly meaning it as someone in Sai Gon could get. Since respecting the family was the highest aspiration of all Vietnamese, stating that a person lacked this deference was incredibly offensive. While Morgan and Hatati wouldn't comprehend this concept, Liu and Nguyen knew I was striking back, revived from my trance. Slowly, I sat up.

"The Chinese have a reputation for trickery," I said. "But you people win the Order of the Brilliant Jade, the highest honor in China."

Mr. Liu bowed, the only one familiar with this rare award.

"All will be explained," Liu said. "Be patient and drink your tea. It will still your soul."

"Enough," Luong said. "We have used him and he has cooperated. Now, it's time to tell him why." This was the pragmatic Luong I knew. The one who had to make something happen and not sit back waiting for the god of destiny, Li Tinh, to control his future.

Hatati was in agreement and said so. "It's time to stop tormenting him. He's done everything we asked."

Morgan nodded.

"You were a diversion," Nguyen said. "You were never a real target. We could have done worse than having Lat pull out a fingernail. Luong wouldn't have it. For some reason, he thinks he owes you a debt. So, we used you the best way we could until we found if you could be trusted. Besides, the other buffoons would never have found what was happening. We knew you would. Better having you on our side."

I scratched my chin and leisurely shook my head, not wanting to betray the raging conflict in my mind.

"That makes absolutely no sense," I said. "You kill an old woman, kidnap and torture me, all the while murdering politicians and past enemies. Then, you fake an escape and take me on one of your massacres, making it look like

Nguyen is after me. I'm enlisted in your scheme and then held by Nguyen again. Excuse me if I'm missing lots of details. The real question is 'why'?"

"We'll never give you all the particulars," Morgan said. "We couldn't even if we wanted to. None of us have the whole picture. We're all being manipulated and compartmentalized. Nutley had the entire picture." He looked at Liu. "And possibly Mr. Liu." He crossed his legs and beamed. "That's normal procedure, and I got to help to Luong get his vengeance. Good enough for me."

"But that's not all," I said, "is it? Killing old enemies wouldn't interest Nutley. There has to be more."

Silence. It was clear no one wanted to take the next step, telling me what was really going on.

By now, the tea was tepid, and I could even imagine the orchids on the Ming dynasty end tables were drooping in boredom. The scent of lavender was replaced by body odor and dust mites drifting from the hardwood floor. Little illumination came from the curtained windows, the light supplied by lamps covered by silk shades portraying fishermen and rice farmers that were probably hand painted in the reign of the Qing. It felt like the jury was trying to decide who would deliver the verdict of capital punishment.

"Have you seen the classic Chinese Magic Stick trick?" Mr. Liu asked.

"Of course," I said.

"The essence is that props and diversions cause the watcher to gasp in wonder," Mr. Liu said. "It is really quite simple. Like killing a number of vermin in the politburo who should have died years ago for the atrocities they committed on Luong and his people, just to list a few of their victims. The true objective is not revealed, while the audience squeals in delight and surprise."

"So this was all a parlor trick?" I asked.

"Hardly," Mr. Liu said. "Unless the woman being sawed in half dies."

"So who's the real target?" I asked.

"As far as I can tell," Liu said, "you're way beyond what the sham Vietnamese courts would need for a death sentence. If we let you go, you'll only last minutes until Lat has you in his ghastly hands again. His joyous times will come just before you're hung."

"What about Nguyen?" I asked. "He must have quite a story to tell if he wants to keep out of Lat's dungeon."

"The tale is quite complex," Mr. Liu said. "Chinese lore provides the answer to all questions. In this case, it's the story of King Fu Jian in the fourth century. His army of nine hundred thousand men was defeated by eighty thousand troops because of trickery. Jian's foe, General Xie, convinced Jian's officers and army to retreat in order for Xie's army to cross the river and the battle commence. Xie's spies spread the rumor that Jian's soldiers were being slaughtered. The ensuing withdrawal became a panic."

"Quaint," I said. "It still doesn't tell me why Nguyen and I are here and what you're trying to accomplish."

"I knew you would quickly figure it out," Luong said. "Especially with the clues we left behind. We understood Nguyen would be put in charge of the case and you'd be his prime investigator. We'd control the flow of evidence if we could get the two of you on our side. Besides, the best outcome is we all either go back to our jobs or leave the country standing up. You can glide to heaven at Ma Jing's and Nguyen can continue his quest for a cover spread in *GQ Vietnam*. There's only one more fish ball remaining in this meal." Another shockingly long tale from Luong's mouth. He must have taken speech classes since we last shared an ant.

"And the flavor is?" I asked.

Over the next hour, the plan was laid out, and we were assigned our roles. The only disturbance was a satellite call from Nutley. Morgan handled the conversation from our side, only passing the phone to Mr. Liu for a short time at the end. When they were finished, both men nodded at each other calmly as if they had just completed the Seven Steps of Buddhist meditation. Obviously, it was a "go," and we had the full support of the queen.

"In the famous words of that great Chinese lesbian actress, Lan Yen, 'a full belly conquers all.'" Mr. Liu said. "I have prepared a feast for us before we embark on this final journey." He clapped his hands and led us to the formal dining room, taking a minute to make sure we were seated according to his wishes.

The first course was *jien duy*, sweet sesame seed balls. Next, came *yu saang*, made with sashimi-grade tuna grilled in white radish, ginger, carrots, chilies, onions, and peanuts. Then was my favorite, *jiaozi*, flour dumplings filled with cabbage, pork, snake, egg white, pepper, and a few other spices. Absolutely tasty. This was followed by caterpillar-fungus-stuffed duck, also reputed to cure tuberculosis. Fried and white rice were always available in massive quantities, steaming in hand-painted antique bowls, the value of which could have bought a high-class Szechuan restaurant in any district of Sai Gon. Unfortunately, no one had room for the heaping plate of Shanghai Noodles that was steeped in rice wine, pork belly, and ginger and sat forlorn at the end of the table. As usual, the meal ended with soup. This time it was egg drop, made with cornstarch, chicken broth, and beaten eggs, followed by a dessert of a variety of Chinese sweet cakes. By the time we were finished, I could have rolled into the living room for the post dinner tea.

"No time for a nap," Luong said, on purpose as always, especially when the chance to kill a few more lowlanders was imminent. "We should be making our final preparations."

Not much chitchat had been exchanged during the banquet; the focus was on savoring the exquisite and exotic tastes. We all realized it could be the last supper for the group unless our planning was carried out successfully. My role was mostly as lookout, no one trusting me with any of the modern weapons and technology that would come into play. This time, being the stupid half-breed meant I wouldn't be on the front line. There were some advantages to my checkered gene pool.

The main objective was a man well above my pay grade or anyone else's in this band of murderers. He would be allowed much more than a cell phone and an old desktop computer like me. Much more. In fact, an entire country more. His name was Nguyen Tan Dung, the Prime Minister. Nutley believed he was supplying the Taliban with Russian-made arms in exchange for opium that he marketed through a syndicate based in the Little Sai Gon area of Westminster, California. Of course it wasn't Dung directly. It was an organization headed by his brother, Le Duc Dung, or Poo Ping as Nutley called him, short for "he dropped a Poo Ping in the loo," in reference to Dung. Poo Ping was rumored to be a cannibal and little boy and/ or girl lover who always wore pink slippers, attributes MI6 tolerated with prejudice, lots of pat-on-the-back joking, and knowing smiles.

Not that MI6 or the cousins in Langley would shirk from the heroin trade if it kept the right people in power. History had shown that policy to be the case many times. It was the supply of military-grade weapons to terrorists that upset the mandarins. Cannibalism, smack importation, poor choice in footwear, and child fetishes could be explained away as "just a little bollocks on the side, old chap," but not the latest AK-47s that might be used to kill anyone including the minders back on the Thames. Greatly bothersome was the ton of Soviet-made PVV-5A plastic explosive Dung had delivered to Sai Gon and subsequently left via Poo Ping's shipping company, Kinshasin. That material could blast another few hundred bodies into jelly doughnuts in the London underground or be left on the side of the road to blow up a passing Bentley on the way to a weekend golf match in Surrey. Besides the fact that Dung was consorting with known terrorists, he was outspoken in his communist beliefs, while he stuffed his Swiss bank account with dong and dollars. Earlier in his career, he'd held the position of Director of the Vietnamese Banking System, so he knew all the tricks. The cousins would cooperate, the Red Scare still raging in the heads of the old guard who still ran the Company.

None of this compared to the intel Dung that had acquired a small amount of fissionable material contained in 2S3 Akatsiya 152 mm self-propelled artillery shells, capable of detonating a small nuclear blast. This was the Holy Grail of all terrorists and worth untold millions to the Saudis who funded the fanatics. One Akatsiya ignited in Piccadilly would kill many thousands and contaminate the area for years.

Our mixture of Chinese, Vietnamese, American, Montagnard, and Malaysian was truly a multinational smorgasbord, united mostly in our common ability to speak English. I was the last to understand that "motherfucker" wasn't a term of endearment, but I mostly got the drift of the conversation. It seemed everything that had taken place so far was a distraction, aimed at getting Dung out in the open. Every resource available to the security forces, police departments, and all governmental agencies, including the secret services, would be focused on stopping the killings of senior politburo members. When it was discovered that all the victims were connected to the photo left on the bodies, and Dung wasn't pictured, all the firepower would be devoted to catching and executing the perps. Us. In the meantime, the nearly impenetrable guard around Dung would be reduced, giving Morgan and Luong a chance to do what they did best.

By the time most of this had been explained, the tea was cold and the light was fading outside the curtained windows. The afternoon rain torrent had ended, and we were all getting into the proper mood for the night's mission. Still, there were a few unanswered questions and I leaned forward, putting my porcelain cup on the end table. There was one thought that was consuming me since it was directly related to any future I might have.

"You believe Nguyen and I will be allowed to return to our positions as if nothing has happened?" I asked to no one in particular.

"Yes," Mr. Liu said. "It has all been thoroughly analyzed and planned. Nguyen was positioned so he would lead the investigation for the security forces and you would be the lead for the police."

"And I would feed selected information to my superiors," Nguyen said, "making sure they understood about Morgan, Luong, and the significance of the cobra and photo, all supplied by you."

"Then you were sent out as bait after Nguyen had you tortured to verify your authenticity," Luong said, merry as he envisioned my pain. "Your kidnap and disappearance played perfectly in the script. Even Nguyen's timely rescue. He'll easily be able to explain how he was protecting you and went into hiding, afraid of more betrayal. He'll spread the blame around, playing right into their paranoia. We'll finish tonight. You should be back at your desk tomorrow, with the fingernails you still have remaining and the queen's never-ending gratitude." He smiled, and it was frightening. Like a corpse had come to life. "You'll be busy. Many gooks will die tonight."

It appeared Luong may have spent time at Sandhurst, the British Military Academy. He even spoke with a hint of the accent graduates often conveyed. I knew because of my hours of watching the BBC on VietCable and the liaison work I'd done with some ex-SAS men from Scotland Yard. No wonder Nutley liked him, if anyone could feel affection for an iguana. Luong stood, making us all aware that it was killing time.

"Relax," Morgan said. "You know the schedule. We're likely still a few hours away, and we have to wait for the call."

"This is too important to me and my tribe," Luong said. "Dung has led the crusade to exterminate my people. He is willing to provide nukes to the jihadists. The Degars and the world have suffered too much. Dung must die. There will never be a time for me to 'relax.'"

Morgan stood and stepped to Luong, touching him gently on the shoulder.

"During the war," Morgan said, "you stood watch while I carried out my assignments. Never did you question or object. I will be with you to the end of this operation. But now is too early. We have to wait. Everything is in place. You'll get your chance. I promise."

Luong went back to his chair, his body still quaking in anticipation and filled with deadly energy.

We waited. Mr. Liu made sure our teacups were never empty. Finally, Liu's cell phone buzzed. He nodded, not saying a word. "Game's on."

While Dung's official residence in Hanoi was a magnificent building designed by French architect Auguste Henri Vildieu and renowned for its acres of ponds filled with pink and white koi, Dung used his own home when he was in Sai Gon. Certainly, it wasn't ancestral, since his fortune was new money made from drugs and selling favors, the modern communist ideal. Poo Ping's villa was near the Botanical Gardens in District One, not far from where we now took turns using the loo to empty ourselves of the gallons of Mr. Liu's extraordinary tea. This was a part of town I knew both Morgan and Luong were familiar with, since it was the area where the son of the ex-vice president was the victim of an assassination I now realized was done at the hands and silencers of Luong and Morgan. We stood, looking back and forth at one another, nodding like the English National Soccer team after the singing of "God Save the Queen," ready to do battle with the hordes. We needed a team handshake, but that would never happen.

My job was simple. I would be in the black SUV, parked along the walls, fifty yards down Nguyen Binh Khiem Street from the entrance to the gardens and a block away from Poo Ping's. There would be little chance anyone would be around the Botanical Gardens, since it was closed at this time of night. It was often described as the "most depressing zoo" in the world. That was manifested by the eight-thousand-dong entrance fee. Thirty-eight cents USD. Not even stupid foreign gaijins would pay more for the chance to see monkeys in filthy cages and elephants in gray rooms smaller than Mr. Liu's flat. Certainly, no one would be interested in visiting this disgrace after dark.

I would be the watcher, ready to sound the alarm if anyone from the outside came to Dung's rescue. Also, the entire team was wired with the latest RedStart 1689 earpieces that both sent and received signals hands free. Winky would be listening to the transmissions, since it was all connected to the open line of a cell phone beamed directly to MI6 headquarters in London. At least I could hear the action, but still felt a little castrated because no one trusted me with an M16, silenced .22, or M84 stun grenade. Even Hatati was part of the assault. Her role was to guard the exterior of the villa once the walls were breached and Luong and Morgan were inside the house.

In the hours spent at Mr. Liu's amid the endless rehearsal, I'd learned much about Dung's residence and the security around the complex. The slayings of the politburo members and Degar killers was more than revenge. The goal was to sidetrack Dung's defensive squad into joining the nationwide hunt for the killers and make them believe Dung couldn't possibly be a target. It must have worked or the agent on Nutley's payroll wouldn't have called in the signal that the op was on.

Now, I was parked just down Nguyen Binh Khiem Street, my earpiece engaged and listening skills totally focused on the few words the team members spoke. A wire led from my transmitter to the open cell on the seat. The sound in London was switched to mute, so Nutley couldn't waste anyone's time with second-guessing from his leather chair on the Thames.

I'd watched Luong, Nguyen, Morgan, and Hatati scale the wall using ropes and hooks that made them look like they were climbing in Ha Long Bay, the mecca for Vietnamese rock addicts. Dressed totally in black and faces smeared with charcoal, they were mostly in shadow. It took them only seconds to breach the fifteen-foot-high, solid concrete fence. They looked like they'd practiced the moves a hundred times. I knew they hadn't and it was a testimony to the thoroughness of their training, no matter what country had paid the tab. That effort was punctuated by a few "*cut*" grunts. Shit. Now, I mostly heard whispers, none frantic.

They would all make a circle around the outside of the villa, hiding in the bougainvillea when necessary. Perimeter guards would be neutralized without hesitation even if that meant a quiet bullet to the head. Nutley had assured the team that any motion detectors or other electronic surveillance had been deactivated. Dung hated dogs, his dossier said, so there would be no Doberman threat. How Winky discovered all this information was no concern of ours, only that it was accurate. While I jiggled my nervous legs, I pushed hard into the earpiece, never trusting I wouldn't miss a word.

The first noise I heard was a *phuppp*. It was immediately recognizable as the sound of a silenced .22 pistol. I didn't know who had fired the shot, since they all carried the Hush Puppies as well as other weapons. Morgan was especially versatile in the use of a garrote and an Ultima fighting knife, both quiet killers. He had carried out many of these night raids, according to Luong, and wouldn't hesitate to shoot a dog or sentry.

Over the next few minutes, the *phuppp* sound was repeated at least five times, often punctuated by an exhale of breath and the muffled noise of a body slumping to the ground. Back in Cholon, Luong had told me most victims immediately voided their bowels and the smell was "nauseating, the worst part of midnight executions." He still said it with one of his horrific grins.

We had figured there wouldn't be more than a half-dozen guards outside, and the body count was almost there. Once the lookouts were neutralized, Morgan and Luong would make their way into the villa, while Hatati watched from near the front door, Nguyen, the back. All of this had been carefully planned, schematics and aerial reconnaissance photos supplied by Nutley and verbal updates from Mr. Liu and his legion of agents. All electronic security had been jammed or shut down through the magic of MI6 I would never understand. The attack had been rehearsed so many times even I was familiar with the nuances of the plan and the layout of the house. At least they'd promised me a Sig Sauer P226 in case it all blew up and I could point it at my head before Lat got another chance to cream his black slacks. Unfortunately, they'd forgotten to give it to me.

The next word I heard was a whispered "in." Nothing else. It was Morgan and it meant he had gone through the French door on the garden side.

"Check," Luong said. That signaled he'd made it into the back of the house. Now, the accuracy of Mr. Liu's intel was critical. There should be several guards roaming the house and a few sleeping, while the night shift protected Dung. Liu hadn't been sure of the exact number of men, since it had been changing rapidly due to the Night Snake killings. Morgan and Luong would sanitize the villa before they headed to Dung's bedroom.

At least I could visualize what might be happening. All possible surprises we could anticipate had been thrown out and planned for, knowing full well that, according to Sun Tzu, it was necessary to "do everything in your power to be prepared, because it's only a matter of time until something goes wrong." Several times in the past, Luong had told me, it was chickens or pigs. This time, it was a girl. And a parrot.

Her shriek startled me. Without breathing, I waited for the *phuppp* sound. It didn't come. That meant it was beaming from Morgan's transmitter, not Luong's, who wouldn't have hesitated. Within a heartbeat, the stifled gag of someone with a hand over their mouth resonated in my earpiece. In the background, a bird squawked, the first one not loud, the next increasing in volume. Then, the screech of a bird's "*du ma, du ma,*" fuck you, over and over, the speed and intensity increasing with every repetition. Another *phuppp* and the noise stopped, the only sound Morgan's whispers to someone I guessed was a child.

"*Su im lang,*" Morgan hissed. Be silent.

I heard just the slightest squeal that had to come from a girl or a very young boy. Liu's intel had said Poo Ping was hung up on little girls even more than boys, like so many of our esteemed national leaders. Vietnamese political and military officials must have been intimidated by the dragon ladies they usually married. They escaped with twelve-year-old children. Or younger. Recently, a high-ranking member of the Vietnamese Communist Party, Nguyen Truong To, had been accused of having "unhealthy relations" with a dozen girls, all under fifteen. Of course, To was released. His position and the Party's reputation were too fragile for this type of investigation and ensuing public mockery. It seemed one of Dung's young prey had gone down to feed the parrot and Morgan had shot the creature, while he tried to quiet the girl. Too late.

Through the mic, I could hear pounding feet and yells.

"Code Red," Morgan barked.

That meant Hatati and Nguyen were to immediately join Morgan and Luong inside. Stealth would no longer be possible and I would need to move the SUV closer, blocking the gate if anyone answered the alarm before the wet work was finished. I was already missing the forgotten Sig Sauer.

Then, the real shooting began. Mainly, the early assault was heard as a series of *phuppps* and groans, punctuated by short comments like "here," "on the right," and "clear," all in hushed gasps. Within seconds, the staccato of AK-47s on full-auto rang in my ear. Those sounds were highlighted by screams and shouts. None seemed to be coming from my new team.

Sitting in the SUV was nearly as tough as having Lat threaten to peel my skin like a mango, starting with my *cac*. There was nothing I could do but watch and listen. Inside the house, the thump of feet racing up the stairs pounded in the earpiece. This meant the lower floor was secured enough that Luong and Morgan could make their way to Poo Ping's bedroom. The element of surprise was gone, and there was no way to anticipate what awaited them inside. For all they knew, he could be armed with an AK himself.

The sound of an explosion. It was a stun grenade, mostly flash-bang, and not meant to demolish a room. It would give Luong and Morgan the few seconds they'd need to kill Dung. Morgan would hesitate, making sure no more girls were there before spraying the area with his M16. Luong wouldn't pause for a heartbeat; more dead flatlanders meant less panfaces to persecute his people, no matter the age or gender. Either way, there wouldn't be time for a face-to-face with Dung. He was terminal.

The noise of sirens wailing and getting closer howled from outside the open window. It was time for me to move the SUV, disable it in front of the gate, and go to Plan B, a hurried retreat that included elephants and monkeys. I started the engine, backing up to the turn-out in front of the villa's entrance, stopping parallel to the gates so no vehicle could come or go. Grabbing the sat phone, I jumped out, making sure to break off the key in the ignition and ripping out the wiring under the steering wheel. Outside, I punctured the front tires with the fighting knife Morgan had given me. Within seconds, I was running toward the Botanical Gardens, realizing if it was more than a few hundred yards, I'd probably have an oxygen-deprived heart attack. Even if I made it without fainting, I had to scale the wall. At least there were masses of fruity vines to help me climb.

At the same time that several blue-on-white police cars swerved to a halt at the gate to Poo Ping's villa, I reached the corner of the fence that surrounded the zoo. Grabbing handfuls of woody liana vines hanging from the spiked peak, I was glad we'd remembered to bring gloves that kept the small thorns from cutting my hands into bamboo slivers. By the time I pulled myself to the top, I was nearly gagging on the pungent smell that rubbed off as I touched the flowers I knew were pink and in full bloom even in the dark. I was older than Nguyen and younger than the rest of the squad, but I figured none of them would dilly-dally thinking about broken bones and immediately jump to the ground below. They'd leap into the void as if they were indestructible and it all was just a bit of fun. Me. I dithered, wondering what the future held for a half-breed detective with a mangled leg. While most Sai Gon policemen made sure their meager retirement benefits were propped up by the daily "donations" of the city's residents, I spent my entire pension at Ma Jing's. The Sai Gon police graciously called the never-ending bribery and corruption a *"trang thue,"* or "white tax," and it included anything from a few dong for a broken headlight on a cyclo to many millions for the murder of a mistress. I turned around and grabbed the top of the fence, sliding down as smoothly as possible. At least I hadn't picked the tiger's cage for my clumsy landing.

Back at Mr. Liu's, we'd all memorized a map of the Botanical Gardens. I'd scaled the fence, ending up in shrubbery just to the east of the War Remnants Museum and west of the main gate. Pausing a second, I listened to the assault raging in Poo Ping's house, the noise of firearms still raging in my ears. My job was to make sure this Plan B escape route was clear, since I'd abandoned the getaway SUV.

No one was sure whether or not a guard would be posted in front of the War Remnants Museum. The building held many treasures from the era of the American invasion like a pile of unexploded ordinance, barrels of Agent Orange, a Huey helicopter with machine gun holes in the skin, and photos of the My Lai massacre. It was mostly a testament to the atrocities committed by the United States military and seemed out of place in a zoo and lush gardens. The current status of Vietnamese–American diplomacy determined whether there would be a sentry and it was impossible to comprehend what that meant or who decided. I was prepared for it either way. Staying in the shadows of the immense tropical plants and trees estimated to number close to two thousand species, I moved slowly past the overhang that covered the entrance to the museum. There was no guard.

Most bothersome was the shooting that continued to crash in my earpiece, every few seconds highlighted by a scream or loud groan. The assault should have been finished by now, and I couldn't tell if the team had become engaged with the police or more military. Or even if they were winning. I moved past the rhino and monkey enclosures, turning north. At least the paved path was bordered by manicured jungle bush, giving me lots of places to duck into if anyone appeared. Beyond the tigers and lions, the trail ended at a huge banyan tree and bamboo forest. Farther on was the Kenh Thi Nghe Channel and the boat we'd used to escape from Binh Thanh what seemed like ages ago, but was only a day or two before. Luong's men had been instructed to leave it tied up on the shore right where I would emerge from the undergrowth. Plan B was that I steer the motorboat quickly to a rendezvous point behind Dung's house that also bordered the Channel. It was then only a short cruise to the Sai Gon River and safety hiding among the sampans and dinghies that dotted the river and its edges.

When I pushed aside the giant ferns, my first thought was Luong's tribesmen had failed. I looked both ways and saw nothing but lantern lights from houseboats moored to the shore and city reflections across the water. But something was bulging from the bamboo about ten yards to my left and looked like a tumor on the forest wall. It was the back of a boat camouflaged with lilies, creepers, and brush. I pushed my way through the foliage and, untying the rope, pulled the boat free. Luong had made sure I knew how to push the starter button and drive the vessel, even if it wasn't done hands-on. I did as I was instructed and was motoring up the channel in seconds. It was less than a half mile to the meeting point and the sounds of battle at Poo Ping's had begun to diminish, only an occasional *pop* of a weapon and a hushed "over here" or "follow me" coming into my head. I slowed within a few minutes at a boathouse and dock where Dung kept his twenty-seven-foot Bayliner Sunbridge cabin cruiser just as described by Mr. Liu from intel gathered by his legion of informers. I backed the boat in and waited, silence now in my ears.

The first to appear was Hatati. She ran down the dock, stopped next to me, and crouched, her body now faced back toward the house that was showing flames dancing in the windows and smoke pouring out of the roof.

"Be ready," she yelled. "They're right behind me."

Next was Nguyen, holding Luong under the armpits and dragging him as fast as he could, an AK-47 hanging from his free hand. Luong's head was slumped on his chest and he looked barely alive. I started to get out in order to help.

"Stay there," Hatati barked. "We'll put him onboard. You take care of the boat and be prepared to get us out of here fast." She didn't move to aid Nguyen, continuing to stare toward the path from the house where Morgan had to soon materialize.

When Nguyen reached the boat, I ignored Hatati and stood, holding my arms out to take hold of Luong's limp body. He was heavy and awkward, especially with the boat swaying in the current. Together, Nguyen and I managed to wrestle Luong into one of the padded seats while the Degar moaned, obviously unconscious and in great pain.

Just as we got Luong settled, Hatati began firing her AK toward the house, and bullets started pinging off the metal dock. Nguyen turned around and opened up with his rifle, aiming up the slope from where a tall white man was running toward us through the thickening smoke. Morgan was limping and only held a pistol. I moved behind Luong, getting between him and any shots that might hit the Degar in the head. I reached inside his shirt and found a Sig Sauer P226. Finally, I was armed, too, but the enemy was too far away for the gun to be of much value. All the same, I sighted in on a man just moving into the open and fired. He went down, and I didn't know if it was a fluke or Hatati's work, since Nguyen was occupied with targets farther up the hill. With all our fire power blasting away, it was loud. The smell of cordite mixed with the stench of a burning house coated my nose in grit. Morgan was close now and Dung's defenders were getting more desperate. I dropped the rifle and made my way to the steering wheel, the engine idling. Hatati waited only a second when Morgan stumbled at her feet, pushing him onto the boat, and jumped in right behind. I shoved the throttle forward and three hundred horses leapt away from the dock, bullets continuing to rattle into the sides. Within seconds, we were into the channel and too far away for anything but a lucky hit.

"Is this the dinner cruise?" I asked anyone behind me who could hear over the roaring engine and the deafness caused by rounds fired in close proximity to ears.

"Get us out of here," Morgan yelled, holding his hand tightly against a wound on his thigh, "and I'll buy you all the filet mignon you can eat at La Villa." La Villa was rated the number one restaurant in Sai Gon. It seemed

Morgan knew all the hot spots and loved to tantalize me with profferings of gourmet meals.

"Sorry," I said, "I'm not into French cuisine. Too much subtlety. How about Baba's Kitchen. The lamb curry is magnificent."

"Anywhere," Morgan said through clenched teeth. "Just don't run us into a sampan."

Everyone knew I'd only driven a boat once, and that voyage ended in disaster. I came into the dock too fast and slammed into the wooden pilings, punching a hole in the small craft and spilling two of my fellow policemen into the dank water. Most of what I knew about captaining was learned from Morgan back at Mr. Liu's and was verbal only. I thought, *how hard could it be* just as we thumped hard over something that could have been a human body, an Irrawaddy river dolphin, or a bloated cow carcass. Whichever, it caused the wheel to spin out of my hands and we began to head straight at the tree-lined bank and a dinghy moored to a tree. The channel was only about thirty yards wide, and we would be sinking within seconds. I grabbed the controls and pulled hard left, almost capsizing. Groans came from the back, and I didn't bother to listen to them gripe about slant drivers.

"You should be careful to keep your mouths closed," I said, shouting over the engine noise. "The water here is quite contaminated. Haven't you been reading about the mystery skin disease that has killed almost two hundred recently? Even the WHO is stumped. Most of the victims lived around our polluted waterways. It causes ulcerous sores on the hands and feet and then spreads internally, finally ending in death from an inflamed esophagus. You suffocate. In other words, talking could be harmful to your health, comrades." I smiled, only wishing the part about the "polluted waterways" was true. The rest was and maybe it all could be spot on. The report caused silence, and when I glanced behind, all of my passengers had their forearms over their mouths, trying to keep the rancid spray out.

A few minutes later and we were in the Sai Gon River, headed toward Binh Thanh. Here, the channel was much wider and I could move between junks and sampans at a slower rate. We had yet to hear the *thwop thwop* of an expected helicopter. If one did emerge, it would be easier to hide among the traffic in the short distance we had to travel.

After passing under the Cau Thu Thiem Bridge, I guided the boat to a dock close to where I'd first met Morgan and reunited with Luong. Two men were waiting, bulges under their shirts barely concealing the pistols at their waists. They had the serious deadpan look of all Montagnards, manifesting the centuries of persecution that rarely allowed laughter. In this gang, I felt like a pirate, not a policeman, and it was a role that didn't sadden me in the least. The question was if I was going to join this lawless crew, continue breathing, or have a return visit to Ma Jing's without being executed. We helped Luong and Morgan out of the boat and were escorted into the maze of Binh Thanh where a van was waiting on Cau Phu My Boulevard to take us to Mr. Liu's safe house in Cholon. Nothing much was said on the ride, and I tried to settle Luong as best as I could. He was bleeding badly from several bullet holes in his shoulder and arm. At least the body-armor vests had kept him from a sucking chest wound.

At Mr. Liu's, the debriefing began immediately while the flat screen on the wall silently played news about the murder of the country's respected and loved Prime Minister. Liu had made sure there was a doctor with supplies on site if needed. It was and Luong was attended to first, his condition being much more serious. Morgan came next, Hatati hovering over him every second. Mr. Liu questioned me before the rest, knowing my part was minor. I sipped a cup of his excellent jasmine tea and told him what little I knew. Then, he turned to Nguyen.

"You were to be sentry outside the back door," Liu said to Nguyen. "What happened?"

"I used the silenced .22 to take out the guard, then hid in the shadows, waiting," Nguyen said. "Nothing until I heard shooting inside and Morgan saying 'Code Red' in my earpiece. I went through the door, past the kitchen, and out into the main part of the house. I only encountered one man and he was facing away. I shot him and joined Morgan and Luong at the bottom of the stairs. Hatati came from out of the smoke in seconds, and Morgan and Luong signaled us to stay while they went upstairs after Dung. There was lots of gunfire and a grenade from above. No one else came toward us. It all took a few minutes and had mostly quieted down when the first of the sirens sounded." He looked away, rubbing a bruise on his hand.

"And what happened next?" Liu asked. He was seated in his high-backed silk-cushioned chair, playing the part of the mandarin he was.

"We knew he had blocked the gate," Nguyen said, nodding at me. "But that wouldn't keep them out for long. It didn't and we could see men approaching outside the windows. They were helmeted and all carried rifles. More were coming every second, and the siren's noise kept increasing. Hatati and I started firing, each from a different window. At one point, we both threw grenades before reloading. It was too loud to hear Morgan or Luong. Eventually, and just before we would have been surrounded, they ran down the stairs and Luong covered us while we sprinted out the back door, dropping a couple phosphorous grenades in farewell. We leapfrogged across the lawn toward the channel. Luong was hit, and I grabbed him before he fell, holding him up as best as I could and taking him to the boat. Hatati went first in case anyone had circled around. Morgan covered the rear. We all made it, not completely unharmed. As far as I know, Dung is in the place he belongs."

Hatati and Morgan had been listening to the tale and mostly moving their heads up and down with approval.

"That's about it," Hatati said. "I did the same except from the front of the house. I'm sure Dung is dead, but Morgan or Luong will have to tell you that part." In her black pants and blouse, she was as stunning as ever. Her green eyes flashed against the dirt smudged on her cheeks and I realized a woman like this was worth more than the entire Nguyen Dynasty carved gold treasures that were exhibited around the world.

Luong was still in no shape to join the questioning, the doctor finishing with his stitching and bandaging, having removed the bullet fragments that remained and administered a syringe of morphine. Hatati had cleaned Morgan's injury and applied antibiotic and a fresh dressing. He was next to speak.

"Upstairs," Morgan said, "the guards were alerted and ready. We had to fight door to door, Luong mostly providing cover fire, risking his life by staying more in the open. I reached what we had been told was Dung's bedroom after we'd neutralized all of his protection."

A smile on Morgan's face. It was a picture of masculinity. Even if he was too old for the cover of *Esquire*, he was the poster boy for the rugged individualist on the senior circuit. He and Hatati would make the flashbulbs crackle even on the red carpet at Cannes. I was jealous, but that was nothing new.

"When we went in," Morgan said, "after flipping a little gift of a stun grenade, old Poo Ping was rubbing his eyes, trying to look mean with his

AK. Usually, I would have made sure the last thing he heard was his own voice pleading for forgiveness as he spilled out his excuses. There was no time and I stepped aside, letting Luong stitch him a new zipper in his belly. We ran down the stairs and joined Nguyen and Hatati. You know the rest. The only real surprise was the girl and the parrot. The girl was left unharmed. Unfortunately, the bird won't fly again."

The sat phone buzzed. Liu and Morgan looked back and forth at each other, Morgan finally picking up the receiver from the end table.

"Evenin' to ya, bloke," Morgan said, trying his best to sound like a Brit.

He listened, grinning. We could all hear the yelling in the background. Morgan seemed to be enjoying Nutley's anger.

"Hold on a minute there, laddy," Morgan said. "All you need to know is mission accomplished and tell me where the Gulfstream is waiting to fly is back to the Kingdom."

The smirk got even wider as he paid attention to the shouts coming over the ether.

"Not my problem, mate," Morgan said. "It's your brief to handle the 'international incident' rumors. We did our part, and Bob's your uncle if I'm gonna apologize for thirty dead commies who wanted to kill us."

Nothing much more except a few nods. He switched off and smiled at Hatati.

"I think we might have stirred the nest," Morgan said. "That's a bag of shite for MI6 to clean up. Not us."

Morgan turned back to Mr. Liu.

"Can you get Luong, Hatati, and me to the airport?" Morgan asked. "The sooner the better. I think you have plans for Nguyen and the captain."

"There's a car waiting," Liu said. "Cheers. And thank you."

No hugs. They gently helped Luong to his feet and, holding him under each arm, moved to the door.

"Good-bye," Hatati said. "Thanks for everything. Take good care of him," she said, pointing an exquisite finger toward me and winking in my direction. I nearly fainted.

They were gone, and I was alone with Nguyen and Mr. Liu, my fate still as undetermined as a cobra's in front of a mongoose.

Epilogue

Ten days later, I was sitting in front of my customized computer, the office quiet except for the hum of the fan and the chirps bleeping from Phan's cell phone. He was absorbed in version 2.0.3 of SpongeBob he'd just downloaded. Phan had been ordered not to let me out of his sight. I was browsing through the hysterical online articles on Dung's assassination, trying to find if there was any hint about who had carried out the slaughter. There was massive speculation, no proof. Lots of theories, the most popular being a revenge killing involving competing warlords, an acceptable hypothesis now that Poo Ping was dead. The final body count, including the late Prime Minister, was thirty-two with a dozen more wounded. I marveled at the deadly accuracy of my teammates and wondered if I had been responsible for even one. Back at headquarters and able to resume my job, I was only still breathing because of Nguyen. Of course, Mr. Liu had helped. His tentacles reached into even the darkest places.

After Morgan, Hatati, and Luong had left Liu's apartment, he'd explained a few things to me. Not the whole story. No mandarin would ever give all the details, making sure everything was left vague and forever unknowable by the peasants. It seemed I had been watched for many years, my Chinese blood being the most enticing factor and the bigotry that hybrid would surely spawn. There was no way I would have risen to the lofty position of "Detective Captain" without the influence of Mr. Liu and Nguyen. And here I believed it was my incredible ability to close cases, forgetting that I could have been a newly-risen god and still be hated by purebred Vietnamese who wanted me collecting rats for the rodent tariff rather than investigating crime.

The questioning had been intense, especially since a half-breed couldn't be trusted as far as a gecko could spit. Nguyen had prompted me and he was part of the interrogation, making sure no one got too close. Besides, he was my prime alibi, explaining how he had rescued me from the ambush in Bin Thanh, then taken me to a safe house where he had grilled me further about my past comradeship with Luong and delved deeper into Morgan's legend. He convinced the other officers that I was cooperating completely, and he hid me away, fearing even an attack on headquarters was possible. The next few days were spent attempting to trace Luong through sources Nguyen had supposedly placed inside the Montagnard community. Since Nguyen had divulged much of this to his superiors after our tea in the Quickly Bang, he had established both of our credibilities. Mr. Liu and Luong had provided witnesses who would also verify Nguyen's story.

While the murders caused a media frenzy in our censored society, the police and intelligence services were putting on a show. Dung's sleazy behavior was always a threat to the reputation of the party. While the opium trade had lined the pockets of many Vietnamese politicians and ranking military officers, the addition of young children and the Taliban was lower even than the politburo's morality. The first five victims were part of the old guard and not well loved by the younger ambitious generation trying to gain power. Over time, the explanation of a war between the historically dominant Binh Xuyen gang and a rejuvenated Nam Cam crew, led by the founder's son, Truong Van Cam, became the accepted script. Cam had notoriously left a severed finger with Dung's famous ring still attached below the knuckle on the steps of police headquarters. This was a few days after the assassinations and was delivered with a note claiming Bay Vien, the Binh Xuyen leader, was next. No one could prove the legitimacy of the finger or the letter, but the police made sure it was well-publicized.

Now, I was back and still considered the snake in the bird's nest. I sighed and picked up a file outlining the arrest of Tran Thuy Lieu, forty-one, accused of soaking her husband, Le Hoang Hung, with gasoline and setting him on fire. The fifty-one-year-old journalist was asleep in his bed on the second floor of their home. Hung was a reporter specializing in crime and corruption issues. There was some suspicion that Hung had really been murdered by the police for not fully supporting the criminal gang responsibility theory for Dung's execution. No one was trying very hard to prove Mrs. Lieu's innocence. I flipped through the pages, marveling at how a burned corpse could look so much like a blackened mummy with protruding eyeballs.

"Did you have your syphilis test yet, Phan?" I asked my watcher.

"That was those other two officers," Phan said. "You told me I didn't need it. The damage was already done."

"Have you heard my new name around here?" I asked.

"No, sir," Phan said.

"Li Kin Dong," I said. "Yours is 'Dum Gai.'"

And so it went.

Mr. Liu's call came a month after. He spoke of the delicate tea he'd brewed and invited me for another tasting, making sure to arrange for a ride that meant I wouldn't be followed. I ditched Phan while he thought I was in my apartment for the night and met the driver a few blocks away outside the Tan Dat beauty salon and casket store. We weaved our way through the evening rush, passing the fierce carved dragons that stand guard at Quan Am Pagoda and a Starducs Coffee Shop in Cholon, turning down the same alley I was becoming familiar with.

As usual, Mr. Liu was waiting at the top of the dimly lit stairs, motioning me up with a smile on his thin face. He was wearing a traditional red silk jacket and pants embroidered in gold. His hands were clasped behind his back. I climbed up and bowed. He guided me inside, where Luong was seated on one of the satin couches, a cup of tea in both their hands. He nodded and stepped close to him, lightly touching his shoulder that was still humped with bandages.

"Old friend," I said. "You are well?"

"Sit," Luong said, pointing to the chair beside him. "We have catching up to do and we're waiting for a call."

I sat, accepting the cup of tea Liu was holding out.

"I thought you were leaving the country," I said. "There is still a manhunt for you."

"Yes, we know," Luong said. "And Nguyen is in charge of the search." He tried to smile. "There is too much here to do for me to run away. The flatlanders continue their genocide of my people. And too many are still eating pho."

The room smelled of jasmine and sandalwood incense burning in an antique flower-shaped gold vase studded with emeralds. It was the most expensive container I'd ever seen and went well with the ethereal tapestries showing gardens and birds that hung on the wall. Everything in the room, including the furniture, serving ware, lamps, and decorations were ancient Chinese artifacts. And priceless. I relaxed, knowing it would take more than a battalion of the Vietnam People's Army to successfully invade this neighborhood.

"Morgan and Hatati?" I asked.

The encrypted satellite phone chimed.

"Perfect timing," Mr. Liu said, pushing the green answer button.

"Mr. Nutley," Liu said into the handset. "I have someone here who would like to speak to you." Hesitation. Then, "I'll let you tell him." He handed me the receiver.

"Is that Captain Fang?" Morgan asked.

"Yes, it is," I said. "And how are you?" I was smiling.

"Just smashing," he said. "We're back in the land of the Redcoats. Hatati sends her best wishes. How have you been?"

Before I could answer, he started in again.

"Because of your influence, I have been studying your great philosopher, Confucius. He once said, 'The superior man is modest in his speech, but exceeds in his actions.' In other words, 'Foolish man gives girlfriend grand piano. Wise man give girlfriend upright organ.' It is amazing, the wisdom of this man."

"Yes," I said, "I have heard all those bigoted sayings before. It's like saying 'The queen must love stupid people. She rules so many of them.' I would rather hear how you've been. Rather, how Hatati is doing."

"You're the one who showed me how valuable the insult could be," Morgan said, laughing. "Besides, I never fight with ugly people like you. They have nothing to lose."

"Stop," I said, for once disgusted with the never-ending boring slurs. I was beginning to sense that the good man doesn't need to hide behind words, a complete reversal of the last thirty years where my only defense seemed to be offensive. It was time to take life more seriously and honor the beauty of my fellow man.

"I only wish I wasn't born so intelligent," I said. "Then I could enjoy you. All of this childish rudeness reminds me that your parents were siblings."

Nothing more from Morgan. Hatati came on the line. I could hear her speaking to Morgan, saying, "Let me talk to him. You're being a pig."

In the background, Morgan said, laughing, "Pig? Just remember, with sufficient thrust, pigs fly just great. And do other tricks too." I could sense him nuzzling Hatati's sculpted neck from thousands of miles.

"Captain Fang," Hatati said, "I apologize for Morgan's behavior. He is American, you know, and that means he has no cultural compass outside a Happy Meal. How are you?"

"I'm very good, thank you," I said. "I've been allowed to return to police work, even though I have a permanent watcher who thinks heaven is getting to the next level of Bikini Bottom."

"Sorry?" Hatati said.

"Oh, it's a game he plays constantly on his smartphone," I said. "SpongeBob SquarePants. His mother thought Agent Orange was a breakfast juice."

"Were you tortured?"

"No. Nguyen and I had rehearsed too well. Between him and Mr. Liu, their influence has been too great. Besides, it seems no one who matters wants to dig too deep."

"That's wonderful."

"How did you and Morgan get out of the country?"

"We drank champagne and ate caviar on one of MI6's Hawker 800 jets. They delivered us right to Nutley's office. Then, we spent a few weeks getting sand in all the wrong places and working on our tans. Now, it seems Nutley and the queen need us again. If you slow down a little with the lotus pipe, we might be knocking on your door."

"How did you know?"

"Don't be silly, Captain. The dossier on you is a meter thick."

"Should I be flattered?"

"Yes. Size matters." She giggled.

"Is that a racial slur because I'm Chinese?"

"No. Of course not." But I could hear her trying to cover a snort.

"It's OK. I've had many years to grow a thick skin. By the way, do you know why Chinese men don't use toothpicks? It reminds them too much of their penis. That was a new one I just heard."

Her beautiful nose must be dripping from the guffaws. Morgan was asking, "What? What?"

"Enough. We wanted to thank you for all your help, something that's not usually part of the pattern here. Maybe they need more feminine mystique in the corridors of MI6. Besides, every time we get on a boat around the islands, we're reminded how important it is to have someone onboard who knows how to run the thing."

"We made it safely."

"Yes, but I've never come so close to getting seasickness. We have to go now. Nutley is blowing cigar smoke into our faces, his signal there's something threatening the empire. Be well, Captain. Cheers."

"*Chao ban,*" I said. Good-bye, friend. "You enjoy whatever adventure Nutley assigns you, and I'll go on insulting as many Vietnamese as I can. And a few others."

I handed the phone back to Mr. Liu, and we began a final wrap-up.

"How is your finger?" Mr. Liu asked.

I held it up, showing the beginnings of a nail at the bottom of the puckered red.

"Jell-O is the answer," I said. "I particularly like the strawberry-banana. The gelatin speeds up growth and makes naturally stronger nails."

"You sound like you should work at the Best Head beauty salon," Luong said. "You and the rest of the girlie-boys would get along just fine."

"We should finish our business," Mr. Liu said. "I have prepared a celebration." He turned to me. "Is anyone other than Phan following you? Do you feel like you were believed?"

"As much as any Vietnamese would ever trust a mongrel like me," I said. "They do know I can solve most of the murders in Sai Gon while they're trying to zip their pants at the Groping Hands massage parlor."

"No visit to Lat?" Liu asked.

"No," I said. "It seems there has been an outbreak of shoplifting at the Ben Thanh Market. Lots of arrests. Lat was busy torturing teenage girls with their nose rings and lip studs and filming it on their iPhones to put on You-Tube. It's gone viral, and he's gotten several million hits."

"No more talk about Dung?" Luong asked.

"Nothing. As Confucius said, 'To be wronged is nothing unless you continue to remember it.' They have chosen to forget."

"Yes," Mr. Liu said. "A man with a clear conscience has a bad memory. There are too many ways to make dong here to waste time on the past."

"Speaking of money," I said. "How's Luong's dong? I mean, does he have the money to carry on?"

"Yes," Luong said. "And I'm honored you would think about the size of my dong. It is very manageable." He smiled. That was a half-dozen times in a few months and I wondered if his cheek muscles would be exhausted.

"Well," I said. "At the moment, my dong is nearly empty. The paltry salary they pay a lowly mutt like me doesn't allow much fun. Or even a good meal at the Hard Wok Café."

"Are you soliciting a bribe, officer?" Mr. Liu said, now serious.

"Of course not," I said. "I did sacrifice a fingernail for you and risk being shot while I lied to Lat and my superiors. And, going forward, I think I could be of great value."

"The size of the dong," Liu said, "depends on what you can do for me."

"I assure you, I will be truly satisfying."

"I will consider the volume of my contribution to your health. I promise not to be premature in my decision." He bowed.

Luong and I exchanged glances, knowing Mr. Liu wasn't finished with us. Attention and respect were required. I sipped on my now-cold tea, amazed that it still tasted smooth, fragrant, and delicious.

"There once was a Chinese general named Trieu Da," Liu said. "In the tenth century, he conquered the land to the north and south of the Mekong, naming it Nam Viet. He fought for many years with the Han mandarins over control of this new kingdom. He eventually lost and the Chinese ruled the country for centuries until General Ngo Quyen successfully drove out the invaders. This country has been under thumb of the Chinese the entire time, allowed to exist relatively independently. Now, the leftovers of the Qing Dynasty want to return to their glory. If they can't do it in China, they want to rule here. And they have connections to terrorists who would do anything to cause chaos." He stopped, placing his hands inside the silk of his sleeves.

"This is a myth I have heard many times," I said. "Just because I'm paranoid doesn't mean the Han Dynasty isn't trying to be reborn. Even though I'm half Chinese, I do not want the entire country turned into spring roll takeouts. What is it you want?"

"First," Liu said, "we eat dinner." He motioned toward the dining room that I could see was already set for three. A whole roasted duck sat on a silver tray, still steaming. We started with shark-fin soup and rice before digging into the duck. That was followed by fish balls and abalone, ending with pan-fried water chestnut cake and glasses of pinyin grape wine.

During the meal, I struggled with the contradictions of my life, religion, training, and breeding. The clash between Confucius and Buddha might never be resolved in my heart, but I knew I would always be an outcast in the Socialist Republic. Even in Cholon, I was a bastard. Years in the police force had shown me I could do good while surrounded by evil. While I'd grown without role models, I didn't need any organization to show me the light. My self-made morality was enough, even if it included hours of reflection at Ma Jing's. Still, I'd made my home here and knew what it took to exist. If I ran away to England or America, there was only confusion and the unknown. I wiped my lips with a silk napkin and cleared my throat.

"I would be honored to join you," I said to Mr. Liu.

That sentence began the chapters that would forever make me question if there was a god or true enlightenment. For now, the episode of the Sixth Man was closed, and I would go on being the bee that gathers honey during its lifetime but doesn't sweeten its sting.